I BRING SORROW

AND OTHER STORIES OF TRANSGRESSION

Patricia Abbott

Copyright on following pages
Stories by Patricia Abbott
Cover and jacket design by Georgia Morrissey

ISBN 978-1-943818-87-7
eISBN 978-1-947993-00-6
Library of Congress Catalog Number: 2018932406

First trade paperback publication: March 2018
1201 Hudson Street
Hoboken, NJ 07030
www.PolisBooks.com

I BRING SORROW

AND OTHER STORIES
OF TRANSGRESSION

Also by Patricia Abbott

Concrete Angel
Shot in Detroit

For Kevin Louis Abbott
For Julie Nichols

On Pacific Beach

You'll find my mom sitting most days on the sun-bleached bench outside Von's Market. She's probably pushing her shopping cart back and forth as if a fretful baby lay inside. Luckily, it's usually one of the small ones so shoppers can get around it without having their ankles clipped. I wonder if she ever rocked me so lovingly.

Even if I don't recognize Mom in whatever permutation she's adopted—a muumuu, cut-offs, a white tuxedo—I'd recognize her hair, a long, reddish-gray braid that's beginning to look skimpy. She must be what, sixty-two now? She's taken to wearing a baseball cap most days—an item easy to find left behind on the beach. Last time, it was a Padres cap, and her braid, mostly reddish-gold in the sun, erupts from the hole in back like a dragon's tongue.

Her cart might look a little lighter than when I saw her four months ago, just five blocks from here at a Rubio's Taco Shop. The '70s TV she pushed around for a year or more is gone. It's hard to imagine someone pinching a useless TV from a homeless woman. Maybe she dumped it herself. Certainly she was thinner than the last time I flew out.

I'm told there's no facility that can keep my mother off the street for long. San Diego's Health and Human Services office has tried many times.

"I'm so sorry, Ms. Delaney," the woman in a lavender pant-suit told me, thumbing through Mom's file. That was probably more than a decade ago—back when I still hoped Mom's problems could be solved.

"Andrea. Call me Andrea," I told the woman, hoping to create camaraderie.

"Andrea, right. Well, your mom outfoxes us every time. She can pick any lock, disarm guards with her smile, and shimmy down the wobbliest gutter."

Ms. Gutierrez chuckled, and then covered her mouth. "She's very inventive. And so affable."

With so many assets, why was Mom homeless?

There was a time when I thought Mom's resourcefulness was a good thing—when it got us the food we needed to survive, when it got the rent paid, or the school authorities off my back for missing classes.

"Audrey's so affable (there's that word again) when we let her alone. Not confrontational like when she's confined. She's been befriended by a group of locals who feed and look after her in a fashion. One called a month or two ago to say she was sick. Nice, wasn't it?" This was more recently.

Nice in its way, but living on the street, a woman's so vulnerable, out there for the picking. I thought of that flying into San Diego recently when I spotted a relevant headline in the local paper.

"Local Girl Found Strangled on the Beach."

I picked the newspaper up long enough to read the story. It reminded me of those deaths on Long Island, but it was too early to know if this girl's associated with the sex trade. Is there something about beaches that make women particularly defenseless there?

Does Mom remember the names of the so-called folks who look out for her any better than she does mine? I still remember the first time she forgot it. Introducing me to someone on the street, she was tongue-tied for a minute, and then called me Suzie. I searched for some meaning in its choice and found none.

I used to get angry when people questioned me —when an EMS technician, a doctor on the phone, or a cop on the street said, "Can't you do something about this?"

If a two-hundred-fifty-pound cop couldn't wrestle her into a van, what chance did I have?

I want to tell them—all those people employed by some government service—some non-profit—not to judge me. None of you know about the days there was no food in the fridge, the nights she set fire to her bed with a cigarette, the occasions she showed up at school wearing a foil hat to protect her from "the forces," the stuff of mine she hocked to buy her booze or Kools. There's no one to tell these stories to.

My mother's cart is different from carts found in a northern state. No need for heavy winter coats, boots, or an ice scraper. You can make out without even an umbrella here. The guy who's staked out my entrance to 1-94 in Chicago has built the kind of tent fortress I used to make as a kid. Blanket after blanket connected in some jerry-rigged system to keep him warm, to protect his stuff. A shovel to dig his way out pokes out of a hole. When I stopped to slip him a fiver last month, several cars behind me beeped.

"You're part of the problem, lady," someone yelled. I gave him the finger, which shut him right up. The possibility of my suffering from road rage douses any follow-up remarks. Oh, yes, I have some of my mother's genes coursing through my veins.

"Know me?" I ask Mom when I finally ratchet up my nerve. "It's Andrea." When she doesn't blink, I add, "Andy?" Still nothing. "Your daughter?" And finally, "Suzie," which gets a small smile.

Though she doesn't usually seem to know me, I think I must represent possible captivity. Or maybe my face or actual name—Andrea, not Suzie—summons up some vestige of remorse. But in the swirling eddy inside her head, my face does not bode well for handouts or a Subway sub. So I rarely get a smile.

Today, she shakes her head and begins to rearrange her cart. She's gotten her hands on a bright blue boogie board, which she strokes possessively. She's a vessel of maternal gestures she never expends in the usual ways. The boogie board is in good shape so it won't last long. But she makes no attempt to hide it under her dirty beach towels, her copies of La Jolla Light, her pile of tee shirts.

"Going surfing?" I ask, trying for a little humor. She considers my remark, her bright blue eyes sizing me up. She is a bit thinner than the last time I saw her—four months ago now. Handouts for the homeless must have its ebb and flow.

These trips to the coast three or four times a year stretch my paltry salary as an EMS dispatcher to the breaking point. They also raise my level of stress for weeks before and after each visit.

"Why don't you just move back there?" my friend, Rachel, asks me every so often. "Gotta be nicer than Chicago."

Why indeed?

A full half-minute passes before Mom laughs, showing me another tooth is missing. The reason for this is simple: homeless people sift through trashcans, and the most common item in a trashcan is the remnants of a sugary drink. Mom's chief diet staple is a Slurpee. That's why both her health and her teeth suffer.

"How about getting some lunch?"

There are several possibilities for a healthy lunch on the

street, but since I can't take her inside, we walk to a taco stand where I order the healthiest items on the menu: a tossed salad, a chicken taco, and a carton of milk. She carefully removes the beans and lettuce from the taco, the cucumber and avocado from the salad, then eats eagerly without saying a word. The milk carton is too hard for her to open, and she executes a nice hook shot into the trashcan before I can intervene.

"Do you know who I am?" I ask again. "Remember me, Mom?"

She gives me her brightest smile, the one she probably offers to anyone who buys her a meal. "Of course I do," she says, getting up. In a second, she pushes off.

She stops at a trashcan half a block away to retrieve a Big Gulp drink, thirsty I'm sure.

I see her again the next day and the day after, doing what I can each time to clean her up, feed her, and finally, fumbling with her in the back of a vacant auto parts store to change her clothes. She hates my touching her; hates my making her step into a new pair of pants; shudders when I momentarily expose her bare breasts to the dark windows above us; wiggles her feet when I try to trim her toenails before putting on a new pair of sneakers. It's frustrating, but there is something curative, for me at least, in the feel of her flesh under my hand.

I used to smuggle her into the showers on the beach or the one in my motel, but no one, including Mom, liked that idea. So any washing or a change of clothes must be done on the street. Over time I have learned how to do this discreetly.

Before I take off, I call the social service agency to talk to Ms. Gutierrez, who still takes an interest in my mother. A harried-sounding man tells me she's on vacation—won't return until the next Monday. Where does someone who lives at a resort go for a vacation, I wonder?

In my childhood in the Encanto section of San Diego, I

never heard of anyone taking a vacation. A trip to the amusement park at Mission Beach was a big deal, a weekend at a grandparents' place in Rosarita even bigger. I left home at seventeen, searching for an entirely different view to look at from my window. At that time, Mom wasn't a street person. Just a woman living on food stamps and handouts from men she picked up. Odd, forgetful, but not completely daft. She sometimes even took the occasional job until her list of deficits became clear to a potential employer.

"Now, keep in touch," she said as I headed out the door that last day. "Send a postcard when you get there."

Did she dream I was going to Hollywood to become a movie star? Did she think I was off to see the Queen? Did she remember I was only seventeen?

I keep up with Mom, or at least the city where she lives, through an online subscription to *U-T San Diego*, the local newspaper. Pacific Beach's in the northwestern part of San Diego. I have never been clear on how Mom found her way there from Encanto. Probably a date drove her up one night and she liked what she saw and stayed. It's a good place for the homeless, not too toney but fairly safe. Do the homeless migrate to the southwest for the climate?

As I click through stories about the mayoral race, the rise in housing prices, an indie film being shot in the Hillside area, the price of guavas and exotic chilies at Whole Foods, a few days later, I find a story that makes me sit up. It's about that dead girl found on the beach— Mission Beach it turns out— just down the Boulevard from Pacific Beach. She was dressed in a wetsuit and found strangled in the sand by a sunrise class in Tai Chi. It gives no name—five days later now—which must mean they haven't been able to ID her. Or perhaps to locate her relatives.

I don't think about this much over the next few days—such

things don't surprise people who've lived in Chicago any length of time. But when another girl turns up strangled a week later, I begin to feel dread.

This time it's in Carlsbad, thirty minutes up the coast. I'm not actually afraid for my mother—these were both girls, after all. The first woman has now been named: Rebecca Sweet. And it turns out she's not a surfer at all but a twenty-five-year-old day-tripper who must have wanted to try her hand at surfing. Or maybe not. There's speculation she wasn't surfing, but had been dressed in the wetsuit by her assailant—something about the size of it being wrong. I follow the story closely in the days ahead, hoping for more information about either case. Is the murderer looking for day-trippers, young girls, surfers, or none of the above?

Maya Velasquez, the second victim, was not a surfer, not dressed in a wetsuit, not a day-tripper, and not under thirty. I find this out three days later. She was a thirty-five-year-old tax accountant from L.A, down in Carlsbad for a meeting. She'd been expected back by eight o'clock but never turned up. There's a photo online. She looks attractive even though the lighting isn't good, but her hair is yanked back enough to see her features clearly—it's probably a picture from a driver's license.

With the third murder, three weeks later, I go into alarm mode. They post pictures of the three victims side by side—large photos now—and the third woman found on Imperial Beach is said to be a sex worker. Felicity Brown serviced the servicemen on the base and was probably abducted from her usual post and taken, still alive, to the beach. She was found under an abutment of rocks, had probably been there for several days. An unusual period of rain had kept the beach empty.

They have a better photo of Maya Velasquez in this edition too, and it's easy to see the one object the three victims have in common. It's not surfing accouterments, nor an age similarity, nor the location of their bodies. It's that all three women wear their hair in a braid, and apparently these braids were used to strangle them. Or suffocate them rather: the hair was cut or ripped off and stuffed down their throats. Pushed so far down, in fact, that strands of hair were found in the lower esophagus of all three women. Did he use an instrument to do this, I wonder? Some sort of barbecue skewer perhaps.

My mother wears her hair in a braid and has her entire life. I used to ask her why, back in the days when she could still answer a question.

"Hair on my face makes my skin itch," she explained, "and a braid's easy to do."

If only I could call her. I've tried giving my mother a phone, but each time it was gone before I even left San Diego. She cannot learn to use one either. People far more sentient than Mom struggle with such devices.

I call Ms. Guiterrez's number as soon as it's nine a.m. on the West Coast.

"I'm sorry," a woman says, "she doesn't work her anymore."

"Is she in another office?"

"No. With the government cuts, she was laid off."

Laid off? She had to have spent at least ten years in that office. I try to remember the first time I called her. How deep were these cuts?

"Has someone taken over her caseload," I ask, realizing as I say this that Mom is not part of anyone's caseload. At best, she's someone who pops up on the radar from time to time. Because she was friendly, no one really paid much attention to her. Could anyone in the state of California ID her in a morgue? How would anyone know where to call me should such a thing happen? I am stunned at my negligence. Stunned at my inability to foresee such a large hole in my plan to keep an eye on Mom from two thousand miles away.

"We're sorting it out now," the woman said. She sounded exhausted and it was only 9:02 in the morning. "What was her name again?"

"Audrey Delaney."

"And her address?"

I sighed inwardly. "She's homeless. That's why I can't get in touch with her."

"We give cell phones to the homeless now. Especially the women. It's a new program. So they can call in for help."

"She's not that kind of homeless person. She wouldn't be able to hang onto a phone." When the woman didn't say anything, I add apologetically, "I've given her at least three phones in the last five years. Even if she could keep one, she'd never use it." Why am I explaining this to her?

Pause. "God helps those who help themselves."

I am speechless after this bon mot from a servant of the state, so it is she who speaks next.

A huge sigh and then, "Well, I'll see what I can do. Might take a few days. Can you give me your name and number?"

Without a shred of hope that I'll hear from her, I give it to her and she promises to get back to me, adding, "Did you ever consider coming out here to help her out? Your mother, I mean."

I hang up the phone.

But that's what I do—fly west.

I can ill afford this trip, and have to use my last three vacation days. If I can't resolve whatever it is that needs resolution, I will probably have to quit my job or take an unpaid leave. And our office has no unpaid leaves as far as I know.

My Fiesta rental gets me to Pacific Beach at around one o'clock. The streets look as benign as ever—certainly not the locale for a serial killer. I don't see a single woman wearing a braid, not that this is a common hairstyle. Perhaps it's more popular on the beach than elsewhere though—a way to deal with wet hair, or to keep hair out of the eyes. But I imagine any woman with a braid has changed her hairdo after those newspaper photos. Except, of course, the sort of women who don't follow the news. Like my mother.

The street in P.B. that Mom favors is Garnet, where ethnic restaurants, several supermarkets, and a Trader Joe's offer the opportunity to pick up food, rest on a bench, and watch the foot traffic. Mom's usually too out of it to panhandle, and if she does, the money probably ends up in another person's pocket. Most of the time, she'll be somewhere on this stretch running from I-5 to the Pacific Ocean. Other times, I can find her on the boardwalk that runs along the beach. Her cronies usually occupy the nest of benches there, and like the birds that badger outdoor diners, the homeless sweep in for discarded food too.

Today she's in neither place. I stop a few people who look like they might know my mother and ask, "Have you seen Audrey? Audrey Delaney?"

I try to describe her, but my words sound insulting. I approach people on benches, the ones shuffling down the street, a guy lying comatose in an alcove, several on the beach, two propped up against the back wall of Vons. Head shakes, frowns, shrugs. Obviously it's not a name they know. But do they know her face?

For God's sake, why don't I have a picture? Why has this never occurred to me before—the idea that I might need such a thing? Do I want to leave her behind—or at least her image—when I fly back east? Or is it that her face, after years of living rough, is just too disheartening to hang on to, to immortalize?

"Check out the food bank," someone advises. He looks like a man who's spent decades on the street too—so tanned that the hue looks like mud on his face, so whip-thin that no size pants will fit him. I offer him one of sandwiches I bought, but he waves it away.

"I'm on disability now," he says. "Save it for—what's her name—Audrey?"

"A reddish braid, a San Diego Padres cap, skinny, about five foot five, a shopping cart?" I pause, thinking. "Although it might not be a Padres cap now."

"Lots of places she could be," he says, "but probably out on the street. Supposed to get a shelter here, but it never happened."

I nod, having read about this in the local newspaper.

"She could be in a thrift shop, or a church, a donation center or a recycling place, a food kitchen, going through the trash somewhere. The cops could've picked her up. There's a guy comes by couple times a week and gives people a lift to a food bank. Try there." His eyes light up. "Maybe she has a boyfriend."

I run across a couple—maybe twenty years old—with a sign that says, "Help send us back to Houston."

"How long have you been here?" I ask, nearly tripping over the tambourine they're using to collect cash. I add a buck. Then another.

"'Bout a week," the guy says, looking at his girlfriend. "Right?"

"Yeah, our break started about then," she says, nodding. They are too attractive to have been here long. Did they set out knowing they'd have to panhandle their way back to Texas or did some bad stuff happen? I don't ask.

When I finally get to the boardwalk, I find an artist doing caricatures nestled between a burger place and a surfboard shop. He's seated on a high stool with an umbrella attached to it, his long legs dangling.

"Think you could do a picture—the way a police artist does?"

"I can give it a try." He picks up a pencil. It takes me an inordinate amount of time to summon up my mother's nose, the shape of her eyes, her chin. I have poor facial memory I decide. Perhaps my mom does too and that's why she calls me Suzie.

But after ten minutes, it's a reasonably close facsimile. The baseball cap and braid nail her.

"This is your mom then?" he asks as I trade ten bucks for the portrait. "Wasn't till I got the eyes right that I recognized her."

"You know her?"

"Seen her around. Folks call her Brady." He looks down at the drawing. "The braid, I guess. Never thought about it till now."

"Have you seen her lately?"

"Wish I could tell you exactly when. One day blends into the next, same blue sky, same seventy degrees." We both look up. "It hasn't been very long though. She and her boyfriend…"

"Boyfriend?"

I don't know why it strikes me as so improbable. Just because she can't hold on to a cell phone or a TV doesn't mean she can't hold on to a man. "Do you know his name—or where I can find him?"

The artist purses his lips. I am waiting for the "one day blends into the next" sentiment again when he suddenly comes up with it. "Name's George. He's usually at that recycling center over on Lamont St. People who run it are pretty cool about lettin' a few of the homeless drop in. Folks like it better than the shelters downtown where their junk gets stolen and they catch head lice. Center is just a backup place—for when someone's hasslin' them. Or if the cops are givin' them a hard time. You know. You can usually just hang on the street. Or the beach, of course."

I thank the artist and drive to the recycling center on Lamont, where an employee in a tiny office at the far end of the huge facility says she doesn't know anyone named Brady but thinks she might know George. "Big guy with a tat on the top of his head?" she asks, and then laughs. "That tat makes me chuckle every time I think of it."

Now why didn't the sketch artist mention this tattoo? Maybe George wears a hat outside? "Why does it make you laugh?"

"You never seen it then, honey?" I shake my head. "It looks like steam—like steam coming out of his head. Don't know how they did it, but that's what it looks like. Like ole George is blowing his top."

"Is George the kind of guy who does that—the sort who gets angry?"

"Just the opposite. Nicest guy in the world."

"Do you know where he might be?"

"Geez, no. I'm stuck in here all day. I don't know where folks go when they leave here. Don't know where they come from either." She laughs harder. "They're kinda like those zombies that just turn up—coming across the warehouse floor real slow."

In the years I've come to check up on Mom, I've never had this much trouble finding her. Is it because of the murders that she's keeping out of sight? Is it because she has a boyfriend? I am halfway to the Olney Street Police Station when something occurs to me. Usually when I get to Pacific Beach I sit down on a bench and wait until Mom turns up. I read a book, have some iced coffee, take in some of the sun that's scarce in Chicago a lot of the year, enjoy the street action, watch the sun set over the ocean. And sooner or later, Mom strolls by. Always. She favors that stretch near Trader Joe's. It's like her home. Why did I approach it differently today?

So that is what I do. I park the car, buy myself a cappuccino, pull out a paperback, and sit down on a bench. It takes about forty minutes. In fact, I am pulling out my map to consider other destinations when I catch a glimpse of her turning a corner. Her cart is fuller than ever. The boogie board is gone, but she seems to have picked up a number of other goodies. As she grows closer, something unusual happens: she spots me and cries out, "Suzie!"

I rise smiling, and wave. As she grows close, I pull out the item I bought in an airport shop as soon as my plane landed. I was so relieved to find it—had worried about its availability the entire flight. As soon as she's near enough to me, near enough to put my hands on her, I reach out. Scissors in hand, I cut off that braid.

Scrapped

"Aunt Marge? That you up there on the porch?"

Quickly raising the window against the spew of March air, Jerzy Fields looked for a place to park. Her aunt's driveway contained more potholes than asphalt, and she'd wrecked at least one pair of shoes and a practically new tire tussling with it. Auntie never did have a car so there was little reason to tend it.

"Who else?" Marge said, her voice muffled by the Happy Meal binoculars held up to her face. Pointing the glasses at her niece, she said. "You gettin' old, girl. Add a little more coffee to the cream and I be lookin' at my sister."

Seated on a balding raffia chair, Aunt Marge wore an elbow-less lilac sweater and a faded Tigers cap. The curly auburn wig under the hat was slightly askew, giving her a loopy look. The electric heater sitting on the porch rail shone orange, its cord pulled tight through an open window.

"What you doin' planted on the porch on a cold day like this?" Jerzy said. "Can't be no more than forty degrees." She shivered to illustrate.

"Watchin' for those boys," Marge answered, training her binoculared eyes on the street again. "Saw 'em cruising by before I was half done with my sugar pops. Drove by a second time when I was fixin' up this heater. They up to no good. Uh-huh."

"Those boys been harassin' you, Auntie?" Jerzy stamped her feet, trying to warm up.

Marge shook her head. "They jus' doin' what they do, which is no-good trashy stuff. Driving too slow to be passing through. They lookin' for something all right." Several clucking sounds followed this observation.

A baseball bat sat next to her chair. There was also an old cot with a broken leg propped up against the porch railing, and a rusty old grill with a layer of mummified charcoal from who knew when. What could anybody want from Auntie?

"Look here, this cord's frayed, Auntie. You gonna set your house on fire."

"Better get me a new one, then, Jerzy. You'll have to do it. If I don't watch the street, who will?"

There were only six houses on a street once home to twenty. None could stand up to a January blizzard or a July tornado. So why the interest from these boys? Someone must be selling crack. She'd seen some skanky girls 'round the corner on John R. Looked like a ho stroll in progress with their getups of high heels, short skirts, bare midriffs, dirty fur jackets. Men like this? Nope, only want what's under it.

Jerzy was abruptly overcome by the craving to have both a cigarette and a drink. It came over her lightning quick sometimes. She'd sworn off both a few years back, but the old lady sitting in front of her in her broken-down house on this God-forsaken street brought back that craving—the itch only certain things could scratch. Bad things. She steeled herself by thinking about how much money such weaknesses took from a pocket. And "the human cost," as they called it at the meetings. Maybe it was time to go to one again.

"Look, Auntie. I'm gonna check things out inside the house long as I'm here. See what needs doin'. Make me a list." There was no one else to see to Aunt Marge since Jerzy's mother died.

Marge nodded slightly and continued watching the street. Good Lord, her teeth weren't in her mouth, Jerzy realized, hoping she hadn't lost or broken the plate. Medicare didn't give a good goddamn about your teeth.

Inside, the house was tidy enough in a peculiar way—piles of folded clothes not put away; cans of food stacked neatly on a counter; magazines, lifted from doctors' offices, fanned on the coffee table. It was nearly as cold inside as outside. A half-eaten bowl of sugar pops sat on the kitchen table next to a cup of half-drunk coffee. Thankfully, Auntie's dentures sat there too, looking ready to take on the cereal. Jerzy rinsed out both dishes, and the dentures for good measure, then made the bed. She pushed a blanket up against the crack in the window; repairing it would have to wait. Auntie appeared to be out of toilet paper, and a lot of the food in the fridge seemed past the sell-by date. She tossed a few of the worst offenders into a garbage bag, setting it by the door. She didn't put too much faith in sell-by dates anyhow.

The thermostat, set at eighty degrees, read only fifty. In the cellar, the octopus, looking to be eighty years old, occupied most of the room. Water puddled in two spots on the concrete floor. The water heater might be broken too, or perhaps it was the ancient washer a few feet away, which would explain the unwashed clothes. How much would a new furnace and water heater cost? Auntie was looking at several thousand dollars to set things right. No way she had that kind of money. Lucky there was a used appliance store in Highland Park.

Jerzy sighed and climbed the stairs, going back outside. "Got a furnace man, Aunt Marge? Your house is fairly freezin'."

Her aunt screwed up her face. "Thought it seemed a bit brisk. Well, just call up Detroit Edison. They'll fire it up."

"It's called DTE now, Auntie, and I don't think they can fix it. You probably need a new one. Or at least a new used one." She picked up her aunt's hand. Pure ice. She made a quick decision. "Better come along home with me. We'll call us some help from my house. Get you nice and warmed up."

"You know I can't do that, girl. Who'll watch the street?"

Her aunt's head continued to swivel back and forth, lips set. Jerzy wanted a drink more than ever as she pulled her aunt to her feet. Two fingers of Jim Beam on the rocks would put some backbone into her. Did Marge's eyes look funny? Her mother died from Alzheimer's five years back. Did Aunt Marge have it now too? Did it run in families or just plain run?

"Easy, old girl. I'll get someone over here lickety-split. You'll be home in a day or two. Soon as we get some of this stuff sorted out."

"Still got cable television over at your house? Channel with all those movies?"

Jerzy nodded. Auntie's unwillingness to leave her spot on the porch suddenly vanished, and the two women went inside to pack a bag.

"Think I need my Sunday dress?" Marge asked, headed for the closet. Her mood had picked up with a vacation in the offing. She shuffled through the wire hangers, pausing to remove a few items. "Like me in this?" she said, holding up a Red Wings jersey Jerzy found for her at a flea market last year. "'Bout the warmest thing I got."

Sunday was five days from now. James would go Nam on her if Auntie stayed more than a night or two. He didn't like outsiders in his house. Didn't like to share his precious commode.

"I want a direct bee-line when I need it," he had told her countless times. "Don't need to be findin' some stranger sitting on my spot."

"I'll come back and get you a dress if you need one."

A lady from the Jesus Tabernacle congregation picked Marge up for church every Sunday. Ladies in bright flowered dresses and extravagant hats filled every pew with the rare rooster crowing his bass. Only black women wore hats to church nowadays, Jerzy thought, noticing several sitting on the closet shelf. Peacock colors. She'd kept two of her mother's. Reminded her of Mama like nothing else.

As they pulled away, Marge looked back at the house, the binoculars still hanging from her neck.

"All by myself," she said. "How I always done it."

Jerzy reached over and patted her knee.

Marge came to Detroit from Alabama in '59, working off and on in upholstery installation at automobile plants for forty years. Never married, never had kids. Made a decent living when she wasn't laid off, and bought her house on Robichaud Street when the neighborhood was still respectable. Neat houses with mowed lawns, a porch on each one. Marge's sister, Mildred—Jerzy's mother—was her only kin in Michigan. Now Jerzy and Jerzy's brother, Rufus, were it. And Rufus was hardcore. Not even good for lickin' a stamp.

James was standing in the doorway when they pulled up, the mail in his hands. He looked at the two of them like he'd never seen them before, his lips a grim line. Shaking his head, he turned and went inside, sitting down on the corduroy ottoman to lace his boots. James worked for the city, spending most of his time in the city's sewers. The city called him an engineer, but he was really a handyman trying to keep those ancient pipes from leaking, holding back the flood. He'd probably circled Detroit with duct tape ten times over.

"What's this all about?" he asked now, eyeing Marge with something close to repugnance. "Why we having company on a Tuesday?" He'd never much cared for Marge, who kowtowed to no man. James liked his women meek.

"Auntie's furnace broke," she told him, ushering the old woman past him and onto a seat. The woman sank down, sighing loudly. "She'll just be with us a few days," she told him in a low voice. "Think you got time to take a look?"

He shook his head. "Already late. And I don't know a damn thing about furnaces." He looked over at Marge, dozing already. "You aiming to be a nursemaid, Jerzy? Looks like that's what she needs. You best start thinkin' what you gonna do with her."

"Just for a few days," she repeated. "I dragged her outta there. She'll be beggin' to go home by tomorrow."

James rolled his eyes. "Tell me that on Saturday."

Proving James right, Aunt Marge had a head cold the next morning.

"A day or two," the woman at Family Furnace told Jerzy. "Maybe three."

"Tell 'im to come out with a used furnace still has some kick in it."

"Just stay here and rest yourself," Jerzy said, handing Marge a cup of bouillon. She hadn't even known they still made those cubes until Marge sent her out for some. And they'd been sitting in the store a while, she thought, struggling to remove the foil.

"Only thing tastes good on a cold," Marge said, watching. "Don't care much if it's beef or chicken, but no vegetable ones, please." She made a face.

"Feelin' wack, are you?" Jerzy asked, noticing the tissues piling up and wondering if she needed to buy herself some latex gloves. Picking the pile up with another tissue, she tossed them in the trashcan.

"Why you gotta use that ghetto talk? So hard to say sick like a civilized person?"

"Are you feeling sick?" Jerzy said.

Her aunt nodded. "But I better get over to my house anyway. Can't stop thinkin' 'bout those boys ridin' around like they was. Can't be a good thing—no neighborhood watch on my street."

"I'll look in on my way into work. You be okay here alone?"

"Always has been." Marge smiled. "And I got me a good movie channel now."

At first, Jerzy thought a fire had ravaged her aunt's house as she pulled up to the curb. The decorative iron front door was missing, as were the bars on the windows. In fact, the windowpanes themselves were gone. The rain gutters had been removed along with the blue aluminum siding. The metal fence enclosing the property had been ripped from the ground, leaving nasty flakes of metal sprayed across the lawn like sparks from a fire. Auntie's little red Bible lay on the grass, its pages fluttering crazily in the stiff wind. Jerzy picked it up and stuck it in her purse. Piles of goods sat everywhere; she picked her way through, trying not to bust into tears.

Inside, anything useful had vanished, and the rest was destroyed. If she didn't know her aunt's sweetness, Jerzy'd swear it was a grudge crime. Every article of clothing lay on the floor. Every can of food had been tossed. The bedroom was impassable, and pieces of paper, bills probably, were blowing out the empty windows. There was not a single item that hadn't been tossed, taken, or vandalized. Even the electric meter was missing. When she tried to turn an overhead light on, she realized the bulbs were gone.

Jerzy sank into the one remaining chair, cushionless with

springs sprung, caught her breath, grabbed the cell from her pocket, and dialed 911. Two hours passed before a squad car pulled up. Two hours when she'd scarcely moved. She'd started to call James, her brother, then Rufus, a friend, but coming up with the words to describe the house's state was too much.

Feebly, she began to protest the long wait to the officer when he arrived.

"Look, ma'am," the cop said patiently, "priority goes to crimes in progress. This one's for the history books." He looked around. "Scrapped her place but good." He sounded like he admired the thoroughness of the job.

"Scrapped?" She'd heard the word before but couldn't put a meaning on it.

"Scrappers come in and take anything they can sell. Metal stuff mostly," he added. "It's why they didn't bother much with the food or clothes. Every empty or foreclosed house in the city is scrapped sooner or later 'less you put a guard on it. A guard with a gun."

She knew this—but it was something happening to other people. Not Aunt Marge. "This wasn't no empty house, Officer. Only been gone a day. One day!"

"Means nothing to the people did this. You think we're talking about human beings with a soul? Gone a day is opportunity to 'em." He walked around, taking an inventory of what was clearly missing. "She got insurance?"

"Hard to get insurance in this neighborhood."

Something else struck her then. "I bet they took all her cards. You know, social security, health, ID, driver's license, bankcard. Maybe they buried out there." She waved a hand toward the heap of trash covering the lawn. "How will I get her some money? How will she prove she's Marge Lennox?"

"We got people who can tell you 'bout it. Victim's rights." He handed her a card. "If they haven't cut those jobs yet. City's broke, case you didn't know it."

The cops wanted to talk to her aunt.

"In a day or two," she promised.

A day later, Marge sat on a milk crate in her front yard. "Must be some stranger's house. Don't know nothin' about it. I'll tell you this though, I'm not going in there ever again."

James stood next to her, scratching his head. "You need to start making a list, Marge." He turned to Jerzy. "Maybe we can hire someone to put things right."

"It looks different 'cause they took down the sidin', Auntie," Jerzy explained, ignoring him. "They took anything they could sell to a scrap yard. That's what the policeman said."

"Not even one window left. Couldn't they use the door?"

"They sell glass too."

"Damn, these are nasty people." Tears were falling now.

"Maybe they needed money to buy food." This didn't sound convincing even to Jerzy.

"Now they got what they need, they won't be back," James said. "Nothing to worry yourself about. You'll be home in a few days."

All he could think about, Jerzy thought, with disgust. Getting Marge out of his john. He'd be willing to have her sleep on the floor in a freezing house.

"Those boys weren't homeless. I saw their big-ass car cruisin' this street. Got an eyeful of the fancy jackets they showin' off. Gang jackets, I think." Marge looked at Jerzy. "I told you I hadda watch the street." She wiped her face with her sleeve, and James and Jerzy helped her to the car. "Should never have taken a vacation."

Over the next few days, Marge steadfastly refused to enter the house, continuing to deny it was hers. "I'd never paint my house a hinky yellah."

"The blue siding covered the yellow paint. Maybe from a

time before you bought the house.

"She needs to file a report," the cop said when she dialed his cell.

"A report means you think you can find her missin' stuff, then, huh?" she asked him. "Gonna pour all your resources into a search for those scrappers." He didn't answer her.

A few days later, Jerzy came home from work to find Marge missing. Also missing was her lilac sweater and Tigers cap. It wasn't even thirty degrees outside and Jerzy wondered if she still had her pajamas on under the sweater. Dear Lord.

"Where you think she is?" she asked James over the phone. "She don't know this neighborhood for beans."

"She got a screw missin'," he said. "Can't take care of herself and this seals it. She has to go into a home. Like your mama," he added.

"That's what you thinking about now? Can't you let up on it?"

Jerzy drove back and forth between her house and Robichaud Street for hours. She called the police and social services. Neither seemed interested in sending out a car until more time had passed. James, for his part, continued wrapping his tape around city sewers. Holding things together underground while people stole what was above.

At first, she didn't see her aunt sitting on the porch. Marge had dragged the milk carton up from the front lawn and her head could barely be seen from the street.

"Them jokers did a job on my house," she told Jerzy after her niece climbed the steps. "I took a good look. They took a hack saw to the furnace, but it was too tough for 'em." She nodded with satisfaction, shaking a fist. "Old boiler put up a fight. Least we don't have to fix it now."

"Aren't you freezin' out here?" Jerzy asked, looking for something to throw over her. "Where you been all day, Auntie? I almost had the cops after you."

"I hadda take a bus over here. And I got scrambled 'bout which one. Routes changed since my day." She shrugged. "Bus was nice and warm though. Think I went back and forth a few times." She stood up. "Let's get me outta here. I'm done with 423 Robichaud. I just sat in on my own—what you call it—wake. Like the boy we read about in school."

As they drove down the street, Marge let out a scream. Jerzy slammed on the brakes.

"Lookity right there, Jerzy. Old brother is usin' my iron door for a table."

Jerzy saw it too. A barbecue grill smoking meat stood right behind it. The door had been fitted with a piece of glass to make a table. "Probably my window glass too. I am decoratin' homes across the hood. Never thought I'd see such a thing in this world." Auntie was almost laughing. Then she was crying again.

"These people are too mean to live. What they call it—scrappin'. I'd like to take them to the junkyard." She paused. "I never want to see this street again."

"We'll find you a new place, Auntie. You have money in the bank. We just need to get to it."

"No, I'm leavin' this whole city, girl. Going back to Montgomery. Can't be worse there. I got a cousin will take me in when I got my monies straightened out."

"Can't she stay with us, James?" Jerzy begged him when they got back. "She's no trouble at all."

"Your mama stayed here for months before she went to the home—don't you remember it? Calling me Horace and tryin' to hold my hand." He shivered. "Then it was your junkie brother trying to kick the habit. Ha! Bringin' all kinds of people to my stoop, sittin' in this very room with those goddamned forties in his lap." He grimaced. "A man needs some privacy, Jerzy. She don't wanna stay here anyhow." This was true, Jerzy had to admit.

Things fell into place surprisingly quickly once Jerzy gained access to her aunt's accounts. Within a month, they were standing at the Greyhound bus station on Howard Street, Marge having refused to fly. "Too old to learn new tricks now."

"I'll send the rest of your stuff," Jerzy promised as the man lifted her aunt's two new Walmart grippes into the baggage hold.

"Just you, ma'am?" the driver asked Marge, turning around.

"All by myself," Marge told him with a trace of the old pride in her voice.

"She transfers to the Montgomery bus in Nashville," Jerzy told him, handing the ticket over.

"I know how to do it, girl," Marge said. "Make the trip every couple years, don't I?

Minutes earlier, on the ride down to Howard Street, a helicopter had loomed over the freeway, almost causing Jerzy to steer into a Hondo Accord. The helicopter pulled a sign saying "Moby's Scrapyard in Hamtramck. Best prices in town."

"They allowed to do that?" Marge had asked. "Show themselves to the world for what they are?"

"Never mind, Auntie. Hey, I heard on the radio they got ole Jefferson Davis resting in a junkyard in New Orleans."

"Wonder who scrapped him?" Aunt Marge asked.

A Kid Like Billy

Everyone knows a kid like Billy. You've seen him at the grocery store bagging food or stocking shelves, or in a pet store feeding the animals and cleaning cages. Or maybe at a nursery in December, dragging a Christmas tree to someone's car. That's the sort of place you find a boy like mine.

When Billy was three, a careening car killed his mother. When I surfaced from the bottomless grief, I counted myself lucky Billy had been off in pre-school and not in Ellie's arms. Lucky too, Ellie had been mine for a while.

The years passed slowly. Billy repeated fourth grade and then ninth. On the night I watched him walk across the squeaking stage to take his diploma, I knew in my heart he still didn't understand what a fraction was or where to find Michigan on a map. But in a town like West Lebanon, any kid who puts his butt in his seat most days eventually gets a certificate. I made sure he stuck it out too, putting his butt there more than once myself.

People advise you to get a boy like Billy into plumbing or carpentry—jobs where you use your hands and muscle more than your head. But Billy's hands weren't his strong suit either. But I called in a favor and got a friend in construction to hire him.

"What're you doing home?" I said, finding him in front of

the TV one day when I came home unexpectedly to retrieve a file. He should've been at a work site on State Street, sweeping up nails or toting two-by-fours.

"I felt like a tuna sandwich today. Came home to make one."

His shoes were kicked off, and the half-eaten sandwich was dried up on a plate. His feet smelled bad, and I wondered when he'd last changed his socks. I probably wasn't on top of that stuff enough.

"I packed you tuna. Did you even unwrap it to look?"

"You usually pack ham Wednesdays."

"Today's Tuesday," I said, grabbing the dirty plate.

Al Ferguson gave him a job at the IGA next. About the only tasks Billy had was to stock shelves, sweep the sidewalk, and help customers tote bags to their cars. But Billy took it into his head to begin organizing the cans by colors—markers he could relate to more easily than the brand names.

"Oh no, you don't," I said, coming in one day to pick up some Hamburger Helper. He was on his knees, sorting the cans. I began replacing them, getting angrier with each one. "Look, just do what Mr. Ferguson tells you. Bear down, boy."

That job fell by the wayside too. Don't get me wrong. There was no meanness in my boy, no cunning or ill will. He wasn't lazy or dishonest. But neither was there an ounce of common sense in his tousled-hair head. I lay awake nights wondering what would happen to him, wondering if a town like West Lebanon was the best place for a boy like mine.

West Lebanon's in the northern part of the Lower Peninsula in Michigan. In summer, the population swells to five thousand, but for nine months a police force of six keeps order for the twelve hundred permanent residents. In my years as chief, we've never had a murder or even a suspicious death. Drug problems, sure, more than enough DWIs, a few marital disputes, one or two suspicious fires, some B&Es, especially in the summer, a bully or two raising hell over at the high school, lots of traffic accidents. But spread over three hundred sixty-five days, it's a peaceful spot.

In the tenth year of my tenure as police chief, I hired Billy. I took some heat for it—both with my men and with two members of the city council.

Patty Harmon, the council president, put it bluntly. "I guess you're the one who'll take the blame if he screws up. Right?"

Gradually, my men came around. Billy turned out to be a pretty good crossing guard at the elementary school. He also saw that the squad cars were washed and serviced, answered the phone, ran errands. These were the chores my men disliked most, and after a few months nobody was complaining. I never sent Billy out on a dangerous or complicated job. He didn't carry a gun or even a nightstick. He didn't do patrols. If he answered a phone call asking for serious help, he passed it on.

"A good kid," Sam Hunter, my second in command, told me. "A high IQ isn't everything, Chief." He laughed a little. "As I can testify."

The winters up north are filled with slow days when a crossword puzzle or crime novel often occupied us. Rummy and solitaire were popular. So was *The Price is Right*.

It was a lousy February, like most of 'em up here, one of those months where it never seemed to be fully light. Cold, snowy. In the second week, four of us came down with a stomach virus. The headache that came with it was crippling. Billy didn't catch it though. He'd never been sick a day in his life.

So it was just Billy and Ed Stuyvesant at the station. Around noon, the bug hit Ed like a missile to the gut. He hightailed it into the bathroom.

"All right out there, son?" he called to Billy between bouts.

Ed wasn't worried. Half the town was down with the bug too so things were even more quiet than usual.

The relevant call was clocked at 12:45 p.m., coming from a house out on Badger Creek Road. Helen Clayton's. She told me later she'd expected Billy to pass the phone on to someone senior. But after hearing her first sentence or two, Billy told her he'd see to it and hung up.

Ed said later he'd heard Billy talking through the john door, but since he hadn't heard the phone ring, he thought it was Billy babbling to him about something. Maybe asking if he was all right. Ed mumbled something back and returned to the business at hand, never dreaming Billy took off to answer a call.

Billy drove out to Badger Creek Road on his motor scooter at 12:55. The roads were recently plowed from a storm the day before. Mrs. Clayton had reported the disturbance as coming from the Ryans' summer home. We'd checked the house for a disturbance as recently as the week before and came up empty. But Helen was no hysteric, and breaking into summer homes is an ongoing problem where houses are deserted for months. Mostly it's teenagers looking for a place to have sex and drink. But not always.

Helen didn't want a long driveway to plow so her place was smack-dab alongside the road. She couldn't see much at the Ryans because their house was set further back. She described the noise as a radio playing at full volume, laughter, swearing, shouting, and a car pulling in and out too noisily. She thought it was teenagers—out of school for President's Day. Skiers maybe. It was odd to have a party at noon though.

The racket finally died down, and she assumed one of us had come out to quiet things, and went back to whatever she was doing. Didn't give it another thought, she said.

An hour or two later, someone stumbled into the police

station saying he'd seen something—probably a body—holding the door open at the Ryans' place.

"I didn't go closer than my car," the fellow told Ed. "Didn't know what I might be walking in on." Embarrassed, he muttered, "Looked like he was past any help from what I could see. Sprawled out and face down."

Ed was wondering what'd happened to Billy by then. But since wandering was one of Billy's most aggravating traits, he hadn't been too worried. He took the guy's statement, asking him how he happened to be out near Ryan's. The guy whisked his hunting license out, told Ed where he was staying, and left, pretty shaken up. Of course, the hunting season for anything other than squirrel and rabbit had been over for months, but Ed had other things on his mind.

After checking the phone log and talking to Helen, Ed called me, trepidation in his voice. We drove out there, immediately spotting Billy's figure in the doorway. It was almost certain someone had hit my boy with the iron shovel lying next to his body. There was blood everywhere: blood and parts of Billy's skull and brains. My stomach, churning all day from the damned virus, went suddenly calm. Ed's reaction was different though: he ran inside, making it to the john in time but defiling the crime scene with his dirty shoes. Me and my men weren't used to the protocol for something like this.

Within a half-hour, the area swarmed with my squad and men from the neighboring town. I put in a call to Traverse City, and they sent over their forensics team and a detective more experienced than me in handling crime scenes and homicides.

"Do you realize these bloody footprints probably belong to your own man?" the detective asked me.

I nodded. "We've never investigated a murder."

"You get the same training we do."

I Bring Sorrow

"It's his kid, you know," Ed told him, going quickly from ashamed to angry. "The body you just carted away."

"Sorry for your loss," the detective said quietly, hanging his head.

Those were the words we'd been taught to say, and for the first time, I realized how hollow they sound. How perfunctory.

I hung back from the start, letting others take the lead, allowing them to turn my son's body over, letting other men carry him away. I never set foot in the house. It wasn't up to me to find my son's killer. Anything I did was likely to screw up a subsequent trial because of my inexperience in homicides and my relationship to the victim.

At least a dozen times in the weeks ahead, Billy's actions were questioned, and I repeatedly admitted Billy shouldn't have been there, shouldn't have been employed by a police department, shouldn't have been allowed to think himself capable of answering such a call.

If I'd grieved plenty over Ellie's death twenty years earlier, Billy's death damn near sent me 'round the bend. Why hadn't he called me? I hadn't given enough thought to a situation like this arising, and Billy paid the price. The only thing keeping me sane was the conviction the murderer would be caught and brought to justice—that I would see him put behind bars for the rest of his days.

But it didn't look like there was going to be a trial anytime soon because the one and only piece of potential evidence was a Spiderman wristwatch, the kind you can buy in any department store. It wasn't even certain the watch—found about ten yards from the door—hadn't been lost by some summer guest months earlier or a more recent passerby.

It'd only been spotted because the glint of the glass caught someone's eye.

"What do you think, Chief?" Ed asked. "Has it been lying

out here since last summer?"

We both looked at the watch. It was in pretty good shape for a watch lost six months earlier. The band was surprisingly long for a kid.

"Do adults wear these things?" Ed asked.

Billy would've loved such a watch, I thought to myself.

I looked at it again. "It may not belong to whoever killed my boy, but it hasn't been here long. It would've been a foot deeper in the snow and a lot dirtier. Nobody would've found it, and I don't think it'd still be running."

We both consulted our own watches and found Spidey kept pretty good time.

"Plus," I said, "if it'd been here since last summer, the time would be an hour off."

Ed looked impressed I'd thought of it; this was the depth of investigation our force could muster: remembering the existence of daylight savings time.

There were other signs people had been there: cigarette butts, beer cans, a few empty chips bags. These items were eventually run for fingerprints but none matched any prints on file. No doubt whoever it was wore gloves for the cold.

I buried my boy five days after his murder, putting him next to Ellie, the spot where I was meant to be. There was nothing to hold up a funeral when a shovel to the head was all there was.

"One quick jab," the coroner decided. "Guy must have been an ox."

The whole town turned out and the folks from the neighboring ones. People are like that up here. The investigation continued, mostly at my prodding. But finally the new leads, the people to question, the timetables to work out faded away. There was no way to keep it going.

I'm a patient man. Billy taught me to be. I knew whoever

killed my son had found another crib—if that's the current term—but they hadn't disappeared entirely.

Small-time drug dealers don't disappear. They're peasants like me. And peasants don't travel well. They like their own john if nothing else. I knew they'd never return to the Ryans' house, but the area had dozens of similar setups.

I waited through spring and summer with nary a report of noise or unusual traffic. Summer fills the towns in northern Michigan, but by October, the houses are being boarded up. It was then reports of unusual activity began to surface, lighting up our phone lines or coming across the Internet. Local kids partying a bit too hardy, odd movement at night, a few DUIs, which didn't seem like the usual beer-induced euphoria. I spent most nights driving or walking the streets of our town and the ones nearby.

"You're not sleeping much, are you?" Ed Stuyvesant asked as we stood in front of the station's coffee machine in November. "Saw your car on Huron Street last night, Chief."

"Just making sure our taxpayers are safe." We watched silently as the machine dripped its God-awful coffee into the scarred pot. "And what were you doing out there, Ed?"

"Marge's sister, Brenda, lives out there. Her dog had some pups in the middle of the night. Ever since I delivered that girl's baby in the squad car, those women think I'm an ob-gyn." He held his hands up. "Do these look like the mitts of a skilled vet?"

I smiled. "She hear anything? Brenda, I mean."

He shook his head. "Sometimes, Chet, if you're looking too hard..." Sampling the brew, he made the requisite face. "But if you come across anything, give me a call—no matter what time of night. I never did care about eight hours sleep."

"I'll give you a call, Ed. I'm not aiming to screw it up now."

"Still hoping to convict someone?"

I nodded. "If I don't see this piece of shit behind bars, I'll never get past it"

"Odds are against it by now. Those cowboys are probably long gone."

"And where would they go? Detroit? Chicago? Bet they can't even read a map."

The week after New Year's I picked up two reports of activity in Duck Hollow. Duck Hollow's fifteen miles down the road. It's even less of a town than West Lebanon, mostly attracting folks who just want to fish or hunt. Loners. There's a general store with a gas pump outside and not much else.

Most of the houses sit deep in the woods. They're really just barebones cabins—not meant for families. Duck Hollow uses the schools, police, and services of the neighboring towns to get by. Off-season population is one hundred sixty-six and most are men over sixty, holed up in tiny cabins they knocked together with a few drunken buddies over a couple of weekends thirty years ago. Nobody tells them how to live their lives in Duck Hollow; taxes are among the lowest in Michigan.

The first suspicious report came from one of the few couples. They reported New Year's Eve had been celebrated eight hours straight at a cabin nearby. The man said it sounded like a machine gun was being fired. It may have been a pump BB gun, but the officer who took the information thought it was probably a semi-automatic shotgun.

Two more reports came in: the sound of windows being broken, cracking branches at night, possibly more gunshots.

When I looked at a map, the locations called in as suspicious lay in a straight line if you traveled through the woods. Maybe someone without a car, who was tramping from house to house, looking for food, opioids, booze, or stuff to steal. Ed and I went up there, scouting every cabin and succeeding only in drawing attention from two men with shotguns.

"Police," Ed yelled. Both times, the gun was silently withdrawn through a crack in the door. No idle chatter in Duck Hollow.

But the third time, we found their lair. Although the boards facing the dirt road were still up when we circled the house, the ones over the back door and window had been ripped off enough to allow entry and a bit of light. Smoke curled out of the chimney and two pairs of dripping boots sat at the back door. Nice, they'd removed their boots before entering the cabin. Someone had taught these guys manners.

"They're waiting for us, Ed."

Ed kicked in the flimsy door and I peered in cautiously. Inside was a barely furnished room with a kitchen at our end. Two guys sat at one of those fifties-era kitchen tables watching a tiny TV. It must have run on batteries since the electricity was turned off. They both looked up, blinking at the sudden light and at the poised Glocks in our hands.

Before they could move, I yelled, "Freeze," which they immediately did.

The older one, a beefy, red-faced guy, was around forty-five; the other, a kid who was even larger, was maybe eighteen or twenty.

"Put your hands where I can see them," I added. The kid's enormous arms shot right up—probably something he'd seen in movies.

"Like this?" he called out in a surprisingly pip-squeaky voice. I could see his wrists clearly, and it nearly took my breath away. He was wearing a Spiderman watch. Red band this time.

"Where'd you get the watch?" I asked, grabbing his wrist and twisting it for good measure.

The kid screamed, nearly falling off his chair. I yanked him back onto it and he sat there, his mouth hanging open, not saying a word.

I repeated the question, "Where did you…"

"Look, he ain't right," the beefy guy broke in. "And all you're doing is scaring him half to death." His voice softened considerably. "His Dad bought it for him when he lost his old one. Right, Johnny?" The kid nodded. The older man looked at me. "What's with the watch anyway? Someone stealing them?"

"Could you be the guys who killed a boy in West Lebanon last year?" I asked. "Left him dead in a doorway."

The beefy guy shook his head. "No way. I was inside Jackson 'bout then. Didn't get out till June." He looked at me, answering my next question. "Stole a car and drew a sentence."

"What about him? He do it?"

"He ain't right," the beefy guy repeated. "He don't remember what he did yesterday. His dad just lets him hang around." He looked around as if the father might be listening, then added, "He don't know what else to do since Johnny's mom took off. He's found some place gonna take him after the holidays. Up near Marquette."

"Ever hit a guy with a shovel? A guy wearing a shirt like mine?" I asked Johnny, knowing I shouldn't be asking questions. Knowing I should call the cops in Traverse City and let them handle it. Knowing I was screwing things up. But I had to know. I could feel Ed flinching beside me.

The kid shrugged.

"I toll you. He probably don't remember," the beefy guy said. "And if he did do it, which I ain't saying he did, he didn't know it would hurt the guy. A kid like Johnny, well, you know how it is. Everyone knows a kid like Johnny. Right?"

"Either of you have guns?" I asked, ignoring his last comment. I nodded to Ed and he started to search them.

"Nah, I'm just a minder, you might say," the guy told me.

"John here gets minded since those events. I'd just as soon stay out of Jackson so it's okay with me. Money's less but it's somethin'. Don't think I'm saying anythin' happened over there. Who knows how scared a kid like John might be to see a uniform come through a door. Who knows what he's liable to do."

"You're not saying it, huh?"

"It's just daycare," the guy continued, in case we still didn't get it.

I looked at the table where the boy sat, head down. A tear slid down his cheek, his hands still up in the air.

"A place in Marquette, huh. After Christmas."

The bigger guy nodded. "No more than a month till he goes."

"Why don't the two of you get out of here?" I said, avoiding Ed's shocked face.

"What 'bout the other stuff going on?" Ed asked me. "The break-ins. You know."

"These fellows won't give us any more trouble. Right?"

"Right. Right! You mean we can go?" The guy was rising, looking for his coat. "Get your coat on, John."

Johnny lowered his arms slowly. "I don't need a coat, Shep." He looked longingly at the TV where Oprah Winfrey was interviewing a female guest. One of those skinny blondes you saw everywhere nowadays. "You ain't gonna leave the TV behind, are you?"

"You do too need a coat, Johnny. It's not ten degrees out there."

Shep helped the boy into his coat, grabbed the TV, and started for the door.

"Get out of this county now," I said from the doorstep. "As far away as possible. Don't ever come near it 'cause next time it'll be different."

I stood at the doorway, watching them head toward the

forest. "I may not remember what it's like for a kid like him next time."

I was shouting the last words and Johnny covered his ears. Just like my Billy would have done.

Pox

Hanna planned on burying the baby behind the house where a gnarly walnut tree had shaded the berry-covered vines that surprised them last summer, their first summer in Wisconsin. This was what she'd decided in bed last night, weaving the fringe on the crocheted blanket between her fingers, sliding her warm cheek across the icy bedrail. She'd get up and do it first thing—before the chickens were fed, the cow was milked, before she washed her face. It wouldn't wait.

But the ground was stone beneath her spade in the morning. A hard frost had settled as she watched winter etch the isinglass and darken the house, felt fingers of cold poke into cracks where the mud had thinned. All of this happening in the hours after her baby slipped away.

A city girl, she'd never thought of the consequence of frozen ground before. Raising the spade above her head, she jabbed at it, the handle coming loose as she assaulted the unyielding earth. It was like chipping a block of ice; minuscule pieces of frozen dirt flecked her face, flew into her eyes. On her knees finally, she scrabbled with numb fingers, but it would not give. Nothing in this wretched place would yield to her. Who but a stubborn man like Claas would choose to live here? Her eyes stung too badly to cry again, but a stray shudder flitted across her chest. Her throat felt like she'd been screaming for hours. Had she?

They came to this place last spring. She wrongly thought nothing could be worse than the wall of fire rushing across the fields in August. Mr. Hatcher, their nearest neighbor, showed them how to dig a firebreak, changing the fire's course as the flames hurried toward them like a rabid animal. The wind's fury whipped the sky with bouquets of burning grass ripped from the ground. They saved their house by hastily erecting a clay armature to surround it, but their precious windows— two of them real glass ordered from Chicago despite Claas' mutterings—shattered from the heat. The reproaches they so often hurled at each other were lost in the wind. Had they fought this often in Chicago?

Afterward, they looked in amazement at the black path zigging and zagging for miles. As if Satan himself had charged through the countryside, leaving a sooty trail to remind them of their impotence. The smell of smoke defied bucket after bucket of lye soap and water, and only Freddie didn't mind a shaved head.

"Look at me! I'm an old man," he said, using a charred stick for a cane. Annie had her mother wrap her head, though only the four of them ever saw each other. Had an evil eye found their homestead? Did she need to fashion one herself?

Tell me it's time to go home, she pled, mostly silently, with Claas. But he continued with late summer chores like the fire was nothing. Like her loneliness didn't matter. But angry silences could melt away when a plea for help with a loose animal or a ravaging storm came along. And sulking or not, Claas couldn't help but turn to her in the dark.

She'd have to bury Martha inside. Put her in the ground near the stove where the earthen floor remained soft. Place

Martha deep inside the bowels of this cursed place. She flung off her shawl and unwrapped the baby again, examining her fingers, her toes, and the perfect, unmarked face. Trying to memorize her daughter's features, she decided Martha had Annie's delicate face in shape, but her own ruddy coloring. This was what she'd remember when she lay in bed on future nights. Sometime later, she set Martha back in the cradle and then looked in the toolbox for the fire shovel. With a start, she noticed the toolbox's size. Dumping the other tools on the floor, she put it aside, wondering if Claas would mind its confiscation. He'd have no idea of why it was needed.

Annie hadn't even wanted to go back to Chicago with Claas. "I don't remember Opa," she insisted two weeks ago, combing the wooly, black hair on her rag doll with her fingers. Almost nine, she'd be putting her doll aside soon. This doll, poor thing that it was, was the only childlike thing about Annie now so Hanna clung to it too, making dresses with any scrap of material she came upon, using twigs for furniture, drying bits of mud shaped like plates and food. Annie would glance at the newest offering politely, stowing it away without comment. Only the doll itself found its way into her hands. It was more habit than fondness, like the blanket babes often clung to.

"Are you afraid to go home?" Hanna asked softly, stirring the porridge. She didn't understand why Claas was silently insisting on taking both children south with him. It would be a wearisome trip; the roads in Wisconsin were little more than packed mud with sudden hills that tripped a wagon, with half-disguised holes big enough to swallow a spilled child. When she finally got up her nerve and asked Claas why he needed to take them along, he looked at her grim-faced, the weeks' old letter, newly arrived, staring at them from the table.

"My mother will be wantin' to see her grandchildren."

"But surely the funeral's over by now." She kneaded the dough without looking up, struggling to keep her voice soft, submissive. A voice more likely to persuade.

He slammed the door behind him and said no more about it, afraid to have his wife make a sound argument. They'd be gone two or three weeks, even with the best of weather. Could Claas care for the children alone on the road? Did he know Freddie was terrified of snakes, or Annie cried easily at a gruff voice? Would he remember to feed them at regular times, to listen to their prattle, to fuss over them now and then? He was a good man, she reminded herself—he would always put his children first.

She put down her spoon and squeezed Annie's shoulder. "Opa's funeral is already over, Annie. You won't have to see… him."

"I've seen dead people," Annie said coolly. Then a pained look flooded her face. "Oh, I'm sorry, Mutti." She hid her face with her hands. It had been her brother, Karl, Annie saw dead. Karl died in the night more than a year ago, already cold in his cradle when Annie got up at dawn to feed him, her screams rousing the rest of them.

"Sometimes it happens like this," the doctor back in Chicago had said uneasily when Claas chased him down, looking Karl's body over for some mark of disease.

Karl's death brought them north. They packed up their possessions after Claas made a short trip to buy land. In a daze, she had not taken his mention of cheap land in Wisconsin seriously.

"Ask my father to go with you. Father has a good head for bargaining." But Claas refused and set out alone.

With his dislike of foreigners, he probably took the first land the agent showed him, afraid to either bargain or say no.

I Bring Sorrow

She had watched him buy feed and other supplies too often not to notice how he shied away from haggling, paying the top dollar when he needn't. Last spring, she saw better land for sale a few miles from here, land sitting on a rise high above rocky pieces like theirs. Their property didn't have a single tree save the walnut.

"More land for crops," Claas said defensively, when she pointed it out. By July, he was cursing their shadeless yard.

"We can plant some trees in the fall," she suggested, taking pity on him. "Mr. Hatcher will give us some cuttings." He nodded in his abrupt way, his chin rising even as he turned away.

She put Annie's cereal on the table. "You'll see your cousins and both omas, Annie. Uncle Pit will give you a pony ride." She would love to return to Chicago if only for a few days, but there had been the animals and Martha to care for. Plus Claas had never suggested such a thing. If all of them left, none would return. She could see fear in his eyes.

"I'm too big for ponies. Vati can take Freddie along."

Annie acted like the matter was settled, taking on a look Hanna had seen often on her husband's face. But Annie's plan seemed the better one. Freddie was seven years old, big enough for the trip and anxious to go alone with his father. And she could use Annie's help in Wisconsin. Martha's birth had been a hard one, the midwife coming too late to do more than clean up the baby, shaking her head over the lost blood, helping Hanna bathe and change her gown, looking the baby over with practiced eyes.

The day Claas and the children left, Hanna, holding Martha in her arms, watched the wagon until it was out of sight.

"Mr. Hatcher will keep an eye on things," Claas had promised, coming as near to a hug in front of the children as he ever did. He seemed less sure about his trip now; she could have called him back with tears.

It was warm two weeks ago; she hardly needed her shawl. She wondered now if Annie's tearfulness, her stubborn attempts to change Claas' mind, came from a premonition she would never see her sister again. Martha was the second sister Annie lost, the first dying at birth when Annie was three. Five children had been born in ten years and only two remained. Claas' plan to take his children south had been the right one—but not for his reasons. If they lived, if they hadn't taken the disease south with them, it would be because of his stubbornness.

She dug a waist-deep hole; she couldn't throw the dirt up after that. Claas would want to move the baby to a proper location next spring anyway. The toolbox was almost too big for her to handle and, in fact, it slid into the hole in the end, nearly losing its lid. She didn't even read a Bible verse over Martha; there would be time later. Afterward, she threw herself on the bed and slept for hours, a strange sleep with dreams from someone else's head. Dreams where wild animals chewed on children's toes and women wearing black dresses with huge silver buttons spun like tornadoes.

Later still, she dragged everything the baby touched outside and set it ablaze; clothes, the cradle, the blanket she had bought a few weeks earlier from the Winnebago Indian who came to her door—every last thing.

It was the closest she'd ever stood to an Indian, and when she told Claas about it, he forbade her to open the door to one again.

"What did you give him in exchange?" Claas asked, looking around for missing goods.

"Oh, this and that," she said, shrugging. "Nothing we'll miss."

Claas was easily persuaded, knowing how well she held on to a penny. In truth, she gave the Indian more than the blanket's worth to hurry him on. She'd piled jellies, the last of the summer squash, eggs, and a live chicken into his arms, nearly pushing him out the door. An Indian in her house!

Her father had put her to sleep in childhood with tales of Indians and their strange ways. In one of his favorite stories, a group of Indians insisted on coming into a recent widow's house each night, parading around with her sons on their shoulders, draping her quilts over their heads, firing bullets into her shallow fireplace so they bounced off the walls.

"On the fifth night, the widow fired a bullet into the chief's head as soon as he walked through the door," her father finished, still laughing years later when the story had grown stale. Suddenly, his eyes would narrow and he'd hiss at her. "Never make the mistake of thinking they're just like us. They'd cut your throat and take your scalp home for their children to play with without so much as flinching."

It always ended with her father grabbing her chin or arm too roughly—with her mother saying, "Enough, Hermann!"

The morning after, Hanna often found a bruise on her arm or chin. She tried to cover them when she could for her mother's sake. And when she married, she married a man as unlike her father as she could find. Too little like him, she sometimes thought.

The Winnebago, tall and elegant, had stood at the doorway politely, holding the beautiful woven blanket out to her. She wondered how they made such rich blue and yellow dyes. Once in her hands, she put her face to it before she realized what she was doing. It was soft and coarse at the same time, smelling mostly of horse. Before she pulled the door closed, she glimpsed other garments made of animal skins hanging over his nag's back. Maybe next time she'd trade for a warm coat for Claas. Maybe next time she wouldn't be a mouse.

A circle of stones outside held the fire in. How quickly it

was over. Soon there was no trace of baby things other than the milk leaking from her breasts and the tamped dirt in the house. She wet down the remaining embers, trickling water over them so the fire wouldn't flare up. Claas taught her these things in their first weeks here, before the house was built.

It was nearly dark now and the sky had an odd cast to it. She hurried inside where, in the last light, she found a rash had begun to form on her arms. Although common sense denied it, she tried to tell herself it was from handling the baby's things or tending the fire, from anything other than pox.

The pox had taken the baby quickly; Hanna heard it was often this way with infants, their bodies kept perfect for God. Until now, no one she knew here had died from pox. Her family turned against vaccination though after her mother's sister died from an inoculation in Bavaria. And her father's cousin came down with smallpox years after he had cut his own skin, rubbing in the toxin saved from a friend's light case.

"If God means you to have pox, you will, and Jenner be damned," Hermann Grueber told his family, "neither my hand not the government's will intercede." He was a man "agin" more things than "for" them, hating the government, the organized church, anything foreign, his neighbors if they tried to tell him how to live his life.

Claas though, had been vaccinated in Illinois two years ago. He was sick for a few days afterward, proving Mr. Grueber's point.

"How is this better?" her father said, shaking his fist. Claas' employer, a paper mill owner on South Stubb Street, made his workers line up for vaccinations.

"I would have given him notice," Mr. Grueber told his son-in-law even before he got sick. "Is this the freedom America brags about?"

Ashamed of being bedridden, Claas decided his family

would wait for a different batch of serum. Only Claas' mother took advantage of Mr. Tyler's offer to vaccinate his worker's families, and when Claas got sick, she came to care for him, shooing Hanna away. They moved north before another outbreak, thinking that the pox couldn't find them here.

Hanna's rash spread quickly, seeking out the places where it hurt most: the soles of her feet, her palms, her face, neck and back. She looked frantically at her hands where pustules seemed to form while she watched, still not believing she could be so quickly overtaken by this disease that blew into their lives through some mysterious doorway. Someone had told her if the pustules connected you would die. With little else to do and still in a fugue from Martha's death, she watched the pox marks chase across her body as she thought about Claas and the children. They must be on the road home by now.

Outside, nature was in revolt too. There was nothing in their yard to bend or blow, but the wind's bawl convinced her of its force. Hanna began to look for something strong to write on. What little paper she had was flimsy, sure to tear away from the door in seconds. Finally, in desperation, she ripped the back cover from Annie's primer and printed in large, black letters:

POX Quarantine-Keep Out

Taking nails from the cupboard and a hammer from the spilled tools, she nailed the sign onto the door. The door flew open before she was finished, crashing into the sod wall, the wind tugging insistently at the hinges. The wind tore at her too, ripping her hair loose from its knot, whipping her skirt up around her waist. Her shawl lashed around her as tightly as a noose as she fought with the door, leaning into it finally to push the bolt across, tears of frustration frozen on her cheeks.

When she checked later, the sign was gone. She found another book cover, Freddie's this time, and made her sign again.

Now she pounded eight of Claas' precious nails in. The pain from hammering with oozing hands nearly overwhelmed her. She wished Claas kept a bottle of whiskey like her father did. It would help her to sleep if nothing else. But surprisingly, she fell into a dreamless sleep seconds after she lay down. Only her parched throat woke her. The pox was a pattern of oozing, rank sores on her face, and when she tried to drink, the pain was excruciating. Her throat was covered with pox, the poison running down her gullet in a thick, choking flow. When she coughed, blood speckled her sputum.

Outside, the world was a dizzying white and the second sign was gone. Any minute now, Claas, Annie and Freddie would return, coming in the door full of tales about their trip to Chicago, shaking snow from their coats, stamping cold feet, bragging about what they had seen on their trip. Maybe the snowfall would delay them for a day, but not much longer. Claas would be eager to get home, the children even more so. The days missed with her mother and sister would trouble Annie especially. She'd agitate her father to come home, anxious to play with her new sister.

Hanna's heart nearly stopped. Claas and the children would never see Martha again. She should have waited a day or two before burying the baby; the cold would have preserved the body and they could have shared the rite. Now she lay four feet deep in their kitchen. Under their feet. Should she tell them this? Would the children insist on bringing the baby out of the box for a last look? With her rising fever, it was hard to think clearly. Perhaps she could make Annie and Freddie believe Martha was under the walnut tree with their kitten, Gingerbread. Claas could move her once the ground thawed in April. How would he react to her decision to bury his child under the hearth? Would it mean another breach between them? Days of slammed doors and red eyes.

I Bring Sorrow

Hanna put up her final sign the next morning, using the last piece of strong paper she could find—the back cover of the Bible, a thick German edition sent to them on their marriage from relatives in Wuntenberg. Sixteen nails, driven in with a fevered strength, held her sign in place this time. When she looked again, forcing the door open against the stubborn wind, she saw the nails had held, but the sign was mostly ripped away.

Sobbing again, the tears burning her face and throat, she made her way to the shed, noticing the black path from last summer's fire was blanketed in white: winter blotting out the scars of summer. Would summer's green hide wounds too? She had yearned to see the black gone, but now missed what had marked a road away from here. Something to follow should her days grow too hard.

In the shed, Hortense looked half-dead, lacking even the energy to nuzzle Hanna's hand. She took the milk in now-practiced pulls, Hortense shuddering with relief. A year ago, she had never so much as put a hand on a cow. Her hands were bleeding again and only the chickens, dancing around her feet, oblivious to the cold and as noisy as ever, kept her spirits from collapse.

Outside again, the snow had finally stopped, leaving only a paltry coating of white for all its bluster. It would melt away within hours with nothing to show for it. There was little time left. Claas and the children were making their way home even as she stood shivering in the shed, even as her temperature rose and the pox tormented her.

Claus would never think to mind a barred door. He would kick it down and bring the children in with him. Her last living children. That was the kind of man he was—for better or worse. She'd known this about him for the outset, liking it until she saw what it was to live with. Stubborn. Silent. Just imagining him forcing his way inside the house with Annie and Freddie behind him angered her. She could be stubborn too. She could do what she had to do to stop him.

Picking up a burlap bag from the shelf, she stuffed handfuls of hay into it, pushing Hortense into a corner so she could steal every piece from her stall, moving the protesting chickens out of the way with her feet. Putting her illness aside, summoning the strength from somewhere, she made several trips back and forth with bundles of wood. Inside, she fashioned a ring like the ones made of stone outside: a ring filled with hay and kindling, then with anything she could find to burn, quilts, clothing, bedclothes, When the ring was complete, she soaked it with lard oil—oil they used to light a single lamp at night—pouring it as generously as barreled rainwater on her summer squash and tomatoes. Finally, she spilled a trail of oil from the stoked fire to the circle of hay.

Looking over her handiwork like it was a new quilt laid out for basting, she stepped into the circle's center broom in hand, prepared to light the trail of oil from the fire. The disease would end with her; nothing would be left in this place to sicken their children. As Hanna lifted her broom to the flame, she heard the sound of wagon wheels. She stretched her broom toward the fire, realizing her reach was not long enough, and she fought back tears. Outside, the wagon had stopped, and a moment later, Claas was at the door. He was shouting something, but his voice was lost in the wind. Were the children with him, only steps behind? She couldn't spare the time to look. Stepping closer to the stove, she raised her broom again. Claas was pounding on the door now. Was it Annie's voice she heard? Be strong, she willed herself.

And then he was at the window, holding the last of her signs in his hands, rapping on the glass. He must have found the sign on the road.

I Bring Sorrow

"Go away, Claas," she screamed through the door. "Martha's dead and I'll be soon too." She didn't know if he could hear her; her voice turned indistinct when she raised it. Where were the children?

The door splintered suddenly as the head of an ax sliced through. She was sobbing again, too weak now to even stand her ground. There was no way to stop her stubborn husband.

"Keep them away from me," she sobbed. "Why must you... be you?" Then he was in the room, standing in front of her, his beard dripping pieces of ice, his face scarlet, his eyes full of tears. Out of breath, he grabbed her to him. She pushed him away.

"Are you mad coming in here now you've seen the sign? Take the children and go. It's not too late."

"They're back in Chicago," he panted, dropping his hands to his sides. "They've had it too, Hanna."

"They have?" She was sobbing even harder. "Why didn't you stay with them?"

"My mother is with them." He reached for her and she stepped away again. Could he carry the disease even though he'd had it? "No, no, you don't understand, Hanna. They're getting better already." He put a hand to her cheek and she allowed it. "They'll be recovered in a week."

"They'll recover?" She couldn't believe it. Would she recover too? "How do you know?"

"The doctor said so. Freddie's already asking for toys and Annie's bossing her Oma. She wants to see Martha." He smiled and looked around.

"Martha's dead, Claas. I put her in the ground yesterday."

He nodded mutely, looking out the window. There was time to tell him more later. Suddenly, she thought of something else. "Then you came all the way back here alone for me?" There must be something else that brought him, but she couldn't think of it. "You drove back here knowing you'd have to turn around and go back for the children."

He nodded. "I can't even remember Martha's face, Hanna." His voice broke. "I didn't think of Martha. I just thought of you—just you."

"It will be all right, Claas." Hanna said, patting his hand. "You only have to look to Annie to see Martha. We'll go back soon and bring them home. When I recover."

He nodded wearily, but then smiled. "You said home, Hanna. You said home."

She had said home. The place she'd been about to burn down seemed like home. Or would—when the children returned—when they were together here once again.

I Bring Sorrow

Is That You?

She saw kids like him every day. Her café sat only a block from the juvie court, and kids and their parents funneled through for a beverage or chips. But this one—hunched in the doorway at seven a.m.—looked a bit older. More worn down than the usual teenager, skeletal and dirty, like he hadn't had food or even a basin to wash in for days. Smelled too. Not outrageous, but damn ripe. He'd probably spent the night in one of the stairwells that snaked through the development. With recent cutbacks, Tucson cops had better things to do than chase down vagrants.

Oh, what the hell. "Want in?" she asked. The boy nodded. "Got money to buy something? I'm not a soup kitchen." He reached into his jeans and a grimy hand came up with a bill or two. She opened the door and waved him in. "Be with you in a sec."

At her divorce settlement five years back, Abby got the café, the cat, Cleo, and her bike. Ned got the house, the car, and the puppy—she'd forgotten its name. Ned never liked working here—or most any place—and the cat made him sneeze. Cleo died three months later, mourning her exile from Ned. A month or two later, a car backed over the bike. And what looked like a thriving little business in a new develop-

61

ment in 2006 became one of the few spaces rented after the crash. Whoever thought this would be a good spot for a travel agency, a shoe boutique or a fancy pottery shop was dead wrong. Businesses that stuck fed off the nearby courts. A barbershop, the city tourist office, a taco stand, a nail salon and a bail bondsman were her only neighbors in a retail space built for thirty shops. The guy shining shoes just had an overhang to shade him so you couldn't count him.

Once inside, the boy slumped down at a table and immediately fell asleep, head propped on his arm. She could see a hole the size of a redskin potato in the sole of his shoe. Frowning, she began preparations for the day ahead.

Sitting across from the Tucson Visitors Center, the café got an unpredictable mix of customers. Affluent tourists mixed uneasily with people meeting a court date. Worse still were the homeless people needing a place to pee. There was no bathroom in the café, but a public restroom was twenty feet away and gave her a less than scenic view and smell. If the courts were closed, she might as well be too.

She began making coffee, though nothing a barista would brew. Price was the top priority for her clientele. Most days she threw half the pot away. Few people needed to warm up in southern Arizona.

During his time here, Ned had insisted every item in the café be marked with its price, and although at first it seemed cheap and dumb—like him—she stuck with it even after his departure. If someone came in wanting a pack of gum, a miniature cactus, or a detailed map of the city and if she was busy, more often than not, they'd leave the money on the counter. Anything to do with heat, cacti, and the sun was bound to sell. And it never hurt to have aspirin, cold remedies, souvenirs, word jumbles, golf balls, comics, condoms, and small toys. On a slow day, she'd been known to do a jumble or two. She also

I Bring Sorrow

had a copier, which came in handy for folks on their way to court. Some days, the copier got more of a workout than she did. She'd considered adding an ATM but it seemed like asking for trouble.

She went in the back room now, relying on the bell to ring if a real customer came in. The kid was snoring, and she wondered if she'd have to call the cops at some point to get rid of him. He was sure to scare off legitimate clientele but seemed harmless. She'd gotten pretty good at sniffing out trouble. Ned had left his gun behind for protection, a relic from his days in Texas. After trying several locations, she kept it in a pouch in the broken microwave.

Coffee, hot water, and a few prepared sandwiches were the first order of business. Often people came in with only a few minutes to spare before their trial resumed so it made sense to have something they could grab and go. She opened the box from Dunkin' Donuts and put them on a clean plate. The bagels were from a local chain. She fried up some bacon because not a day went by when someone didn't want a BLT, and then put a half-dozen eggs on to boil for her other standby: egg salad. After a few half-hearted tries, she gave up the idea of a taqueria and stuck with typical café grub. Local favorites were a luxury she didn't have time for.

He was stirring when she came out at 7:20. She walked over to his table. "What can I get you?"

"Wha..." he said, only half awake. He looked around, seeming surprised to find himself here. But after a few seconds, his eyes focused and found the menu on the whiteboard. She knew he was looking for the cheapest item he could order and hang on to his seat. There were only three tables and she never filled all of them. But he didn't know that.

"How 'bout—ah—some coffee and a Slim Jim." Their eyes simultaneously lit on the jar on the counter, the price marked on the glass in turquoise.

"Not really sitting-down food, kid. If things get busy…"

He nodded.

"Might as well throw in an egg or two. 'Bout to go bad." She cursed herself. If she'd ever had a kid of her own, he would've run all over her.

"Hey, thanks." To her surprise, he pulled out a cell phone—one of the old flips social service agencies gave the homeless—and dialed a number.

She broke three eggs in the pan, ears open. He was calling what seemed to be a former employer, asking if there were any landscaping jobs. Painting to be done? Flyers to be distributed?

"I can get out there by bus," he kept assuring them. "Wouldn't take a half hour."

Sounded like he had a cold, and her suspicions were confirmed when she turned in time to see him run a sleeve across his nose. Jiminy, did her good luck never end? She'd have sniffles by the weekend. And she'd hoped to drive up to Ironwood on Sunday.

If Abby had her way—and she knew it sounded crazy because Ned had told her that enough times—she'd ditch this place and become a pot-bellied pig rescuer. She'd gone up to the sanctuary a few times when Ned was still around and sharing the café duties. Ironwood, an hour north of Tucson, had as many as six hundred pigs at a time. People thought they were cute, bought them, and then ditched them when they grew to be pig-sized. Teacup-sized, they called them in brochures and shops. Ha! The work was hard, just lifting the bags of feed was crippling for a one-hundred-ten-pound woman. And there was no pay in it; most of the workers had regular jobs. You did it out of love—or for some other fucked-up reason. Being out at the sanctuary full time, well, that was a pipedream. A café

64

up there would do less business than Adam and Eve's apple stand in Eden.

A couple came in, saw the boy, and looked at each other.

"Get you something?" Abby asked quickly. She turned the burner off and faced them.

"We're waiting for the tourist office to open," the man said. "Printed the wrong opening time in the guidebook." He pulled off his cap and wiped his forehead with a handkerchief. "Surprising how many mistakes these books make. Wrong addresses, wrong opening times, prices…"

"I guess they can't visit every tourist spot each year," his wife said, trying to console him. "Stuff changes."

Abby continued to stand there, expectant.

"Guess we'll have a cup of coffee and…" The man looked at his wife.

"Iced tea?" His wife wore one of those visors—the kind that didn't mess up your hair. Sunglasses took up half her face. She looked at the plate of donuts. "And maybe we'll split a bear claw."

"We just sell the bottled stuff." Abby nodded toward the cooler. Five years alone and she still said we, but it never hurt to let people think someone else was around.

"I'll have a cup of Earl Grey, then." They sat down at the table nearest the door and pulled out their guidebook.

"First time in Tucson?" Abby asked the couple as she set the eggs on the boy's table.

He was talking to someone else now, saying his mother had kicked him out when a new boyfriend came along, and his father was long gone.

"Think a father would want to see his son once a decade," he told the person. "And I paid all my traffic fines, so I wouldn't be tempted to hit him up for any dough. Just wanted to…"

"Been here once before," the man said, playing with the

brim on his Red Sox cap. "Back in the nineties."

"We're here on business this time," his wife said. "Sort of looking for opportunities in the southwest. We're sick of the winters. Right, Hugh?"

"Right." Hugh sounded less sure.

"And neither of us likes Florida. The rain, the insects, and everyone's older than Methuselah."

Abby carried the bear claw and drinks over to their table. "You mean like investing in property?" she asked. She'd just heard on the news last night that one in three houses in Tucson sold for under one hundred thousand now. Investors could scoop them up and wait for things to pick up. Three years since the crash and things still sucked.

"Something like that," the man said. Simultaneously, they each took a sip of their drink and grimaced. Abby kept the water super hot, thinking it could cool off but not warm up. She usually managed to warn customers in time, but her mind was on that kid.

The woman cut the bear claw in half, but Hugh waved his portion away.

"Sure must be hot in July," the woman said, taking a bite.

"You bet," Abby said, responding to a comment she heard several times a day.

"If I could get a few bucks a day, I'd do almost any work," the kid was saying into the cell. "Even turn tricks, come down to it. Done it before." His voice rose in pitch with his misery, and Abby could feel the couple bristling behind her. "Yeah, but mostly I like to work with live things—maybe work at a plant nursery or in a park," he continued. "If I could just get somethin'. Even five to ten bucks a day would do me. I don't mind living rough."

He slammed the phone down and slurped up some coffee. The Slim Jim lay unwrapped on the table, but the eggs were gone. Abby watched as his eyes lit on the cash register, then on the couple across from him.

"Nice little spot you have here," Hugh broke in. "Do a lot worse than owning a café by the courthouse and not two blocks from the library and art museum. Probably get a lot of tourists with the bureau right over there."

"That was the idea."

"Didn't turn out that way, huh?"

"Things been pickin' up lately," she lied. "Worst of it's over, they say."

The boy was on the phone again, explaining in a low voice why whoever it was couldn't return a call. "Phone's only good for making calls."

The three adults were transfixed by the negotiations.

"Okay, then. Well, just in case. The place is behind the courts in an adobe mall. Kinda blue-green." He looked up at the window. "It's called the Stop-in Café." Snorting, the kid tossed the phone down and put his head back on his arms. But one eye opened, fixing itself on the cash register again.

In the years she'd been here, Abby had always feared a robbery—especially after Ned took off. Or some sort of incident she was ill equipped to handle. Someone bursting through the door and demanding something from her—something she couldn't possibly provide. Something Ned hadn't put a price tag on. It was inevitable, wasn't it? But maybe not today. It was possible a relative was coming to pick the kid up. Maybe a parole officer, a priest. Someone harmless.

And she had the gun. When Ned first gave it to her, he insisted on taking her to a target range in Apache Junction where she could practice shooting.

"Not bad for the first time," he said, examining the target afterward. "You could really be something if you wanted to."

"Like what?" she'd asked. It'd be great to really be something.

"You two ought to try it out," she said suddenly to the couple.

"Try what out?" the woman said, finishing her tea. Her hands glistened with spilled sugar in the bright light.

"Running a café. See if it suits you. I can walk you through the place some day. I've had about enough Arizona for this life." She turned to the boy. "Hey, kid. Gotta name?"

He stood up, looking confused—like she'd asked him a difficult question.

"Got a job for you working with live things. Pay's not great, but they'll have a place for you to sleep. Food too. You good with animals?"

"You mean like dogs?"

She could picture someone coming through the door, someone with a gun or a grudge or a gripe of some sort. The gun in the microwave might not even work by now. Probably needed to oil it more than once every five years. Ned had said something about maintaining it. Faster she got this kid out of here, the better. She'd been wrong when she thought he was harmless. When she didn't pick up the scent.

"I think you're going to like this job I have in mind. There's a sign just before you get to Ironwood that says, 'We are looking for a dedicated person who is ready to commit to the care of unwanted and abused pot-bellied pigs. Is that YOU?'"

He seemed to think she was asking him the question rather than quoting the sign and said, "Yes." A pause. "Is it a real thing? What you just said—pot-bellied pigs?"

"Sure, it is. Place is about an hour north of here." She scrambled in the drawer for the card she kept handy. Sometimes she solicited donations for the place and stuck the card on a jar.

"There's a pig out there with your name on it," she said.

"I'd need a bus to get out there." He paused a minute. "And

the fare."

She was looking for the bus schedule when Hugh butt in. "We can give him a lift. Right, honey." He put a ten on the table, stashing his guidebook in his knapsack. "Planned to wander north anyway."

Abby slammed the drawer shut and handed Hugh the card. "Sure it's not out of your way? I got a bus schedule around somewhere."

The woman—Abby never did catch her name—said, "We're just trying places out today. Looking for an opportunity. Maybe we'll want to rescue dogs."

"Pigs," Abby said. "Pot-bellied pigs."

Hugh smiled. "We've done worse in our time." He looked at the boy and then at the card. "Ready for Ironwood, son?"

"Tell them I sent you," Abby said. "They'll know who Abby is."

The boy looked like an underfed twelve-year old walking out the door between them. The man, sensing this perhaps, took one arm. His wife took the other. Abby watched as they passed a trashcan where Hugh tossed the card she'd given him. They passed the tourist bureau without a sideward glance, closing in on the boy so she could hardly see him now. His disposable phone still lay on the table, she noticed. She was about to run after them when the bell rang and a customer came in.

Maybe he'd come back for the phone. She put it behind the counter and stuck the Slim Jim back in the glass jar.

"Won't You Pardon Me?"

Ron was pulling guard duty on the perimeter of a firebase in the A Shau Valley when his doorbell in Detroit rang. As the mountains faded and the line of suspicious-looking soldiers on the Ho Chi Minh Trail disappeared, he jerked awake. The bell rang rarely because of its odd placement on the doorframe, and almost the only person who could be leaning on it was his son. But Nat was in Afghanistan, a terrain that would, no doubt, be his son's dream landscape for the rest of his life. But Nat was not due home for three or four months, and he would've texted if his plans changed. A good kid, though at thirty-seven—or was it thirty-eight—kid was probably the wrong word. And, of course, his son had a key.

Ron's feet searched for his slippers as he shouted, "Just a minute." He had no idea if someone at the door could even hear him. Pressing down hard on the arms of the chair, he hoisted himself up. His knees threatened to buckle, but they manned up just in time. He'd grown skinny quickly. After years of toting around an extra thirty-five, it fell off in three or four months. He made his way to the door, stopping to rest along the way. It was only twenty-five feet, for God's sake. The doctor had said a year, possibly eighteen months. But didn't they always double the time it took for the cancer to kill you? He'd heard that once.

Someone had gouged the peephole out—probably him in

a drunken rage—so he had to open the door without looking. A tall woman with long gray hair tied up on her head stood there. He peered at her, thinking she looked an awful lot like Sally Pastor, his former mother-in-law. But Sal must be long gone.

He said her name anyway. "Sally? That you?"

The woman laughed sharply, almost a barking noise, and then he knew who it was. His ex-wife, Carmen, Sally's daughter.

"You've gotta be kidding," he said before he could stop himself.

"Do I really look like my mother?" she said, stepping inside before he'd even moved out of her way. "No one's told me that till now."

She still wore the same scent. Something spicy. He'd thought women gave up perfume long ago, but Carmen always was one for candles, flowers, and brewing herbal tea. The only person he'd ever known to remove perfume samples from magazines and stick them in drawers.

"She's dead. About six years now." When he said nothing, she added, "Heart."

He'd forgotten Carmen's sparse speech.

He shook his head. He'd always liked Sally—the only gringa in Carmen's Ecuadorian family. But he was in shock. Did things like this just happen? Carmen was standing two feet away from him like it was nothing unusual. He pulled himself together. "And Hector?"

Carmen looked at him quizzically. "He died before...before I left. Remember?"

He didn't remember. Or maybe he did. It must've been in the days of wine and doses—when he was lit most of the time.

"Car accident," she said. "Or truck, in his case." She looked around. "It's been twenty years."

"Deb call you?" he asked. And then suddenly, he added, voice rising, "She been keeping track of you all this time?" If she had, he'd have to strangle her, knowing as she did how hard he'd tried to find his wife.

"I got in touch a few months back. Thought I should know what was going on. Hear Nat's in the Middle East."

Nat was Ron's son from his first marriage, a union lasting a much shorter time than his second. Nat had lived with his mother in Traverse City growing up, visiting Ron and Carmen only occasionally.

"He'll be done with his tour soon."

"Right," she said, looking around. "Well, this place looks like it belongs to an old man, Ron." She sniffed. "Smells like it too."

"About right," he said. "I am an old man, 'case you didn't notice."

The amazing thing—he realized this on some level—was they were talking to each other like normal people. Despite their history, despite not seeing each other in twenty years, they sounded civil. He didn't even feel particularly angry about her telling him he smelled. It was exactly what he'd expect Carmen to say. And she said it easily—without rancor.

She went into the kitchen, Ron following her at his snail's pace. He wished he were wearing shoes instead of slippers. The shuffling put him at a disadvantage. Carmen, as if to highlight his inadequacy, looked great. She wore rust-colored boots with four-inch heels, her jeans tucked in; a flowing blouse in a vibrant green; dangling, amber earrings. He wondered if those loose threads still concealed a perfect body. Thirty years ago, you could look all day for a single imperfection. And look he did. Then and now.

God, if only he still could. Could he? Not that she would.

"Place is a mess, Ronnie. Someone needed to blow taps for

your refrigerator years ago. I bet it doesn't keep things cold enough."

She turned to look at him, stared for a few seconds, and then shut her mouth. First time he'd ever seen her do that, and it was unutterably depressing. What she saw took all the fight out of her. She turned around and began to clean, shaking her head at the smelly sponge, the empty bottle of cleanser.

"Got any baking soda? Vinegar?" she asked.

"What do you think?" he said, deciding to be feisty. Maybe she'd be too. "Hey, nobody said you had to do this. I'm going to get someone to come in. Just haven't gotten around to it." He slid a chair out from under the table and sat down. "So what are you here for? In Detroit, I mean." Before he could stop himself, he added, "To gloat?"

Shaking her head, she looked at her watch. "I only have a few hours. Let's see if I can get things into shape."

"A few hours to what?"

"Before my plane. It's at eight-thirty."

He looked at the kitchen clock. It was three p.m. "You flew in just to do this? To clean my kitchen." Flew in from where, he wondered? Where had she been for the last twenty years?

"It's just a layover. When Deb told me what was going on, I changed my flight so I could change planes in Detroit. See how things were going here." The sponge fell completely apart, and in desperation she grabbed a dishtowel.

"Not as bad as you think," he said, looking around for an explanation. "Even before I got sick, the place looked pretty much the same. Never was a great housekeeper."

She was throwing half of the food in his fridge away. "Hey, some of that stuff is fine," he said. "I'm not a millionaire, you know."

She held a container of something up to his nose, and he blanched.

"Where you been all this time?" he asked. Couldn't help himself.

"Lots of places," she said. "I ran until the money gave out. Then I got a job and settled in. Out in Oregon for the last ten years." She set a cup of coffee she'd made for him on the table. "Drink up. I still make good coffee."

It wasn't his regular mug, but he picked it up. She looked like a hippie. Always had. "If I had had to guess, it would've been Oregon."

She smiled.

"Did it help? All the running?"

"Nope. But somewhere along the way, the anger sort of wore off."

"Smoking weed a lot?" he asked. "That'll do it."

"Why do you think I picked Oregon? It's a forgiving part of the country. But it's an occasional thing nowadays. Something about gray hair and grass doesn't mix."

"Oh, I don't know," he said. "There's plenty of stoned gray-heads hanging 'round the VA."

"Still on John R?" She was tensing up, and he regretted bringing it up, reminding her.

"Yeah, but they built a spankin' new hospital. Looks like a hotel for toddlers."

He looked at her for a long minute as she swabbed out the bottom bins. Her arms were still strong—her skin smooth. She was—what—fifty-eight? He was over seventy. Before he could stop himself, it was out of his mouth. "So, along with getting rid of the anger, did you forgive me?"

She didn't say anything for a minute. Then, pursing her mouth, she answered, "Think you deserve forgiveness? I'm going upstairs to clean the bathroom. Why don't you wait here?"

Damn, why had he gone and brought it up? Not a day passed he didn't go back over the day of his daughter's death, his part in it. Surely it was the same for Carmen—not that she shared any of the blame. But they'd just gotten off on the right foot today and he'd gone and messed it up. As her feet climbed the steps, it began to run like a tape in his head.

Julia didn't know any of the other kids yet, and they'd talked her into going to a homecoming float party. She'd been a student at St. John of the Apostles parochial school through eighth grade and was shy and insecure in her new public high school. But eventually she agreed. She was excited when she learned the freshman float would be based on the movie *The Goonies*, one of her favorites. Carmen dropped her off on her way to the coffee hour for new parents, with Ron scheduled to pick her up at nine-thirty. Kids didn't routinely have cell phones then, but he had the address and telephone number of the host.

He'd gone over to the Vet's Hall around seven like he did most Friday nights, had a beer or two, then lost track of the time amidst the inundation of war stories passed around as readily as cigarettes and beer. By the time he arrived at the party, it was after ten-fifteen and the number of kids had thinned out. No one knew where Julia was—or even who she was. He turned out of the driveway and drove about a half mile before he saw the flashing lights, the smashed car, the sobbing driver. Julia, or her body as it turned out, had already been loaded into an ambulance and was on the way to the hospital. Carmen had already been called and was waiting at St. Joseph's when he arrived.

In a few terse sentences, Carmen told him what happened—something she'd just learned from a paramedic minutes before and hadn't yet absorbed. Julia, tired of waiting for Ron, had attempted to walk home down a dark road with no sidewalks, barely even a shoulder, and was hit by an elderly woman. Her car skidded on the wet autumn leaves and hit Julia, a tree, and a mailbox. Julia was probably killed on impact.

The recitation of these facts was Carmen's last words to him for days. But she told no one he'd been late to pick Julia up, allowing everyone to believe Julia decided to walk home for some reason. For a long time, he believed this deception was a good sign—protecting him had to mean Carmen would eventually forgive him.

But it didn't work out that way. Instead, Carmen's anger increased as the days passed. Her initial instinct to protect him faded, and she came to blame him for not stepping forward and acknowledging his culpability. She waited; he was silent. Would telling everyone he was responsible for his daughter's death bring her back? Would they feel any better about it? Would hating him alleviate anyone's pain? This is what he told himself in his more self-pitying moments. When he was cold stone sober, he told himself he was a coward since his silence made Julia look irresponsible.

Six months later, at the end of a period of pure misery for both of them, Carmen took off, and he completely fell apart. If Nat hadn't moved in with him, he'd probably have drunk himself to death. And then came the months, no, years, of looking for his wife. In those early Internet days, looking for someone was not so easy. He quit his job at Dodge to launch a search, and each job he replaced it with paid less money. Finally, he had to give up.

Carmen was standing in front of him when he woke up. Was it normal to fall asleep at the drop of a hat? He'd have to ask the VA doctor he'd been assigned.

"Sorry," he said, starting to rise and then stopping. "Can we talk before you go?" He looked at his wrist, but he hadn't worn a watch in months.

She sat down.

"So what have you been doing all this time?" Obviously,

she'd taken care of herself.

"You mean jobs, hobbies, friends?"

"All of it."

"I've had a lot of all three over the years. I have a few friends in Salem. Hobbies—well, gardening is great in Oregon. And right now I'm a vet's assistant. I took some courses a few years ago. Pay isn't great, but I like it. It's enough for me."

"Didn't even know you liked dogs."

"It was you who didn't like dogs," she said with a sigh. "Can I make you something to eat? There were a few salvageable items in the fridge."

"Don't have much appetite."

"So I see." She looked at him, head cocked. "Do you want to make love?"

He'd forgotten she'd always called it that. Never "have sex," or "go to bed." No four-letter words. It was always "make love." He was astounded she'd suggested it. Amazed. Reluctantly, he said, "Doubt I can."

"Well, we can fool around a little. See what happens." She put a hand on his thigh.

"For old time's sake?" He had trouble remembering the last time this had happened. Not just with Carmen—with anyone. Maybe with a waitress in the vet bar in Corktown. Would've been more than a year ago. Perhaps two. "You'll be able to count my ribs."

"Oh, I can think of better things to do than count."

He was starting to feel aroused already—it might work out. It'd probably be the last time—would certainly be their last time. The way things were going, he wouldn't make it until Nat came home. Nat has said to let him know when things got bad, but what was the point? He'd lived alone and now he'd die alone. But at least he'd have this. Or maybe he would.

In bed, it was almost like old times. He wondered if she'd

slipped something into his coffee. Well, that was okay. He didn't mind having a little help. She took the lead, straddling him in such a way her weight wasn't on him—spending a lot of time on touching, kissing, whispering. Had she always been this leisurely? There was always Julia in the next room to worry about back then. It inhibited him as much as her. But now, there was no reason not to moan, talk, whatever.

When they were done, when success was theirs, he tried to talk her into canceling her flight.

"I can't, Ronnie. I have to be on the flight." She was sitting up now—fooling around in her purse like women always seemed to do. What did they keep in there that called to them so often?

"Disappearing again. Carm? Running somewhere new." He shut his eyes and threw an arm over them to block the light. Tears were welling up.

"More or less."

"Leave me here to die alone, huh?" He sounded over-emotional, which he certainly was. He had very few ideas on how to keep her here, so he went for the first one that came to mind.

"Not exactly," she said.

"Then what?"

As he said it, he felt a prick in his leg.

"It's pentobarb, Ronnie. It'll just take ten seconds or so."

"You mean ten seconds to die? Now? Here?" He had no idea she was still this angry. "It ends with you murdering me? Because you never forgave me, right?"

She slipped the case back in her purse and stroked his brow. "No, baby, because I did. I did forgive you." The last thing he felt was her hair, loosened and soft, draping his face like an angel.

"Um Peixe Grande"

Though his eyes were squeezed tight against the morning light, Gas could hear Loretta in their bedroom doorway, his lunch bag crinkling in her hand. He also knew from a variety of signs and smells what the day outside was like: cloudy, damp, cold. He'd no desire to do what his wife had in mind, though he'd been a fisherman all his life— like his father and grandfather before him. The money earned from throwing a line or net in the water no longer put much food on the table, and Loretta was after him to get a job at one of the tilapia farms if he was determined to stay in the fish business.

"Take a good look, Gaspar," she'd said, stretching her arms out. "This place is fallin' down 'round us 'case you hadn't noticed. Fish from a Dish pays a livin' wage. Nobody makes it sittin' in a chewed-up boat anymore. Termites own more of it than you. If you'd signed onto one of the big operations—like the Buster Bragg crew—maybe then..." She was at it again, before his feet hit the ground.

Even the name of the tilapia farm made Gas cringe. He belonged out on real water, not in one of those huge structures where his job would be hauling out fish, or delivering them to a slaughterhouse or treatment facility. That wasn't about fishing at all. He liked to imagine every fish he caught had enjoyed a full, free life before he landed it in a fair fight. There was mutual dignity in this time-honored contest. Taking part in the butchery of trapped fish—that had never known a minute of liberty in a sea or lake or river—was disgusting.

"You're turning into a sentimental old fool," his wife said. "What do fish know about freedom? You know how big their brain is?"

About the size of yours, he felt like saying.

But instead, "The domestication of fish through farming is an environmental disaster." The pamphlet was in his pocket, and he patted it. "It's no better than how chickens are kept."

"Fancy words for a man with a leaky boat and a leaky house."

"You'd better get cracking," she said now, shaking the paper bag harder. "The ice-out's nearly over. You might even make a decent haul if you get out there early."

Loretta rolled her eyes as she said this—making it clear there was no chance of such a thing. She lost all respect for him years ago when he quit going out on the Atlantic with Buster Bragg. Their noisy camaraderie and rough behavior hadn't been his style either. What kind of fishermen drink beer all day and lunch on the pier's fast food, pock-marking the ocean with aluminum and paper trash?

"No breakfast?" he said. Eyes open now, he looked out the window glumly. What was that poem about November? 'No sun' was one of the lines. 'No comfortable feel in any member.' He didn't know what any of it meant exactly. And anyway, it was May, wasn't it?

"It's in here," she said, shaking the bag again. His Sam's Club breakfast bar was probably in pieces by now. "Your thermos is on the table, and there's a beef pasty for your lunch—if

I Bring Sorrow

you need one."

This was a slap at his early departure from the river yesterday. How long could you sit waiting for what wasn't going to come? He grimaced at the thought of the coffee—probably from yesterday's pot if a drop remained. She'd been known to hold the used grounds under the hot water tap in a pinch. He'd give anything for plain instant.

Tossing the bag on the bed, Loretta left the room, her feet heavy on the bare wood. She'd become stocky in the last few years. Of course, who was he to talk with his face wizened from the years on the water? On the day they married, people sighed at her beauty when she came down the aisle on her Dad's arm. But forty years had passed, hadn't it? Loretta never was able to have the children they both wanted, her job at the jeans factory had gone overseas, and all of her brothers left Maine long ago for better opportunities. She held that against him too.

"If Gil and Jaime had the gumption to move across the country, why can't we? California has an ocean. You can stick a pole in the Pacific if you have to fish like that."

But California was another country. With its movie stars, orange trees, and surfers. He'd sooner take off for the Azores.

Fifteen minutes later, Gas headed for the St. Croix River and hopefully some salmon. Maybe some bass too. He'd never been much of a saltwater fisherman, always preferring the inland waterways. The Atlantic was too vast—you could get lost in it. Instead, he usually headed for a lake, other times a river. He could fish there in solitude—a condition he preferred.

Half-drowsing, half-puttering along in one of the little alcoves he favored, Gas was thinking about the Red Sox's chances when the water suddenly grew choppy. A large motorboat approached. The wake was sizeable because of the boat's speed, and Gas slowed to a standstill to compensate, pointing his boat toward the wake to save it from overturning. Clearly, the man at the helm hadn't even noticed the small boat on its port side in the weeds. The name, The Clytemnestra, was painted on the boat in blood red letters. What sort of name was that for a boat? A far cry from the Lady Lucks you usually saw around here.

Seconds later, as the boat sped around a bend in the water, Gas heard an enormous splash. Perhaps a large catch fell overboard? Or even one huge fish? This happened occasionally. Inexperienced fishermen—like the idiots likely to be on that boat— didn't always secure their catches adequately, and the fish skidded back into the water. But in the inland waterways Gas knew, there were no fish big enough to make so much noise. Sturgeon—fish that might splash that way—were only in places like the Kennebec River.

He spotted the object. Whatever it was—and it looked like a single fish as he drew closer—was undulating madly, thrashing about. He pulled closer still, wondering if he could possibly catch the fish without capsizing his own boat. The thing had to weigh two hundred pounds. On closer inspection, whatever it was seemed to be wrapped in dirty tarp and tightly duct-taped every foot or so. Then he heard screaming, and it became obvious there was a man inside the bundle. Holy Mother of God!

Without considering the wisdom of his action, Gas grabbed at the canvas, succeeding in grasping an edge on his second try, and yanked it as hard as he could. After considerable effort, the squirming body was in his boat along with several gallons of river water. The boat rocked violently, then shuddered to a more controllable sway. Catching his breath, Gas slit the tarp open cautiously. The man inside was unconscious now. Water streamed from his mouth: a gaping hole in a gray face appearing lifeless. It was hard to decide whether to expel the water or supply him with oxygen first. Gas flipped

him over, pushed his head to one side, and began forcing water from the man's lungs. After a minute or two, the man's left
eye popped opened.

Minutes later, he was still wheezing, and occasional pieces
of tarp and seaweed as well as brackish water continued to
seep from his mouth. Gas pressed on his back until the flow
stopped. Then he turned the man over, did a minute or two
of old-fashioned mouth-to-mouth, and helped him to sit up
against the bench. The guy's color began to return; his panting
slowed. Gas grabbed a towel, a bottle of water, and a heavy
blanket from his dry box. The water temperature of a Maine
river in May was in the forties. The guy could go into shock—
and he was plenty old enough to have a heart attack. Gas dried
his head, wrapped the blanket around him, and offered him
the water.

"Drink." It was more a command than an invitation.

Looking at Gas skeptically, the man finally obeyed, still
shivering so intensely his teeth chattered. Gas looked around
for another blanket, finally coming up with a piece of dry canvas. Then he waited—his hands and feet under attack by pins
and needles—for the man to recover. In all his years at sea,
nothing equaled this.

"Someone trying to murder you?"

It sounded like a joke when he said it aloud, but what else
could it be? The man continued to pant and shiver, and Gas
waited.

"So it would seem," the man finally said, rubbing his head
with the towel. He coughed up some more debris. "If you
hadn't come along, I'd be swimming with the fishes."

Neither man laughed. In fact, Gas had no inclination to
discuss the event beyond this brief exchange, and neither, it
seemed, did his passenger.

"Where should I take you?" Gas said, starting up the motor again. "You need to get out of those wet clothes pronto." The man's shivering continued.

"Anywhere on the shore. Have a cell?"

Even a poor fisherman didn't travel without one, and Gas tossed it to him.

"Not much of a signal," the man said, looking at the phone.

"We'll be ashore in five minutes."

"Hey, thanks." The man paused as if considering his words. "A thank you isn't enough, of course. What could be enough after what you did?"

Neither of them wanted to say what that "something" was. Gus looked out onto the river; the other boat was gone.

"Give me your address and I'll send you a check," the man said. "A check big enough for a long vacation. Or whatever you want. Something anyway."

"I don't want your money." And Gas certainly didn't want to hand this man his address. He was anxious to put a wide berth between them. And an even wider berth between himself and the other boat—whatever its crazy name was. Men like that would have guns onboard. And not be afraid to use them.

"Well, what then?" The man stared at the phone as if an idea would come from it. "You have to take something." He coughed and shook his head. "I can't be in your debt."

"Nothing. Nothing at all." All Gus could think about was that speedboat reappearing on the horizon. What would happen to a witness of an attempted murder? "And you're not in my debt. Anyone would've done the same."

The man shook his head. "Not the men I know."

"Then you know the wrong men."

The man said nothing, but from the look on his face, Gas knew what he said was the truth.

Dockside, a few minutes later, Gas helped him climb out

of the boat.

"Look, take my card at least," the man said, reaching for his pocket. But he'd been stripped of any identification. In fact, to both of their horror, his pockets were filled with stones.

"Well, if that doesn't beat…" The man shrugged.

Gus thought again about the boat that sped away. Had they spotted him? If they had, they certainly would've returned to see to him. See to them both, no doubt. The weeds and water plants in the boggy alcove must have hidden his boat. Did they believe this guy was at the bottom of the river? The stones suggested they must.

"Make your call," Gas said, nodding toward the phone.

After a brief discussion—and Gas couldn't help but overhear the name "Pinto" twice—he was back. "Okay, my name's Pasquale Trota. I'm putting my number in your contacts." He punched it in. "If I can ever do anything for you, give me a call. I mean it," he said. "Something might come to you later." He paused. "I have friends in lots of places."

And enemies in others, Gus thought. But he said nothing.

"I won't ask your name. It's probably better I don't know it. Look, could you hang around for a minute or two?" When Gus didn't respond, he added, "Not gonna lie to you. I'm kinda spooked." Gus nodded.

A dark SUV picked him up in five minutes. The man turned back and nodded before he climbed inside. Gas held up a hand, glad he'd never given Mr. Trota his name, glad Trota hadn't asked. This affair, strange and worrisome, would end right here.

Back home after another disappointing day fish-wise, he thought about telling Loretta about Mr. Trota. But she had a way of making a good deed or something innocent seem foolish. And the more he ran through the story in his head, the more he could imagine her saying he was dim-witted not to have accepted a reward. It'd be hard to make her understand the terror the enormous splash and the quick departure of that boat had filled him with. He'd done nothing brave—hadn't even known what it was he was pulling out of the water.

Instead, he got a tongue-lashing for returning with only enough fish to make a trifling dinner. The next day, when it poured rain, Loretta insisted on Gus going down to the human resources office at Fish in a Dish and filling out an application. As he sat in the HR room with several other fellows, all decades younger than he and twice as muscular, he was filled with despair. Why would anyone hire him when clearly these younger and stronger fellows would make better employees? So even here—at this terrible place—he would fail. And, predictably, the man behind the desk hardly bothered to read his application once he took a quick look at him.

"My father did commercial fishing when I was a kid," he told Gas. "Takes the stuffing out of you. And look, Mr..." he looked down at the application, "Rios. You wouldn't like it here. It's not like fishing at all. It's back-breaking work even for a young man."

"But it pays a wage, right?" Gas said, feeling he had nothing to lose.

"Probably not much more than you can earn on your own."

"Any luck?" Loretta asked before his right foot was inside the door. She was darning his wool socks, an activity she only engaged in when she wanted sympathy for the hard life—or fate—Gaspar had dealt her.

"The guy who interviewed me said I'd have to wait and see," Gas said, not wanting to go into it with her now. She'd blame him for not convincing HR he was a man who could haul a half a ton of fish out of a tank. "Looked good though," he added, trying to get a few hours peace. "I got the feeling..."

She smiled, but he could tell she wasn't convinced. "You

did go down there, didn't you?"

He reached into his jacket and threw his copy of the paperwork on the table, then strode off, trying to look like a man who could pull half a ton of fish out of a tank.

"Mr. Trota?" he found himself saying into his cell phone a few weeks later. He hadn't planned the call at all—but somehow ended up making it, bringing up the contact and pushing the button.

"Who wants to know?"

It was the lowest pitched voice he'd ever heard and not Mr. Trota's. "He won't know my name."

"He knows everyone's name," the man said.

"Yeah, but I…"

"Look, if you want to talk to him, you gotta tell me your name. Go ahead, I'm not gonna tell anyone else."

"Okay, well, it's Gaspar Rios."

"What kinda name is Gaspar?" the man asked. He didn't sound curious as much as he seemed to be preparing the information for Mr. Trota.

"Portuguese. I fish in the St. Croix. That's where we—"

"Oh, sure. You're the guy who pulled him out of the lake. Right?"

"River."

"Right, river. Told me about it. Okay, then. He'll be right here."

"Gaspar Rios, huh?" Mr. Trota said a few seconds later. "Spanish?"

"Portuguese."

"Sure, sure, I shoulda figured." He paused. "Things okay with you? Didn't hurt your boat, did I?"

"Boat's good."

"Well, how can I help you, Gaspar?"

"Gas," Gas said. "My friends call me Gas."

"And I'm gonna be your friend, huh." Mr. Trota paused. "Well, you deserve it. I wouldn't be sitting here drinking this beer or smoking this Robusto if it wasn't for you. Pulling me out of the water like you did. Like the biggest fish you ever caught, huh? So, how can I be your friend, Gas?"

Gas took a deep breath and plunged in, still not knowing exactly what he wanted.

"I wondered if you might have a job for me. Doesn't have to be anything fancy…" Gas felt as awkward as he had at Dish of Fish or whatever it was called. What in the world would a man like Mr. Trota have for him to do? Why didn't he think of something definite before calling?"

"A job for a fisherman?" Mr. Trota laughed. "I don't even eat fish, Gus."

"Gas."

"Gas, right. You wanna sell me fish. That's what you're saying? Maybe you think I have a restaurant. Louie, do I have a restaurant?" Both men at the other end of the line laughed.

"No restaurant, I'm afraid, Gas."

"Maybe I can watch the river for you."

"Watch the river?" Mr. Trota paused. "You mean the St. Croix? Like watch the current move the water?" He laughed again. Gas had never known a man to laugh so much. Especially one nearly murdered a few weeks before. Before he could answer, Mr. Trota answered his own question.

"Of course that's not what you mean. Just yanking your chain. You mean watch the river in case someone tosses me off a boat again? Hey, I got Louie here. And a couple other amici. Look, that's not the way it works, Gas. If they come after me again—which they will—it'll be some other way. Unless they're dumber than I think."

Gas heard him say to Louie, "We can only hope." Both men

laughed. Gas got the feeling they used laughter in some other way than he did. He couldn't remember the last time he'd laughed. No one he knew laughed. What was there to laugh about?

"How much do you earn a year hauling fish out of the lake, Gas?"

Gas told him.

Mr. Trota whistled. "You actually live on that? What's your wife, some corporate bigwig?"

"Nah, she takes care of me and the house." Gas thought of the lunch waiting in his paper bag. He'd bet anything it was last night's meatloaf. Loretta put pickle relish on it when she made a sandwich—like it was an added treat. Forty years on, and he still hated sweet pickles on his meatloaf sandwich. But nothing stopped her.

"At Our Lady of Guadalupe's, they rave about my meatloaf sandwiches," she told him.

Mr. Trota sighed now. "Hold on a sec, Gas." Gas heard him talking to someone else—probably Louie—again. "Look, Gas, tell you what. I'll match your earnings for a year. So you can go out wherever and fish, and I'll equal what they pay you for fish down on the docks. Maybe by the time the year is up, something else will come along. Or maybe we'll come up with an idea."

Gas thought about it. "So you're gonna pay me just to do what I've always done? Just sit on the water and fish?"

"Sure. You can keep an eye out for the other boat. You might save my ass twice. Never know. Right, Lou?" Lou murmured his assent. And, unsurprisingly, they laughed.

Gas could tell Mr. Trota didn't believe such a thing would happen, and neither did he. He thought he'd recognize the boat, but he couldn't remember the name anymore. Mr. Trota must've read his mind because he said, "The Clytemnestra,

Gas. Must be a Greek—that cattivo in the boat—wants my ass in a sling. Everything's global now, isn't it? Want a hitman today, gotta call Serbia or Cambodia. So you keep an eye out. Not that I think Pinto's boys are still out cruising the waterways of Maine. But you never know."

Weeks went by. Every time Gas sold fish to the wholesalers, he went to the library, copied the receipt and mailed it to Mr. Trota. Mr. Trota deposited money in Gas' account. As summer came, the daily haul picked up. He finally broke down and showed the bank numbers to Loretta, thinking to improve her opinion of him.

"Guess you were right to stick with the old ways of doin' things," she said, staring at the figures. "Sure the bank didn't goof it up?"

"You think a bank ever makes a mistake in my favor?"

She kept nodding, but he felt like she was really shaking her head, convinced he was pulling something over on her.

The St. Croix River runs seventy-one miles in length and forms part of the Canadian-U.S. border, and Gas usually fished either the river itself or one of the lakes lying along its path. He was just a few miles from the ocean and yet it never drew him.

"It's like you're afraid of it," Loretta once theorized. "The big bad ocean. Ooh." She rolled her eyes and wiggled her fingers.

"No, but I give it the respect it deserves," he told her. "I'm comfortable where I am."

"Comfortable," she'd said. "That's all you ever think about. Well, I'm not comfortable where I am."

He'd grown slack and lazy over the winter, telling himself he was too old for the sort of jobs he could find. He even turned down the church's offer to plow their lot, an easy couple of grand.

I Bring Sorrow

For the first time since his arrangement with Mr. Trota, a month had passed without a bank deposit. He feared he was at the end of the soup line and began to look at the prospect of a forced retirement.

Seven bridges crossed the St. Croix, but Gus wasn't near one of them in May when he saw the boat again. The Clytemnestra. It was slowly making its way up the river, hugging the Canadian bank. Gas, on his boat, was sitting inside a marshy alcove half a mile south of the larger boat's entry point from a canal. It was a good place to fish and a good place to spy, although, truthfully, he'd long ago given up any idea of spotting the boat. He'd long ago concluded Mr. Trota only gave him this assignment to justify paying him off for his good deed.

Gas watched the boat drop anchor at a point where a rusty old truck with a beat-up trailer was waiting. Couldn't even tell the color of either one. It was certainly not a normal place to either load or unload cargo. There was no beach at all, and the incline was such the nose of the truck was nearly in the water. In fact, the man who got out of the cab had his hands full not sliding into the river. Clearly something was wrong with this operation. Before Gas could think about what exactly felt wrong, another man climbed out of the truck, and together the two men opened the trailer and dragged five women—no, make that girls—out. All of them were bound at the hands, blindfolded, and gagged. Each wore a very short skirt, was preternaturally thin, and staggered in high heels. From their uniformly dark, straight hair, Gus thought they were probably Asian girls, although they could have been wearing wigs. Today looked to become far worse than the one with Mr. Trota. Gus was shaking so hard he worried the boat would tip.

Within a minute or two, the girls were loaded onto The Clytemnestra. The next-to- last girl fell, losing her shoe. The man holding her arm seemed ready to strike her. Then he grabbed the heel that was stuck in the mud, pushed her down, and put it back on her foot. Although Gas couldn't hear anything, he knew she was sobbing from her shaking shoulders. Even from this distance, he could tell they were very young girls—perhaps fourteen. It could have easily been his niece, Theresa, getting loaded on the boat to hell.

Stomach in his throat, he picked up his cell and called 911, telling the dispatcher what he'd seen.

"And where was this?" the officer asked.

Gus gave him the coordinates, the name of the boat, and information about the truck and trailer making the delivery. The boat was practically out of his range already and the truck had pulled out of the drop spot, the trailer moving in a jerky fashion as the driver tried to back up.

Gas also gave his name and number.

"Do you want me to wait here?" he asked.

"Is the boat still in sight?"

It wasn't. So the dispatcher said he might as well go home and wait for an officer to show up and take down his story.

"Might have saved four lives today," the fellow said. "Who knows what those men had in mind for those girls. They probably picked them up in Toronto or Montreal. They could end up anywhere in the States." He paused. "Leave it to us, Mr. Rios. We'll get the guys who did this."

"Five," Gas corrected him. "There were five girls."

"Right. You probably saved five lives today."

Gas debated going home to tell Loretta. But it would take more than an hour so he called his friend instead. He'd called him once or twice over the last few months, mostly to thank him for a few deposits he made when the river was frozen and there were no fish to be had. When Gas had let the man's money put food on their table.

"That was real nice. You didn't have to do that."

I Bring Sorrow

"What do you usually do for cash in the winter?" Mr. Trota has asked him.

"Plow snow for people I know. Chop wood for some shut-ins. Doesn't pay much but it covers my oil deliveries." Except this year when I got lazy, he thought, but didn't say.

He'd resisted calling Mr. Trota last month when no deposit turned up. How long could he expect such an arrangement to last? How could he hold his hand out again?

Today, he expected he'd be warmly thanked. Surely this would put the crew of the boat behind bars. Mr. Pinto's goose would be cooked. His friend wouldn't have to worry about taking a dive off that boat ever again.

"Hello," he said, recognizing Louie's voice but not wanting to chance using his name. Maybe he wasn't supposed to know any of these guys. "It's Gaspar Rios. Is Mr. Trota in?" Then his excitement broke through. "Guess what, I saw that boat today. You know, The Clytemnestra." He wasn't certain if he'd pronounced it correctly. "Know the one I mean?"

"Yeah, sure," Louis said. "Funny thing you should call. I think he forgot all about how you were out there looking for it. But it's okay 'cause he's out on the boat himself. Weird, huh?"

"What?"

"Yeah, he bought the boat about a month ago from Mario Pinto. Decided a nice little boat with a crackerjack crew might come in handy. He decided to turn his enemies into friends for some deal he had goin'." When Gas didn't respond, Louie added, "His business sometimes works like that." He laughed. "But more often, its vice-versa. Friends turn into enemies."

Gas had never felt worse in his life. More than anything, he wanted to ask Louie not to tell Mr. Trota he called. But instead, he hung up quietly, sat thinking for a minute, and then got some of the California brochures his wife kept forcing on him out of the hold. As he slipped the rubber band off, he wondered if the car was too old to make a cross-country trip. Or if he and Loretta were. He guessed they'd find out.

> "Lie thou there; for here comes the trout
> that must be caught with tickling."
> -William Shakespeare

Doe in Headlights

Exit MI 53 at Cass City, and then hook a left on the gravel road across from a yellow Caddy.

Doe looked around. The question she'd been asking herself for three hours—how could Feck know the car would be parked there—was answered when she saw a sun-bleached Cadillac up on blocks. She wouldn't have known the color if the directions hadn't said yellow. The house behind it was mostly bare wood. Just strips of an undeterminable color remained. How much time had passed since the last paint job?

She shivered and turned up the heat. November in Michigan, right. Just one hundred and fifty miles northwest of Detroit, but she was in another zone. This area—and she could easily picture its position on the hand Michiganders held up to point to a spot—was a popular summer destination. But on a gray, late autumn day, there was no sign of mini-golf, tee shirt shops, fudge or kayaks. Where was the lake anyway? She made the turn, paper map in her mouth, and crept along looking for:

A banged-up pre-fab boathouse.

There it was, and "banged-up" was putting a good spin on it. It looked glued together—like the popsicle-stick log cabins she made as a kid. She took the next right and the gravel gave way to dry, sandy dirt covered with pine needles and decaying leaves plucked from the trees towering above. It was just like the setting in that goofy horror movie—the one Feck tried to explain when they were high on something.

She'd been working for Feck for nearly two years, starting

95

immediately after Ruthie took a flyer and moved to Vegas.

"She's got the legs for it, Doe," Feck said, throwing Ruthie's scrawled note on the table. "Showgirl gams."

"She's cleaning hotel rooms," Doe told him. "Or toting a tray. She may have the legs, but she doesn't have the feet." Ruthie was the most graceless person she knew.

Up until Ruthie's surprise flight, Doe's name had been Delores, and it took her a minute to realize she'd been renamed.

"How do you spell that?" she asked him. "How do you spell Doe?"

He spelled it for her, and that was that. They had sex for the first time that night—like an initiation or something. She could still smell Ruthie on his sheets. And it wasn't perfume, since Ruthie didn't wear any. Ruthie on the Sheets, as she thought of that scent, was soon replaced.

Doe waitressed at a bunch of dumps outside Detroit before Feck took her on. She supposed her job with him wasn't much better, but there was more variety. He was good at mixing things up, even if he wasn't anything special in bed. He had to be nearly forty, so what could she expect? He'd probably memorized his moves twenty-five years ago and saw no reason to change them now.

Feck paid her to clean and cook, deliver and pick up an assortment of packages, pretend to be various people, have sex with him about twice a week, answer his phone, make bank deposits, place bets at the track, make phone calls using her knack for accents, and take care of his fish, although she could hardly count that chore because she'd killed them within a week. His mother, her next charge, fared better.

Mrs. Feck had one of those diseases—Doe couldn't remember the name—where she could hardly lift her head. So for the last six months of her life, Doe took charge—wiping her ass, feeding her oatmeal and scrambled eggs, even holding a tissue to her nose, and changing her Depends. She learned how to inject insulin, and bathe her without soaking the sheets. She even—and this was the worst of it— inserted suppositories. The two of them watched television about sixteen hours a day. The old woman couldn't speak in more than grunts so figuring out what she wanted—and it was mostly about shows on TV— was frustrating. She'd been particularly incensed when the network cancelled her favorite soap.

"Work out a system," Feck told her when she complained. "Maybe she can tap things out, like with Morse Code. Or blink her eyes, yes and no." For his part, he saw his mother as seldom as possible. "She wasn't exactly a mother-of-the-year," he said. "I was never sure she could tell my brother and me apart."

"Are you twins?"

"No, and he has six inches on me."

Doe duct-taped a pencil to Mrs. Feck's palsied hand once, but the old woman shook it off, nearly hitting Doe in the eye. Despite these minor issues, she grew fond of the old lady. Having someone depend on her turned her on. Like she was Mrs. Feck's mother in some sense. She wasn't clear on the reason for it.

"I think I might want to have a baby some day," she told Feck after his mother passed. "Or maybe a puppy."

"Good luck with that," he told her. "As long as you're not thinking I'll be the daddy."

Actually, she'd already ruled Feck out as father material. But he paid her a better salary than she made at the Weekday Café or Tudge's Pub, so as employer material, he'd do. Once in a while, she caught the whiff of something bad going down, an event giving her pause. One too many Serbian or Bosnian girls turned up on their porch last spring, for instance. And there was the time she heard a man screaming with pain on Feck's cell.

The thing Doe did most often was wait. Wait for a phone call, for a car to show up, for the bank to open, for food at a drive-in, for a clerk at the post office, for Feck to call her, for him to finish up in bed. Wait. She'd become very good at waiting.

She'd no idea what was in the cards today. Feck said he'd call at two and fill her in. Looking at her watch, she saw it wasn't even noon. The next marker on her map was:

Look for a big-ass sign saying Todd's Cabins.

She found it a minute or two later. A Closed for the Season sign hung in front. Skiing would begin in a month, but Todd's was not the sort of place skiers stayed. She doubted hunters would find their way here either. Todd's Cabins probably closed for the season after Labor Day—as soon as old Todd needed heat to keep warm, as soon as he cleared winter beer money.

There were eleven cabins—a number that made her nervous until she realized that one was Todd's office so it didn't count. Odd numbered things always seemed like a jinx. She looked for number four. Four was the only one whose windows weren't boarded. She put the key in the lock and pushed the sticking door open.

Something had died inside. But other than the smell, it wasn't a bad place—two tiny bedrooms and a main room with a kitchenette at one end. A bathroom that was reasonably clean. Todd or Mrs. Todd had made the place kind of homey with plaid slipcovers and curtains, a lacy tablecloth, although it turned out to be plastic. A couple of prints of the northern woods. She could picture spending a week here with your kids in the summer. Kids—that thought kept returning. Had her parents ever stopped fighting long enough to take her sister and her to a place like this? She couldn't remember a single vacation. Bible school was the furthest she got from home.

I Bring Sorrow

The ladies who ran the Bible school knew they were babysitting Sheila and Delores and made them memorize Bible verses while the other kids got to color Joseph's coat.

A dead mouse was in the bathroom, and another in the drawer of the stove. Using fireplace tongs, she threw both outside. Several dead wasps lay curled up on the windowsills, but other than that it was okay. Smelled like mildew, suntan lotion, insect repellent, and burnt onions once the odor of death was removed. Someone had been by recently because there was fresh food in the cabinets and more in the fridge. It wasn't like Feck to think of things like this, which made her suspicious. There was a space heater in each room that she immediately fired up. Maybe enough stuff onhand for a long weekend. It'd better be enough because she hadn't passed a store for miles—maybe not since Lexington. Even the house with the Caddy was four or five miles back.

Cabin four was the furthest from the road and Feck told her to park her car in the back even though there was no road there. As she looked out the window, she began to get worried. Obviously, he didn't want anyone spotting her car and nosing around. What was she doing here anyway? What did he have in mind? It couldn't just be a drug pickup. Someone must be coming up here for a few days, and she was going to stay too because Feck had made her pack a bag. She hoped she wasn't expected to sleep with whoever it was. Probably not, or Feck would've had her pack differently.

"Just some jeans, tee shirts, and underwear," Feck said. "You won't be goin' out on the town." He looked at her face and said in a wheedling tone, "Nothing's open 'round there now anyway."

"What will I be doing?"

He hated it when she asked him things like that—preferring not to let her in on the details unless he had to, and only then when it was unavoidable.

A good example—she hadn't known she'd be caring for Mrs. Feck until the night before.

"Her nurse took off," Feck had said. "Do me a favor and stay with her till I can find another minder."

Ha!

"Just wait for my call," he'd said this morning. "Things are a little fluid." Still in bed, he'd run a nervous hand through the hair on his chest. "Better get going, honey."

So she did, used to doing whatever she was told.

There was a small TV in the cabin, but no cable. She was only able to tune in one channel, so she watched Family Feud and some dopey talk show. Hungry then, she heated up a can of tomato soup using half water and half milk, ate some crackers, and made a pot of coffee.

Two o'clock came and went. She found a Robert Parker book on a shelf in a bedroom closet and began to read. She'd become more of a reader now that she cooled her heels so often.

At three thirty, she heard a car pull up and ran to the bedroom window. It wasn't Feck's Tahoe but a non-descript Dodge. It sat there for a few minutes, and then a man she'd never seen before got out, opened the rear door, and lifted out a sleeping kid. The boy was maybe about eight or ten, she decided, as the man tossed him over his shoulder like a sack of flour. Had this guy rented one of the other cabins? The man was younger than Feck, maybe thirty or so, and big. He was bearded, but it was neatly trimmed. He wore a hunter's getup with big black boots.

She figured he might be here for deer season, but then he headed straight for cabin four and kicked the door open. Why hadn't she locked the damned thing, up here all alone? She had a feeling a lock wouldn't have stopped him for more than a second or two anyway. Inside, he looked even bigger.

"You in here?" he whispered. "Doe, right?" When she didn't answer, he added, "Feck said you'd be here."

She walked out of the bedroom.

"He never filled you in, did he? Damn limey." He walked into the second bedroom and placed the kid on the bed.

"That kid isn't dead, is he?" Doe asked, her voice shaking.

"Of course he's not dead. Boy, Feck really did keep you in the dark. Kid's our little honey pot, and we're going to take real good care of him." He looked at her. "Or you are anyway. Feck said you were like a nurse."

She stared at him. "I'm not a nurse. What's your name anyway?"

He shook his head. "I'm just here to drop off the kid along with some stuff he'll need. You don't need to know my name." He headed for the door. "I'll get the rest of it."

"I can't take care of him. What's wrong with him?" The kid still hadn't moved.

The guy turned around and shook his head. "Damn, Feck didn't tell you squat. Kid's knocked out, and you'll have to keep him like that for a day or two. Till his parents pay up."

A funnel of cold air swept from her throat to her stomach. "What do you mean keep him like that?"

"Keep him unconscious. Just wait till I get the rest of it." The man trudged back to the car, opened the trunk, and removed an attaché case along with the kind of box that paper comes in. She watched, trying to decide quickly what this all meant. Trying to get a jump on things. Her brain was dead though. Terror did that.

"Okay," he said, returning, "the box has some stuff you might need—kid's clothes mostly—in case he pisses his pants, I guess. But the attaché has the important thing." He opened it and took out what looked like a medical kit. "This kit has about a half-dozen or so prepared shots in it." He counted them slowly and aloud. "Eight of 'em."

"What…"

"You know syringes—I guess." He glanced at her. "Hypodermics. You should know, bein' a nurse and all."

"I'm not a nurse," she almost shouted, but then lowered her voice. "I am…nothing."

He shrugged. "Well, whatever you are, you gotta give him one of these injections about every six hours." He paused dramatically. "'Cause if you don't, the kid's gonna wake up, and then where will we be?"

"You mean he's kidnapped, don't you?"

"Well, duh! Think I brought him here to go to the water park?"

She was speechless.

"Oh, and Feck sent a mask along." He opened the box and removed it. It was rubber or latex and looked like Snow White's face. "If the kid wakes up for some reason, you should put this on. So he can't ID you later." When she didn't say anything, he continued. "He's old enough to be able to do it too." He looked her over closely. "You look ordinary to me. But you never know."

"Whose kid is he?"

"Some fat cat works at GM, I think. Feck didn't tell me much. We're at the bottom of the food chain, you and me."

"Not even a name?" she asked. "The kid's name, I mean."

The guy let out an exaggerated sigh. "Look, you don't want to be talking to the kid, Doe Re Mi. Get it? You want him out cold till his daddy pays up. Don't be thinking you're gonna have cookies with him or something." He looked at the syringes in the kit, putting a hesitant finger on one. "You know how to do this, right?"

"I guess." What was the point in denying it?

She was trying to understand why Feck thought she'd be up for such a thing. Nothing she'd done could touch this. She'd show him. She'd be out of this cabin as soon as the hairy joker left. She could be in Canada in a couple of hours. Or did you need a passport for that now? Damn 9/11.

He must've sensed her line of thought. "You know Feck's got all kinds of stuff on you, right? Keeps a file on all of us. If you think ole Ruthie's living the life out in Vegas, you don't understand him at all."

For a minute, she couldn't remember who Ruthie was. "What do you mean a file?"

The man reached into his pocket and removed a small envelope, handing it to her. "Said to give it to you if need be." Inside was a photo of her exchanging money for drugs in a park in Detroit. Another showed her removing the license plate on a Camry out in Warren, the GM Tech Center looming behind her. Bent over, her ass looked as big as a basketball. Why had no one told her this? She swallowed hard.

"Feck's been setting you up for bigger stuff ever since you turned up. Testing you in little ways. But don't worry about this escapade." He nodded toward the bedroom where the boy was. "This one's gonna go off like clockwork." He paused, looking at her carefully. "Kid gets his next injection at seven p.m. Then one every six hours after that. Can you remember that? Know how to set the alarm on your phone?"

"What if something goes wrong?"

"Nothin's going wrong, worrywart. Just wear your mask if he starts to come 'round—wear it when you give him his meds too. Don't be a hero. If he yells, no one can hear him out here. But keep him asleep. A doctor fixed it all up. He'll be fine. This doc fixes tranqs for dogs on plane trips all the time—big dogs even. This is the same deal."

"Tranqs for dogs," she repeatedly numbly.

On his way out the door, he grabbed her car keys from the table.

"Hey," she started to say.

"Don't worry. You'll get 'em back when I pick up the kid." He shrugged. "Look, you could bolt, and we can't have him here all by himself. Don't want him to wander into the woods and get eaten by a bear. You got your phone, right?"

"Right."

She was in this—whatever it was—up to her neck. Her second thought was had she brought her charger? Third, who would she call anyway? Feck cut her off her from everyone long ago. Not that there'd ever been a big social scene in her life.

"Oh, and one more thing. Feck might call you to take a picture of the kid. Know how to do that? Take a picture and send it to him?"

She nodded.

"Practice by taking one of me now."

What world did this bozo think she lived in? Dully, she pulled out a phone and complied.

"Now send it to me. Just for practice." He gave her his cell number and in seconds, he had the photo.

"Good. Wow, I could use a haircut," he said, looking it over. "Now I'll take your picture." He made her pose with the kid on the bed, making her put a hand on the boy's cheek, hold his hand. Nurse Doe.

She did all of this numbly, not taking it in right away. Not figuring it out.

After that, he erased his number from her phone and took off. "Doesn't matter, of course. It'll be in the trash five minutes after Feck has it. Guy doesn't miss a trick."

For the next three hours, she sat staring at the kid, thinking about how dead she'd be if anything went wrong, leaning over him every few minutes to be sure he was breathing. She googled missing kids. Nothing fitting his description. She plugged her phone into the charger then and crept around the house, looking for something, though she'd no idea what. She gave the kid his next injection and continued to watch him, only leaving the bedside to pour some cereal. She could've guessed Feck would choose Fruit Loops. The milk tasted like cream. She finished the coffee from earlier.

She needed to stay awake, but around ten, she fell asleep anyway, waking to find the boy staring into her face. It looked like he wasn't fully awake. She realized after a second or two he couldn't really see her clearly between the effect of the drugs and the darkness of the poorly lit cabin. She considered putting on her mask just in case, but his eyes were fuzzy and unfocused. It was too early for his next injection so she kept still, and gradually his eyes shut.

Where the fuck was Feck? She dialed his number and left a message. "Call me, you jerk." She began reading her Parker book again, remembering the ending sixty pages in.

The kid started coughing about six a.m., a few hours later. His forehead was hot, really hot. Shit. Would it be safe to inject him if he was sick? She called Feck again. Still no answer, so she left a detailed message, trying hard not to sound too angry, too dangerous.

Another hour passed. She found some aspirin in her purse, and after grinding a tablet to a paste, held a finger to the kid's lips. Perhaps intuitively, he licked her finger. It was probably just a simple cold, but she began to worry more. She put on her mask and woke him up.

He didn't seem surprised to see a woman in a Snow White mask. Perhaps his life was filled with events like this. Hers had been.

"What happened to Obama?" he asked sleepily. "Where'd

Obama go?

She wasn't sure what he meant until she realized the guy who dropped him off probably wore a mask too.

"Back to D.C., I guess. How do you feel?" She put a hand on his forehead. "You're burning up."

But he was already sleeping again, his breath more ragged than before, his face glowing red. Now she wondered if it was the virus rather than the drugs knocking him out.

She yanked her phone out of the charger, noticing the power read less than five percent. The outlet must be disabled. If she called 911 for help, they'd have a record of her cell phone number. She knew by now that there was no way this was going to end well. She could end up with Ruthie—probably in the ground—or she could end up in a cell. But she would not be responsible for letting the kid die.

"There's a sick kid here," she told the woman who answered her call. "Sorry, I'm not sure of his name. Yeah, I know it's strange." She gave her location and the woman knew the spot right away.

"Todd's? Sure. Just stay where you are," the dispatcher told her. "It'll be a little wait. Our funds were slashed and we have to use the EMS from Caseville. We'll do our best. Hang on tight."

She knew the woman would not be so conciliatory once she found out what was going on out at Todd's, but it was nice to hear a friendly voice for now. After she hung up, she gave some brief thought to fleeing on foot, to even holing up in that Caddy. But snow was beginning to fall and it was miles away. Since she had nowhere else to go, she dampened a cloth and put it on the kid's head. She listened to his pulse. She covered him with a warmer blanket. She ground another aspirin. She tried to be his nurse.

And she waited. She was good at waiting.

Mad Women

"Come this way, miss."

Like Paul Winchell, the ventriloquist on television, the man's lips hardly moved at all. "Don't want to make a fuss now, do we?" His head swiveled toward the crowd of shoppers threatening to engulf them.

Eve Moran, his prisoner, appraised potential paths of escape, and then, head down, went along. The grip on her arm bordered on assault. She wondered if the Belgian lace sleeves on her pink linen suit jacket would bear his fingerprints forever.

The uniformed operator in the elevator shot her a sympathetic glance as the apparatus delivered them to the top floor. Her capture played out efficiently because the sophisticated security procedures of this august store detained shoplifters and miscreants every day: women who couldn't keep their hands off the merchandise; agile men who picked pockets; scoundrels of both sexes with stolen charge plates; boys who broke things, then ran; teenage girls who sneaked into dressing rooms and exited resembling polar bears; females who ransacked makeup counters, dropping tubes, pencils, and nail polish bottles down their blouse or into their pockets; teams of professional boosters who made a science out of defrauding stores. It was 1962 and store theft was becoming professional-ized.

No one spoke or even glanced at Eve as she passed down narrow hallways, walking up a final flight of narrow, uncarpeted steps. The detective, if that's what he was called, showed her inside a gloomy office, holding the door open without saying a word. The room was dark, tiny, and windowless except for a slit of light from the hallway. A battered walnut table, two chairs, and cheap paneled walls greeted her. It smelled of tobacco, burnt coffee, Dentyne chewing gum, sweat. It was not the sort of room where suburban women were coddled, pitied, or forgiven. Not a place where sympathetic gestures were offered, nor where men in off-the-rack suits looked the other way if a pretty face smiled back at them.

She couldn't think of how to turn this situation around. Her brief detentions with inexperienced clerks in shops in South Carolina or Texas, where Hank and she'd lived on military bases, were no preparation for the security staff at John D. Wannamaker's Department Store in Philadelphia. Eve had no leverage to use here, no husband wearing bars or stars on his chest on a base a mile away to offer up excuses, bribes, charm.

"I think you misunderstood what happened…downstairs," Eve finally managed to get out. "I fully intended…"

He put a plump hand up. "Not a day goes by when someone doesn't say those words to me." He motioned to a chair. "Tells me they were about to pay for it. Tells me I misunderstood. That they have relatives in high places." His eyes fluttered toward heaven and his hand waved dismissively.

"I'm sure I have the necessary receipt somewhere in my bag." She began to stretch for her handbag, but he pushed it out of reach.

This man, this security guard who looked like an M.P., had heard it all before from the look on his face. She couldn't think of anything to offer him—anything to charm him. He looked far too tired and bored to trade absolution for a grope or a kiss. There was some relief in this realization, though, in knowing she'd been outmaneuvered and could await her sentence without discussion.

He gestured again toward a wooden chair, and once she was seated he proceeded to remove the items from her bag, one by one, shaking his head at the variety of store tags: Gimbels, Lit Brothers, Strawbridge's, Wanamaker's—the four grand dames of Philadelphia shopping—finally saying with a hint of a chuckle, "You went wild, didn't you? Had to have yourself a memento from every store. Was it a dare?"

She was silent.

He tossed her hard-won booty back in the bag. "Half of your haul is junk, lady. A dish probably selling for two dollars and ninety-nine cents? Crissake, there's dust in it. It's a display piece." He held up his dirty finger, and she felt heat rising on her face. The charm bracelet from Wanamaker's, with its dice and rabbit and one-armed bandit, still lay on the table. "This is something a twelve-year-old girl buys. Not a woman like you." He fingered the dice charm. "Kind of a sign? You like taking chances, right? Have to have your souvenirs even if they're worthless."

He asked to see her driver's license, wrote a sentence or two on his pad, then picked up the stolen goods and headed for the door.

"Part of the kick, isn't it? Seeing if you can get away with it? Guess what?" She looked at him blankly. "You can't." He shut the door behind him.

His suggestion that seeing if she could get away with it was part of the kick was ridiculous. She sat for a long time wondering if they'd called the police yet. What the fine or punishment might be. Could she cover it herself?

How would Hank react? She could picture his red face—though it turned purple whenever she crossed swords with him. Maybe he could be kept out of it. How much money did she have with her? She hadn't planned on needing more than enough for a quick sandwich at a counter or the automat. She reached for her purse.

Something similar to this—an incident where things spun out of control—happened when she was fifteen. She'd taken a lipstick from Woolworth's makeup counter. Well, okay, a couple of tubes of lipstick and some eye shadow on the theory "in for a penny, in for a pound."

The clerk caught her, grabbing her wrist as she reached for a third tube. The woman—only a few years older than Eve, which somehow made it more galling— called Eve's father after demanding his phone number in such an authoritative voice that Eve couldn't refuse, couldn't help but fumble in her wallet until she found his office number on a yellowing piece of paper.

The clerk then dumped the purse's contents on the counter, attracting the attention of a number of shoppers as items crashed on the glass. Cheap, worn-out possessions, which looked ridiculous on display. The whole incident might've been forgotten if her purse's interior hadn't branded her as shabby.

Her father showed up after what seemed like hours. Grimfaced, stoop-shouldered, scuffed-shoed Herman Hobart, hat in hand. Leaving his cubicle at the Philadelphia Naval Yard to travel across the city, he paid the dime store clerk with nickels and dimes and quarters. The one bill he pulled from his pocket fluttered to the floor, and when she retrieved it, the dollar felt like velvet, folded up as it was and probably had been for years.

"I guess that'll do," the clerk said doubtfully, finally scooping Eve's things up from the counter. After making a face, she returned Eve's pocketbook. Her father didn't speak to her once on the bus ride home.

Sometimes it seemed like there was nothing but a long line of dour-faced men in her life: fathers, husbands, school principals, security guards, cops. Disapproving doctors her parents had consulted after incidents at school. All of them avoiding her eyes, disappointed in her.

The episode at Woolworths hadn't changed her behavior, but it'd made her more careful. No one likely to make a fuss had caught her again…until today.

And no one found her with a pocketbook full of dross after that. Never again would someone dump its contents on a counter and find used tissues, dirty combs, tampons, worn-down lipsticks, half-eaten boxes of Good and Plenty, stuff she'd taken from other girls' lockers in school, snapshots of movie stars from Hollywood studios, autographed by a machine, or so she'd been told.

There was less than fifteen dollars in her purse today. She counted it twice to be sure, checked the little pockets, unrolled the white hanky, and dug around in her suit jacket pockets. Too little money to pay a fine or bribe the guard—if it came to that.

She'd come downtown today in a fog. Could she tell this to whoever came into the room? That she hadn't known any of this would happen? She hadn't meant to take those things, hadn't considered her heart's desire until it was tucked inside her purse. Would they care she'd set out this morning in her pretty pink suit with nothing but a jaunt into the city in mind—a lunch downtown to break up the tedium of her life, some window-shopping at most. She looked so nice in her pretty pink outfit. The conductor on the train had smiled at her. So, too, had the ticket seller, the woman across the aisle, the man who gave her a hand stepping down from the train. It had started out so well.

Then, suddenly, she had to have one or two of the beautiful things she saw, articles she'd wanted her whole life. She didn't understand it herself. It was like she was in a dream, doing these things as if sleepwalking. There must be a name for it. A name for this condition that overtook her.

She got up, stretched, and looked out the tiny window and down at the people on the street, people free to walk around, to have lunch, to make a purchase. Only an hour ago, she had been one of those people. Was the window no more than a slit so imprisoned people like her couldn't jump out?

Occasionally, someone opened the door, never saying a word despite her hopeful smile. Making sure she hadn't magically stuffed herself in some bag or box or drawer and found her way out of the office, out of the store, much like the stuff she'd tried to take. But there was no escape, only long, sinewy hallways lined with the offices of the people who'd spot her. An hour, perhaps more, passed. It was like waiting in the doctor's office without the posters about various diseases to examine, without the eye chart.

Suddenly, Hank stood in the doorway, looking more tired than angry. His face was ashen. "Come on," he said, offering his hand. "Let's get it over with."

Although the gesture implied some feeling for her—some pity—his voice was cold. Not even inquiring if she'd done what they said. He led her out of the room, and down the hall. No one stood in their way; no one peeked from drawn blinds or through open doors. She was in a fog, absolutely terrified. Get what over with? What had Hank meant? Hadn't he taken care of it? Wasn't that what he did? Wasn't that part of the deal?

Hank led her to a larger and brighter office in the famous Wanamaker's Department Store, the mother ship of emporiums in Philadelphia. It was too bad she hadn't been caught at

Lit's, she thought, following him. Lit Brothers didn't have such an exalted idea of itself. It knew its place. She'd have been able to bluff her way out of the lower-rung stores. Their security wouldn't have made so much of it—so much out of the paltry stuff in her bag.

The windows shone transparent here, the room was carpeted with a richly colored, thick rug. A slight odor of stale cigars hung in the air while she waited next to a too-silent Hank. She wasn't going to be put in the Eastern State Penitentiary, she realized. People charged with a crime didn't get ushered into offices like this one. Hank probably gave them a deal on their printing needs for the next fifty years. Men like Hank, president of his retired parents' printing firm, didn't have wives incarcerated in the Eastern State Penitentiary. It was simply not done.

The store manager came in, Bill Harrison, a fellow St. Joseph's Catholic High School graduate. Suddenly loquacious, Hank began a rush of glad-handing, jocular remembrances of St. Joe's, memories about which priests were still teaching, talk of cafeteria food, of theatricals with all-male casts; the punishments dispensed by the principal—a man of uncommon strength; a few mutual friends. This took five minutes, during which she stood like a convicted felon awaiting sentence. The two men eventually ran out of high school remembrances, agreeing quickly once they got to it that Eve would get professional help.

"I've something in mind already," Hank told the store manager. "A place for Eve, that is. I've heard good things about it. We talked to the administrator there today."

Eve wondered who "we" was.

"It's a sickness," Bill Harrison said, nodding his approval. "I think of it as girl trouble. We see it every day—women with too much time on their hands."

Looking at Eve's abdomen for signs of nature's remedy to this, he pumped himself up and waved his arm around, a representative of the great Wanamaker's Department Store, and looking obliquely at Eve, shook his head. "Men, when they steal things, it's tools or something they need or can sell. Girls, well, they take the pretty stuff, the trifles." He looked at Eve. "Can't help herself, you know, Hank. And she'll keep doing it until she gets some counseling or goes to jail."

Eve held back the urge to slap him. She could imagine the satisfaction of feeling her hand on his heavily whiskered cheek. Did he think she was deaf or mentally deficient, speaking to Hank as if she wasn't in the room? Probably some boys' school behavior he'd learned at his costly Catholic high school, where girls like her were looked on as suitable for child-bearing, as dance partners, hostesses, but not much more. For that matter, why had no one spoken to her for the entire hour she'd sat in the dark office? Why must her husband be brought here to tend to it? Why must he speak for her, take care of her? Who was "we"?

If it'd made sense when she was fifteen, it didn't now. There was woman in the Senate, for God's sake. It was the 1960s. Her gynecologist was female.

"Won't do you any good to smack her around either," Bill Harrison added suddenly, snapping her out of her stupor. "It's a compulsion she's got." A bead of sweat suddenly mustached his lip. Hadn't he said this only minutes before? "You'll have to ask the men in white coats what to call it."

The heat in that office rose as he calculated his power over them. He must live for minutes like these.

Hank must've seen the dangerous flash in her eyes then because he began edging her toward the door. "Well, thanks for giving us another chance. There won't be another incident, I can assure you. She'll stay away from Wanamaker's in the future. Right, Eve?"

Even now he didn't look at her. No one was looking at her. She nodded anyway.

"Forget about it," the man said, finally released from the need to dominate the room. "I know you'll take care of the little lady. Make sure she gets the kind of help she needs." He looked at Eve directly for the first time. "Our upbringing, you know. The Church made us responsible men who take care of our women."

This responsible man with good upbringing and fine schools who now was a department store cop.

"I've expunged the record, Hank. Never happened."

She still felt something bilious coming from Bill Harrison as he was about to release them—to send them off into the world chastened. If he hadn't found out that Hank Moran was her husband—hadn't recognized the name—would he have come alone to that dank office and done something to her?

Like her father, ten years earlier, her husband never said a word on the ride home. It was a Buick LeSabre rather than a bus, but that was the only difference. The silence was the same: scorching and horrible. There were always grim-faced men in charge of her, she thought again. Men who guided her around by the elbow, steering her like an unwieldy ship into port. Men who were ashamed of what she'd done—at their association with her. She'd have to turn it around somehow. That's what she thought as they began the drive home, to the house she'd filled with baubles and merchandise—some stolen, some charged to her husband's accounts.

"You didn't mean what you said, did you? About an institution?" she asked him suddenly.

"It's more like a country club," he said, reaching into the glove box and throwing her a pamphlet. "Dad played golf there in the forties, in fact."

Hot air funneled up her throat, forcing her mouth open. She looked at the slick colored pictures blindly. This was a real place, then—Hank hadn't said it just to put the fellow off.

"I'll stop doing it. I'll never..." What could she promise him? What words would derail this idea?

He nodded. "That's true—you won't. After you get some help. Ninety-day observation period." He poked a finger at an early paragraph on the brochure. "That's the mandatory period."

"You are, you are...what do you call it? What you're doing to me?"

"Committing you? Yes. Mother and Dad and I talked it over...." Hank tipped his head to the side and frowned. "It's not like your little stunt today was the first time, Eve. Or even the tenth. It's not like our house isn't filled with things you had to have, things you never bother to unwrap half the time." He pounded the wheel. "Actually, Dad suggested sending you to Norristown State Hospital the last time this happened. Remember when you took that gold pen from the stationer's?"

Had she? Had she pinched a pen? She honestly didn't remember it. "Norristown. That's a snake pit. You wouldn't send me there?"

Stories about Norristown had been part of her childhood. Any kid who acted up was threatened with it. It was practically a chant to skip rope to on the sidewalk.

Cinderella
Dressed in brown
Got carted off to Norristown
How many shrinks
Did it take? 1-2-3...

"They'll be waiting for you when we get home, Eve. I made the call before I left my office, although I've talked to them several times. Mother's come over to pack an overnight bag. I can bring other things later. This is going to make things better. Give it a chance."

"Why can't you take me there, then? Why these men?"

He swallowed loud enough for her to hear it. "They have their own procedures, Eve. They were very clear about it on the phone."

They, they, they. They were in control. His voice was shaky for the first time. "Just go along with it. Give it a chance." He kept saying that—like she had any choice.

The two men were waiting in the driveway, looking eerily like the men at Wanamaker's. Her mother-in-law stood at the door, suitcase in hand, trying to squelch the smile slithering up her face. Eve wondered if they'd chase her if she tried to run. There was nowhere to go though.

She would've just had lunch downtown and come home if she knew what the day had in store for her. Been content with window-shopping. She straightened up in her seat and looked at the smiling men head-on.

The Annas

October 12, 2097

My name is Anna, and I am one of fifty females duplicated in the months before the world went to shit. I'm speaking into a recording device, hoping for the possibility rather than the certainly that future humans are listening to me. The ones on Earth—save for we fifty—are gone. As the oxygen grew scarce, this experiment, modest though it is, was the best idea scientists came up with.

Thinking back over the last decades, there were surprisingly few clever ideas. Years of denial that a problem existed wasted costly time. Futile attempts to launch select groups of humans into space literally went nowhere. It's hard to determine the success of space missions when no communication from anyone has ever been received. Perhaps the mapped destinations were far beyond our reach in more ways than one.

So at long last, fifty of us were duplicated, each one fifty times. The Annas I mentor have their own first names: Alicia Anna, Abigail Anna, Ashley Anna, and so on. It was thought important that the gynoids think of themselves as individuals—up to a point—so a distinct given name along with a shared surname seemed essential.

Each "founding mother" keeps an audio notebook on a

digital voice recorder, documenting events, observations, opinions. I am not a reflective person, but I see the usefulness in the task. A precise record of what transpired is necessary.

Why no men? Superior genetic material has been saved, but a male presence, at least in the early days, was thought to be unnecessary, if not dangerous and distracting. Women are better at nurturing and less likely to destroy each other. Or so we hope.

October 14, 2097

There is scant time to prepare the gynoids for their role in the new society. Annas are to be mediators. I was an attorney in my former life, handling negotiations between marital partners or business associates for only a few years before the idea of both marriage and business partnerships faded away. Until people began to die in frighteningly large numbers many years before the best predictions.

Women who can settle small disputes and maintain order are useful. Not a day passed before I was called in to mediate a dispute over the inequity of pod locations. Rotating pod sites was quickly suggested—by me—and accepted. Its inconvenience seems a small price to pay for harmony. Although none of the Annas came up with this solution, they saw its even-handedness at once. They could formulate the pros and cons with admirable speed.

I have approximately six to nine months to train my Annas before my supply of oxygen is gone. Each mother has roughly the same amount of time to train teachers, engineers, counselors, and so on. These were contested issues—what professions would be necessary in the new world, how many women should be duplicated, what occupations took longest to train. Dentists, for instance, were considered unessential since gynoids would never need them. A broken tooth could be repaired by an engineer or mechanic. And the expertise could be relearned if human life became supportable again.

The Annas must become self-sufficient—able to survive in this new world. They have been designed with the skill set they need to perform their tasks. It's the inner self that needs development. This is my charge. I am driven by the need for their eventual success. Do the other mothers feel this responsibility? Surely we were selected for such traits.

October 20, 2097

I never had a child. That option was no longer available by the time I was of childbearing age. Even if I had wished to procreate, Peter, my husband, disappeared with most of the males. I was never sure what or who took him, but such occurrences were common, if not rampant, in the final days. Perhaps he rocketed his way to that distant star. I will never know.

I love my Annas, and I think they can intuit the idea of love if not the actual feeling. Although androids cannot feel emotion in the same way humans do, they thrive, in their own way, from the expenditure of attention and care. When I recently chastised Allison for a lack of patience when settling a dispute between the street cleaners and the tram drivers, I detected a blush. Androidal research, a hot area in the final twenty years, allowed for some improvements in such areas. Can a future generation of gynoids mother humans without such ability? For as much as humans mentor the gynoids now, the hope is that gynoids will mentor humans at some future time.

October 23, 2097

When my Annas and I sit in a circle—as we do most days—my face reflects back at me like a hall of mirrors. I feel more nurtured and embraced than I ever did in my former life. And this comes after only a few weeks. Many of the other mothers bond only with each other, but I am more at home among my Annas. We are in synch, as they once said.

"Don't you want to come out with us?" Penelope asked me the other night.

The Penelopes are cleaners and certainly not the sort of women I want to spend time with. "Ella and Madeleine are coming along," she added, as if that was an inducement.

I shook my head, citing an emergency to sort out. "Sorry. Maybe some other time."

She nodded. "But it makes it bearable, doesn't it? The times we can let our hair down and put our feet up. Shrug off the pandering quality of companionship from the androids."

She turned away, her knap-sacked oxygen tank adhering to her back like a tortoise's shell. Many of the mothers are unattractive. If I'd been in charge, good looks would have been a requirement. When the population is small, physically pleasing characteristics rise in importance. Why replicate unattractive women? One needs some beauty in a place as barren and featureless at this one.

We were trained to treat each group equally, but I know I would never have interacted with a Penelope or an Ella in my former life. I can't think of why they even thought to invite me. Did I seem lonely amongst my Annas, perhaps? Was there something they wanted from me?

October 29, 2097

I quickly began to detect subtle differences in temperament and skills among my Annas. Within a month, I could discern twelve superior Annas among the rest. Each time I pinned the correct name on an Anna, she was thrilled. This dozen showed leadership skills and became my head girls, as the British used to say.

"None of the other mothers know their girls," Adrienne told me. "They don't even try to tell us apart." She frowned. "We may not be human, but we are not without feelings."

November 1, 2097

I insisted on rigid adherence to physical uniformity. Gynoids from other groups began to drift into a corporeal individuality I saw as dangerous. Some chopped their hair off; others inked tattoos on their arms. At a meeting of the mentors, I mentioned this.

"I think it's important to keep them functioning as distinct groups," I said. "I saw a Heather gynoid the other day who could just as easily have been a Carrie. We don't want them to blend into each other."

"Cousins," Heather said. Carrie nodded. "We're cousins." I hadn't noticed this before

"There must be allegiance to one's own group. The girls should not be encouraged to mingle until their group identity is fixed. Until they understand their place in our society." My voice sounded shrill in the silence of the cavernous hall.

"How can their identity not be fixed when they are identical?" Heather said after a moment. Heather looked to be a potential troublemaker in the months to come.

November 4, 2097

The other mothers made numerous mistakes and I came to understand why. Because a woman has talent as a mathematician or a teacher, there is no reason to assume she'll be able to function as a leader. Why didn't the architects of this society see that? Marian might have been an effective social worker in her former life, but now she spent increasing amounts of time having sex with Bonnie and allowing her Marians to drift. Another example. No alcohol had been allocated for our use, but Hannah, a chemist, was able to formulate a facsimile. At least five mothers spent most nights imbibing at her bar. Their duplicates misbehaved similarly, thinking such after-hours behavior was permissible. Environment still counts for something, and ours was faltering.

"We are still in mourning," Edith, a psychologist, had the nerve to tell me when I approached her about the matter. "Grieving the loss of home, family, friends. We are not perfect, Anna. It will take some time."

"Mourning is a luxury," I said. There was no time for frivolous behavior in our experiment. Our months of mentorship, of mothering, were running out. Six of my canisters of oxygen were already on the recycling heap. I looked with apprehension at the remaining ones.

November 7, 2097

My girls are perfect. Perfect. The head girls inspire the rest. They encourage trust, devotion, and fidelity. They will have to depend on each other so I feel no jealousy in my emerging secondary role.

We have meetings most afternoons and evenings now to discuss our strategy as facilitators. Sometimes I lead the discussion and sometimes one of the gynoids takes charge. I stay behind to allow them the autonomy they need. Arlene is especially skilled and, of all the Annas, most like me. Every parent likes to imagine her children surpassing her, and I'm no exception.

If I were a lesser mother, I would eavesdrop on these private sessions, but I have complete confidence in my Annas. They are made in my image, aren't they? No other group rivals us in discipline, loyalty, adherence to our mission. I—they—might have been military leaders in another life. None of we Annas can bear to watch the anarchy the other groups take part in. Orgies every night, for instance. Did someone believe a single-sex society insured lust would diminish? The behavior we believed to be male-coded occurs in females if given a chance to take root. Did they ever watch the death dance of bumblebees in the autumn? Is this sexual experimentation a similar phenomenon? Annas are ashamed to be associated with it. I long to root it out.

November 11, 2097

I have been thinking I am one of the few mothers fit to govern. And the allotted six to nine months for mothering was an error in judgment. It will take years for the non-Anna gynoids to be ready to run this society. If there were only one mother, she'd have enough oxygen for two dozen years or more. Almost half a life. So many of them deserve a quick death.

November 15, 2097

We talk about the mistakes the creators of this society made, agreeing it's within our means to correct them. It is not me who comes up with the solution to the mayhem around us. It is Arlene, of course. The Annas will stage a raid and seize the stockpile of oxygen tanks, bringing them back to our pod. In this way, I can lead all of the gynoids for the foreseeable future. My Annas love me—it's as if they are handing me a crown when they tell me their idea.

Do I feel any misgivings about sentencing the other mothers to death? I only have to look around me—to see the moping, wailing, screwing, drinking, and lack of discipline the others suffer from. If our task was to give birth to a new society, only I have what it takes to do this.

November 22, 2097

I Bring Sorrow

Ironically, today is my birthday, and thus all of the Annas' birthdays. The plan is to wait until midnight to attack the other pods. For once, the excessive drinking my peers engage in heartens us. It should make our plan of attack easier. I must confess, I tipped a glass or two in nervousness at how it all will transpire. We are not warriors, after all. No soldiers were included in the group of women duplicated.

I wait and wait, pacing my pod. Arlene suggested I remain here so as not to arouse suspicion. I fancy I can hear the feet of my Annas marching down the hall, entering the rooms of sleeping mentors, taking the oxygen away in the carts used for trash removal. It's not necessary to lay a hand on anyone. The oxygen in the sleeping tank each mentor uses will run out by morning. I have seen this happen enough times to know how it works. It won't be a violent death—for most of them. Their lungs are no longer well-functioning organs. They will sleep more and more deeply until they expire.

November 23, 2097

They are coming. I can hear their feet in the hallway. My Annas! I leap up, opening the door. The Annas are not carrying tanks of oxygen after all. What have they done with them? Their arms are empty, swinging at their sides. Their shoes seem heavy in the silence. Thunderous even. Their faces are stony masks of purpose.

Where are those tanks? I try to peer around them, but their number blocks me. An Anna, one that I can't name, comes through the door first. Who is she? Anastasia, Alice, Ardys? I know she's an Anna but I never learned her name. Why didn't I? She didn't seem like head girl material. Her face looks frozen. She stares at me coldly as she seizes my tank of oxygen. Rips it from my back, from my clutching fingers. They swarm about me now, like birds waiting to feast. I am whispering into my recorder as I realize this death will not be pain free. Not the calm extinction I expected.

Not at all.

What Baghdad Did to Us

US Army Specialist, Ronnie Bixby was shipped to Baghdad in 2004. She'd become a member of the US Army Marksmanship Unit before her rotation began, but never fired her weapon, except in target practice, during her entire stint. Guarding Halliburton trucks never drew direct fire on her watch, and she was asleep in her bunk when one of the trucks was carpet bombed, killing two soldiers.

Ronnie was quartered with women and developed a close relationship with several. Most had a husband or boyfriend at home, someone waiting for them. Neither she nor any of her closest female friends were lesbians despite the ubiquitous catcalls.

Her CO created camaraderie among the men by humiliating the women. But it wasn't the sort of hazing that could be grievanced. The CO never laid a hand on a female soldier or encouraged a male soldier to do so. Never used the more vulgar euphemisms women in some units complained about.

So the women in Ronnie's company felt like pussies for complaining about his tactics. Most had experienced far worse in high school—being the sort of women they were. It was trivial, wasn't it; the sort of teasing that went on in their unit. It seemed too insignificant to get upset about.

A point of agreement among the female soldiers though

was that trips to the latrine at night were a risk. Few drank liquids after three in the afternoon, so late-night urination became a remote concern. It was difficult in the summer heat, but necessary.

Unfortunately, it was diarrhea that sent Ronnie to the john one night. She considered asking another woman to go with her but rejected the idea since it was nearly dawn. Cramping badly, she barely made it to the latrine, and when she exited a few minutes later, someone grabbed her.

"Are you a bitch, a whore, or a dyke?" the man asked when she struggled with him. The noise from the idling Halliburton trucks masked any sound.

When he was finished, he wiped himself, saying, "I've had better lays than you out back at Flo's Escapades in Austin."

It was dawn and Ronnie had gotten a good look at the soldier's face; thin, hatchet-like, as pale as the moon disappearing from the morning sky. She considered the rest of him as he walked away: the height, the build, the physique, his peculiar way of walking. Later, she saw him on the base and managed to catch his name. PFC Loomis. Hal Loomis.

She didn't report the assault, but filed the information away. None of the women who'd been raped got anywhere with their charges. Two women had died of dehydration in the heat the summer before and still been ignored. Reporting such incidents only brought shame on the tattletale. It interfered with camaraderie and the esprit de corps, one woman was told.

Ronnie didn't re-up, and back in the States, it took surprisingly little time to find Flo's Escapades on the Internet. She rented a place in South Austin and got herself a job cleaning the cages at an animal shelter. She was good at the work, good with the animals. Soon she was offered a better job. But advancing in the shelter was not the point. She was waiting for the return of PFC Loomis. She knew he'd be back. The directo-

I Bring Sorrow

ry was filled with probable relatives. She cruised their houses, saw yellow ribbons on a few trees.

It was a nearly a year before Loomis swaggered out of Flo's.

"Loomis," Ronnie called from her car. Loomis looked up. "Are you a corpse, a casualty, or a dead civilian?"

He looked at her as if she were crazy, which she probably was. She pulled the trigger on her gun and killed him with one shot, proving her inclusion in the U.S. Army Marksmanship Unit was merited.

Burned the Fire

"Coming out with us tonight, Pearl?' Sam asked, poking his head inside her trailer. He caught a glimpse of her in the hazy moonlight, seconds before the gauze curtains blew inward, obscuring her. The candle on the dressing table shivered. Her hands looked unusually white, but then he realized she was wearing elbow-length gloves. How many months had it been since he'd seen her without specialty makeup, long-sleeved blouses, outsized veiled hats.

He blamed himself. It was he who discovered Ray in Miami and brought the two together. Ray wasn't like her other partners; he had a hair-trigger temper and acted on it. But Pearl liked his volatility, insisting it complimented her more docile demeanor in the ring. They looked perfect together too. It had seemed like a good fit.

"I don't have the heart for a party tonight, Sammy," she finally answered. "But tell the gang to have one on me." She reached for her handbag.

"Come for a little while. Do you good to…" He tried to peek inside, to catch her eye.

"I couldn't—not tonight." She stepped further into the shadows.

"Let me see all of you. What he did to you," he said, voice shaking.

"What happened was between us."

"You shouldn't be defending him."

"We had a lot of good years, me and Ray." She looked around for reminders, but someone—Sam, perhaps—had cleared Ray's things away. "You can't fight what's natural, can you?"

"When did we ever keep the bad stuff from each other?"

"Maybe tomorrow I'll get dolled up and we'll walk the boards. Ride the Ferris wheel. After dark—when it's magical."

"You ain't been out in the sunlight in years, Pearlie."

She laughed, lighting her gas lamp. "Some folks say too much sun ain't so good for a fair-skinned gal. Those bathing beauties, letting their faces brown, are just a passing fad." She shook her head. "I've never liked the sun. It's too real." She reached out a hand, as if to pat his cheek.

They listened as their friends assembled outside. "You two comin'?" someone yelled.

"Go ahead with 'em, Sam."

"You're putting salve on those wounds, right? Don't want more scars."

"I don't really mind the scars."

"What…like war wounds?"

"No, like medals." There was some pride, or perhaps defiance, in her voice.

Shaking his head, Sam closed the door behind him.

It was then she raised the light on her lamp and methodically stripped down to her naked fifty-year-old body, still as slim as on her eighteenth birthday. But there the resemblance ended in a frightening display of ruined flesh.

Ray, and the six that came before him, had made a mess of her. The older scars resembled tattoos. Raised tattoos where flesh had been sewn back together inexpertly: sometimes by her own hand, sometimes by an amateur surgeon. Once by poor Sam, in fact. But it had never been like this before. She was raw meat.

Ray had gone crazy in Iowa City last month. It wasn't his fault. She'd slipped on the mud brought on by a week's worth of rain and fell on top of him in the ring. In a rage, he almost ripped off her leg, lacerated her in a dozen places, and tore her left eyelid off.

He'd been shot on the spot. A man in a straw bowler hat rose in the bleachers, let out a roar to rival Ray's, and fired a gun. She'd hear the screech of the bullet from some faraway place, somewhere the pain had taken her. Their ten years together came to an end in an instant as Ray slumped to the ground. The crowd cheered, then booed, and then a low keening began. That was her voice as she looked at the cat. The last tiger she'd ever own. The last cat she'd share her trailer with, the ring, the road, a life. She really hadn't minded the scars—but Ray's carnage—that she couldn't live with.

The one possession she'd salvaged was his pearl-studded collar, which she put around her waist now. Reaching out, she toppled the gas lamp and threw the candle into the curtains. In seconds, fire rushed across the small room.

She didn't mind when the fire began to nip at her satin slippers, the hem of her garment. Ray had prepared her well.

Ten Things I Hate About My Wife

I'm laid up at the minute—several weeks past a right knee replacement. I took a medical leave and that absence made it clear I'm no longer the indispensible company man. Oh, sure, a flurry of impersonal cards and emails came the first week or two, wishing me well, but that soon dried up. Day after day of television, spy novels, and computer games becomes trying. Even more tiresome is the constant harping of my wife, insisting I hop on the recumbent bike to put in my hour. Or her reminder that a recovery spent in my pajamas was not on the instruction sheet the hospital provided. She's confiscated the pain meds now and doles them out as stingily as she supplies the dog with treats.

I've begun to work up a chronicle of sorts—a record detailing my wife's principal deficits—which have become glaringly clear over the past month. It's given me an unexpected thrill—laying it all out. Nothing's in plain sight though. I'm no fool. Ten things I hate about her. That sounds a little harsh, doesn't it? So many, then why remain married? Out of habit, commitment, financial reasons, ennui? Perhaps getting it off my chest will serve as a balm.

Number one: no one knows more about almost anything

than Kerrie. No kidding. You might think your degree in social anthropology makes you an expert in gang practices in modern L.A, but I'm telling you that Kerrie, despite only being in Los Angeles once, knows more about the subject than Mayor Garcetti. She can spew out the history of tags, explaining comfortably what terms like "all-city," "pull a jab," and "a job man," mean. She's also an authority in such unrelated fields as woodworking, how to stop the spread of Ebola, the history of badminton, and the proper way to make bananas foster.

This is especially hard on our children. Oh, yes, we have the requisite two. When Ella joined the Girl Scouts, Kerrie went right along with her, wrestling the leadership of the troop away from poor Nancy Mellon, a childless woman who'd devoted herself to Troop #1381 for two decades.

"Do you know how long it's been since a girl in her troop has earned a badge requiring venturing beyond the stove or sewing machine?" she explained. "I thought it strange until I realized her handbook dated from the forties."

When Max began Little League, Kerrie learned to keep score, becoming indispensible to the team. Her demonstration of the proper way to bunt with a runner on third base is legendary. Max accepted his lot, inheriting his docility from me, I'm sure.

Number two: her worst trait might be her refusal to engage in oral sex. After nearly twenty years, she continues to see it as aberrant behavior. Despite the fact that legions of fifteen-year-old girls put any dick in their mouth, Kerrie has only twice allowed mine entry to hers. Likewise, she has no interest in my pleasuring her. Any attempt to sidle downward is met with an upward thrust of her pelvis, a signal she's not happy with the direction things are going. A discussion of my wishes in this area is usually shrugged off, winced at, and once or twice, was met with a stinging slap.

I Bring Sorrow

"I am more than happy to have normal sex as often as you like. Do I ever deny you? I like to think I'm pretty skilled at it too." Which is true—she has her tricks, after all.

"I'd be happy to sterilize it," I say, thinking perhaps her fear of germs might be affecting her enthusiasm. "I don't mind dipping my wick."

"You're sick, Robert Bayer." Her face spasms with loathing. It's fascinating to watch her pretty face go through the contortions necessary to achieve a look of pure hatred. But it's a practiced move.

Number three: Kerry has considerable difficulty with losing. Early in our marriage, before tiny screens captured our attention, we played a fair amount of bridge, tennis, and Scrabble. If you'll notice, these are fairly disparate pastimes, and although you might understand a need to win in one or two of them, needing to win in all three—and several more, like Canasta and horseshoes—indicates a competitiveness you can't judge attractive. Take tennis, for instance. Kerry was the beneficiary of countless tennis lessons in childhood—something I, living in the rural Midwest, was never offered. Tennis was as exotic in Americus, Indiana as lacrosse or water polo, but Kerrie never acknowledges her privileged youth. In her mind, it is only from a lack of ambition or laziness that I lose game after game.

"You just want to run a bit more," she shouts when I miss her well-placed volley. "You're twisting your wrist again. What happened to that brace I bought you?" She shakes her head, disgusted with such poor competition. I won't even bring up the years I competed as her doubles partner—our bickering nearly had us banned from the club. In Scrabble, she's luck itself, drawing every S and the highly valued X and Z. She has statistics to back up the argument that over time a Scrabble player will be dealt a fair share of the better letters. And years

135

of doing the NYT crossword puzzle with a timer set to ten minutes has ratcheted up her knowledge of obscure two-letter words.

She cares so much about winning, and I so little. What seemed like an ideal match has soured.

Number four: although Kerry accuses me of suffering from obsessive-compulsive tendencies—"OCD this, Batman,"—she's unable to allow a dirty dish or crusty pot to sit on a counter for more than a few minutes. Last week, she invited the Ryans over for dinner. The Ryans are easily my least favorite couple, but Kerry finds them tolerable—I'm wondering if she sleeps with Tom. Tom Ryan's prone to droning on about his portfolio, and Melanie's sure to pull out her iPad to show photos of their latest trip, their garden, which I can see from my window, or her dog, Bullseye, who tramples my flowers and veggies whenever he gets loose. While I listen to their drivel, first him, then her, in some sort of maddening syncopation, Kerrie is cleaning the kitchen, making sure no evidence of any meal preparation remains. She shuts the door firmly, saying, "I don't want to disturb your conversation."

"You should see this too, Kerrie," Melanie calls. "Kerrie! It's Venice! VENICE!"

"She's a wonder, all right, Bob," Tom says.

I'm not sure which woman he means, and as he reaches inside his jacket pocket, a small sigh leaks from his spouse. Melanie has started her slideshow—Venice in two hundred forty shots—and doesn't tolerate interruptions well.

Is Kerrie deliberately skipping out on a part of the evening she dislikes? No, her absence is actually about the maintenance of our kitchen. She won't return with dessert until every dirty plate is scraped, rinsed, and loaded into the machine; until every counter has been wiped with her vinegar mixture; until the floor is mopped with her wet Swiffer. This isn't Kerrie's worst habit, but I loathe it.

Number five: I am telling Kerrie about the new fellow at the office, laying out my reasons for regarding him as a threat to my position, when I see she has surreptitiously added a word on her Words with Friends app. My wife often has as many as ten games going at once, all with players she has never met. She's also moved up a level or two in that ridiculous game based on pieces of candy. If I were to challenge her about a lack of attentiveness, she'd assure me she'd heard every word and, in fact, probably has. But a man likes to think he's worthy of his wife's complete attention when he's baring his soul.

Kerrie has never paid complete attention to anyone as far as I know. She can be speaking in court on behalf of a client at the same time she's eyeing a pair of shoes on a juror, calculating how she can best approach the woman about the place of purchase without jeopardizing the outcome of the trial. I've watched her in action, and nothing, not even the most spectacular piece of evidence, commands her full concentration in a trial. Her client might think she is scribbling away madly on his behalf when she is making a grocery list or writing a note to an irksome teacher at the kids' school.

Number six: okay, this is going to seem trivial, but it's one of my wife's most annoying traits. Kerrie cannot allow any object in our house to sit parallel to a wall. Every chair, items on a tabletop, articles on the kitchen counter, every tool on the basement corkboard has to be angled. She doesn't have a preference for a left or right slant, but slanted it must be.

Each morning, I line up the items in my bathroom in a nice straight row, and every night, I find them angled. Lest you think I share her compulsion, it never bothers me when she angles everything else in the house. But I think I have a right to place the items in my own bathroom where I see fit.

"Sorry, honey," she says when I confront her. "I do it without even thinking. I'll stop at once." But she never does. And to eliminate such a trivial source of friction between us, I let it go.

Not to go on too long, but I have even seen her rearrange items at the homes of our friends. If I follow her into their bathroom, I immediately recognize her handiwork.

"I can't help it. Things look stiff and unfriendly when they're lined up like suspects in a lineup. A chair at an angle invites conversation. Things placed on a slant look homey."

Could the placement of an object invite intimacy? I eye the jars of moisturizer, eye cream, and exfoliant, angled on our neighbor's sink after a visit from Kerrie Bauer, and doubt it.

Number seven: a lot of the conversation used as illustration here highlights Kerrie's seventh bad trait. She makes excuses. "I didn't mean anything by it," is a phrase she uses whenever I point out that someone's feelings might be hurt.

"I was just trying to help," or, "That's just me," are two of her favorite defenses. A recent fender-bender was the other guy's fault even after an eyewitness refuted this notion. The hurt feelings of her secretary after Kerrie's six-month evaluation spread virally was met with, "I didn't hire her; she was a legacy."

Her go-to defense for everything is, "Well, that's the way I was raised." She was, apparently, taught to be mean, petty, a bit of a racist, and vindictive, although I've never seen these traits in her brother, Brad, who works with mentally challenged kids, or her sister, Sister Marguerite.

Number eight: Kerrie manufactures information to back up her points. She lies, to be blunt. She's able to do this without skipping a beat. For many years, she claimed it was Martha Stewart who recommended a combination of salt and vinegar to remove carpet stains. I took her at her word. When she quoted the ADA as saying that water picks were actually more effective than electric toothbrushes, I bought one at once.

I Bring Sorrow

When she said that sociologists had data proving most men urinate sitting down, and, in fact, sitting improves the strength of their stream, I sat. When she told Max, our son, that seventy-five percent of the National League batting champs routinely took a pitch, he took one—even when his coach was flashing the hit sign. Her advice is often sound, but she's convinced she needs to back it up with the words of an expert.

"You want me to pee sitting down so none of it lands on the floor. Admit it."

"That would be an added bonus, but, really, I'm thinking of what's best for you."

"I won't be one of those men who scuttle into a stall, afraid other men are eyeing them."

"I won't be following you into any stalls. But at home…"

"I have my own bathroom, and I clean it myself."

A shrug. "Of course, there's the powder room to consider. A plumber told me stray urine is responsible for much of the mold under bathroom floors. Don't you have a mold allergy?"

Number nine: you're going to wonder why I took so long to get to this one. Kerrie murdered her mother. She doesn't know that I know this, but I do. It was back in the first decade of our marriage, after Max was born but before Ella. Kerrie's mother, an annoying woman to be truthful, and one who hadn't shown much interest in her daughter from birth on— well, who would with the other two headed for heaven—was diagnosed with a debilitating disease and came to live with us. There was no one else to take care of her, and not enough money to pay for a suitable facility. Kerrie took a leave from her law practice to get her settled in, gave the situation a two- or three-month trial, and when things didn't work out, covered Helda's face with a pillow. It was surprisingly quick due to the breathing issues her mother was dealing with. I watched from the stairway—knowing in my heart that she'd spotted me there. I believe this to be Kerrie's only murder, but I can't be completely sure.

Every so often in the months following Helda's death, I'd see Kerrie looking at me curiously. Did she wonder why I didn't confront her? What good would that do? I was saving up the clout the knowledge earned me. In those early years of our marriage, her other bad traits weren't so blatant. I felt sure I would eventually get my dick in her mouth or at least beat her at backgammon.

Number ten: I'm more and more convinced Kerrie is getting ready to kill me, so I guess this would qualify as something I hate about her. She's mentioned several times that my job seems to be in jeopardy. My days at home too?

"Studies show that men over fifty are rarely creative in business," she quotes from one of her specious sources today. "Those who have absorbing hobbies fare best in retirement." She is mopping scattered drops of urine from my bathroom floor as she says this. Being unsteady on my new knee is understandable, no? I like the view of her on her knees and prop myself to observe better.

"Perhaps you should begin thinking of a second career." Kerrie scrubs every inch of tile with my new toothbrush.

"Say, while you're on your knees," I suggest, shooting up an eyebrow. She shoots back that look. "Well, it could be therapeutic," I finish lamely. I watch as she puts the brush back in the holder, giving me a smirk.

It is this tenth item that brings me to the decision that I must kill her first. If she divorces me, I lose seventy percent of the income I'm used to. I'll also lose my children. In a divorce…well, Kerrie looks very good on paper—the woman who, despite her lucrative and demanding law practice, is a Girl Scout Leader and coaches Little League. Also, she keeps a spotless house, is a gourmet cook, and a powerhouse intellectually. Who could wrestle custody or alimony away from someone like that?

A bit later, as I'm holding her head down in the tub of water she's just filled for my bath, I remember something that makes me loosen my grip. I've taken on too much with this method of murder given our respective conditions. Why didn't I opt for poison? Why didn't I plan it carefully instead of jumping into it? Impetuosity had always been one of my worst traits.

I will fail in this attempt since Kerrie's hoisted weights at her gym for ten years, uses a rowing machine when the river's too frozen for competition, lifted me from my bed daily over the last month. And I am easily overturned these days, much like a table with uneven legs. Like old Humpty Dumpty on his wall.

This lapse in concentration insures my downfall, and in less than thirty seconds our positions are reversed and she looms over me. As I struggle fruitlessly—my feet can't make purchase with the wall tile, my ass sticks annoyingly to the tub's bottom, and I have put on enough weight to make me clumsy—it occurs to me that Kerrie must view this as one more competition, one last chance to best me. Beneath the roiling bath water, I can hear her chastising me for not trying hard enough, for splashing water on the newly clean floor, for trying to position my dick in her mouth, for filling the bath water with the flatulence brought on by my fear.

But I do have her full attention now, if only for a minute or two more.

I Bring Sorrow to Those Who Love Me

Serious study of the cello begins with Bach's Cello Suite No 1.

Prelude

When he first spotted Nanette de Fiore, she was seated in one of the practice rooms at Oberlin College. From his oblique perspective, the instrument seemed to be playing itself, its shadow falling sharply on the white walls. Only a few smudges suggested a presence behind it.

Her hair looked sculpted, drawing attention to a perfect skull. Her neck was long and delicate, her back perfectly straight—cello-like. A pair of unfashionable ochre cat-eye glasses teetered mid-nose. It was the glasses that pierced his heart.

Once recovered, Eli realized her bowing technique needed work; there was too much tension in her wrist, producing minute but discernible breaks in the music—the skittery sound he'd heard disparaged by musicians at his home in Northampton.

"Look, would you mind if I corrected your position?" he

asked when she paused.

"More experienced people than you haven't found my position wanting." She squinted up at him and suddenly seized the tottering glasses, stashing them in the music stand. Her scowl singed from across the room.

Back away, a voice in his head warned him.

Ignoring both her comment and the voice in his head, he continued, "And, while we're at it, I really don't care for your thumb placement." He moved closer. "Make a ball of your hand—like this."

He demonstrated, and when she didn't move, he took her hand—her very cold hand—and closed it, placing the correct part of her thumb in the proper place between the frog and the grip.

Eli Hauser didn"t play the cello. He wasn't even studying music. But both of his parents were in a chamber group—violin and viola—and he recognized good technique. He'd been raised in the company of fine cellists.

Reluctantly, Nan drew the bow across the strings. She looked unconvinced for a split second, but then, liking what she heard—a smooth, continuous sound—she looked up and smiled. "How long have you been playing?" She drew the bow again and grinned.

He paused, wondering how to answer that without losing the slight edge his role as teacher had won him. The door to freedom lay only twelve feet away, but he turned his back on it.

***

Allemande

Nan was so devoted to the cello that it was difficult for Eli to lure her away in the following weeks. Ignoring interested glances and even explicit overtures from other girls on campus, he hung around Nan's practice room as if it were a hive and he, a drone. He admired, resented, and misunderstood her commitment to the cello, lacking devotion to any pursuit himself. Except, perhaps, to Nan.

His situation reminded him of his childhood, the years when he was dragged across the globe to stand in the wings or wait with non-English speaking child-minders in hotel rooms while his parents performed in the great concert halls. Perhaps he'd been trained for this task—standing and waiting—and nothing more.

"Is she good?" he asked his mother when his parents came to the campus to give a recital. Mother and son were standing outside a practice room, eavesdropping, while his father took his afternoon nap.

His mother frowned, patting his shoulder. "Ah, Eli. Well, she'll never be a soloist, certainly. But she might find a position in a second, or perhaps third tier orchestra. Or with a good regional chamber group." She listened a bit longer. "She has a certain feeling for the music. Bach's Suite No. 1, I see." She nodded approvingly. "That's a good starting place."

Was her judgment too harsh? Her son knew about harsh verdicts.

At age twelve, Eli awoke one morning to find his violin missing. In its place was an expensive camera, one he'd been privately coveting for months. He never asked about the missing violin, and no one ever mentioned it again. In fact, when he saw his former teacher at a recital, each of them averted their eyes—as if deeply embarrassed by their joint failure. Neither of his parents suggested he try piano or clarinet—something he expected but dreaded, which probably meant he lacked the proper feel for the music, rather than a specific skill. This was a criticism his parents leveled at many of their private students just before dropping them.

His disappointment was eventually soothed by his proficiency with the new camera, and he turned its lens toward his parents and their coterie. A lucrative business took shape before he'd finished high school. His musical knowledge, his eye for placement of musicians and their instruments, his intuition of what would please, guaranteed success. By his senior year, he was designing flyers and taking photos for professional programs.

"Hey, you." He'd crept into Nan's practice room between movements. "I have tickets to a concert at Severance Hall." He waved them in front of her eyes. "Tempted?"

"Yoyo Ma?" she asked.

He nodded.

And later that Friday night, for the first time in the many months he'd pursued her, she gripped him as enthusiastically as she did her cello. He pushed down the tiny knot of panic that swelled inside him. He'd dreamed nightly of those legs opening for something more than her cello.

***

Courante

Progress was measured. When Nan wasn't practicing the cello, taking required classes, or attending peer performances, she listened to important recordings on her CD player. Or she studied videotapes of technique. He could sometimes lure her away for a concert or a movie with an interesting musical score. Bergman's *Cries and Whispers* was her favorite. But any suggestion of a football game, a Hollywood comedy, or dinner was met with little interest.

"I can't spare the time," she said unapologetically. "I'm hoping to be invited to perform at a church in Chagrin Falls next week. Their regular cellist has mono."

Sometimes his patience was rewarded with a quick tryst. But those times were often more depressing than gratifying.

He could feel a symbolic chucking of his chin, as if she were saying, "There now, that's done. Off to rehearse."

He also sensed a certain rhythmic quality to her sexual performance—as if she were mentally playing her instrument while permitting entry from his.

"Has she improved?" he asked his mother in his junior year.

"Oh, yes," his mother said. "Nanette's doing nicely."

"So she'll be invited to play with a good orchestra or chamber group after all?"

His mother shook her head. "She wouldn't be a candidate for a position at a major orchestra, I'm afraid. Times being what they are." She listened for a minute, droopy-eyed.

"Still working on Suite 1, is she? My goodness."

"Sometimes I imagine, or even hallucinate, that her hand and the bow are one," he said, squinting. "Do you see it?"

He'd read hallucinations were not necessarily a sign of mental illness, and he clung to this hope.

"See how they seem to merge on the forward movement?" He nudged his drowsy mother awake. Nanette's effect on him was seismic. He could feel a shift in the room.

"See what?" his mother said, not really listening to him—as was so often the case.

He wondered if Nan knew she wasn't first-rate. Had her new instructor, a Korean named Dr. Seung, warded off high expectations?

"So is this Seung any good?" he asked Nan later.

"We are very simpatico," she said.

He wondered if that meant she was sleeping with him. It was unlikely she'd risk the purity of the student-teacher relationship with a dalliance though.

If her hand and the bow were one, shouldn't she be first-rate? Shouldn't perfect unity with her cello mean something?

I Bring Sorrow

It was only when she stepped away from her instrument, out of its orbit, in fact, that he saw her clearly, without the tremor of cracked spacings—a concept in art that explained the phenomenon. Cracked spacings occurred when a painting was split after completion, leaving impressions of the original composition in both halves. Nan without her cello seemed incomplete—a loss of the centaur moment. Her hands looked bereft without a bow, a fingerboard. All of it.

***

Sarabande
They married soon after her master's degree was complete.
"You understand?" she said on his proposal. "You understand how it is?"
He froze, expecting some distressing confession to pour from her mouth.
"You understand the music will always come first." Her foot tapped rhythmically on the floor.
He nodded, relieved. This was how it'd always been, and in some way he was drawn to it; he wasn't sure he'd know what to do with a surfeit of devotion.
Eli was often on the road, following classical musical groups and occasionally a pop one with his camera. He placed a photo in Rolling Stone and another in Spin. He had a gallery show in Chelsea, another in Chicago. Overnight somehow, they became affluent—not that she was impressed or even seemed to notice.
"I'm home," he yelled from the foyer, dropping his overnight bag on the tiled floor. Her one request in their search for a house had been a music room. Here she spent most of her hours.
He could hear music. The location of the music room insured any piece played would swell throughout the walls of

the brownstone. Like her body's relationship with her cello, her music occupied every crevice of their home. She was playing Britten today. Sometimes it only seemed like she played Bach continuously. Despite his weariness with the Bach, he was wary of a change in atmosphere and the possibilities it might signal.

"Nan," he yelled again. The music stopped and he heard her sigh. The acoustics were good enough to pick up even a frisson of displeasure.

"I was nearly finished. Now I'll have to begin again."

For a second, he wondered if she'd forgotten his name. And why did she have to begin again? If she erred, even on a final note, she started fresh.

"Wait. I've brought you a present, Nanny." Silence. He bounded up the steps and found her fiddling with her pegs. "Did you hear me? I brought you something special."

He'd been in Munich for ten days and had missed her every minute. He searched her face for a familiar expression, a sign. Had she noticed his absence? He held out the bright blue bag. When he wasn't home, did anyone stop her from playing night and day? Sometimes he cursed the thickness of their walls, which hid her obsession from their neighbors. Only an open window gave her away.

Nan looked up and smiled, finally seeing him. Pulling out the wrapped gift, she opened it excitedly. Usually, he brought home rare CDs or autographed sheet music. Gifts she loved. But this was something special, he hoped. In seconds, she was holding up the music box. Hesitantly, she opened its lid. He knew she was worried that the music would be a violin piece, an instrument she barely tolerated.

"Can you really abide that screeching sound? I know your mother plays violin, but…" She'd said such things on many occasions. Brought up on the violin, he didn't hear the sounds she apparently did. Both instruments—when played well—were similarly melodic to him.

"It's Dvorak," she said a second later, the gift-wrap at her feet. She sounded puzzled. Puzzled and a bit annoyed.

"There's a shop outside Munich, which has quite a selection. Even Philip Glass."

She giggled nervously. "Surely not Glass!" She listened a second or two longer then shut the lid.

"Thank you, Eli. Very artfully made."

He knew she was referring to the case and not the music inside. The case, decorated with a Bavarian woodlands scene on a lovely cherry wood, was nothing special. The music itself was a recording by Jacqueline du Pres.

She saw the look on his face. "Well, I can't help but wonder, Eli—why not Bach?"

Why not Bach indeed?

***

Minuet

Five times in six—no, perhaps, nine times in ten—Nan practiced the Bach suite. Eli seldom entered the house without hearing it cascading down the stairs, spilling into the dining room, tumbling into the kitchen. If she wasn't playing it herself, she was listening to her many recordings.

"Cellists spend their whole life deciding on the correct reading of this piece," his mother explained to him in a hushed phone call. "Attaining a correct balance between the romantic and the scholarly interpretation—and what exactly that interpretation is—is the constant debate. Some say Bach wrote his suites much like one would publish mathematical theorems." She paused. "Is she playing it now?" He held the phone up. "I think she's leaning toward the more aesthetic approach. Interesting but predictable. No one can say she suffers a lack of restraint."

"We've been married for three years," he said. "In all that time, she has never once played outside this house, Mother. If she only plays for herself, is it anything more than self-gratification?"

He could feel his mother freeze. "I don't think we can consider Nan's music in those terms," she finally said. "You don't understand, Eli. Not being a musician. And although you're a talented photographer, I don't think you share our obsession." This was clearly meant as a slight, but he was long inured to such observations from his mother. "Maybe Nanette is your obsession."

He shrugged this off. "I do understand what complete self-absorption is. When I picture her, it's always with that instrument in front of her." He thought again of Nan as a centaur—of an illustration of cracked spacings. If he found a way to separate Nan from her cello, would she lose the thing that defined her? Would she be irreparably incomplete, broken?

"Maybe it's you who has the problem," his mother repeated. "Be glad she cares about something more than shopping trips, decorating, or making obscene amounts of money." She sighed. "And I think you need to examine this: how is Nan different now from the girl you were attracted to eight years ago? Didn't you, in a sense, create her? Are you incomplete without her? Is she the product of submerging your own ambition to someone else's?"

She babbled on about how they shouldn't have taken away his violin, shouldn't have sent him to Oberlin, should have introduced him instead to a nice fourth grade teacher

"I think you should look for a job," Eli told Nan later. "You could teach, work for a non-profit even. You need to get out of the house. Live more in the real world." Having children was beyond her capacity for nurturing. He understood that.

I Bring Sorrow

"I didn't realize we needed a second salary," she said, putting down her cup of Oolong. "I thought we had an understanding…"

"That understanding was based on the idea you'd perform. I had no idea—"

"And I will perform," she snapped at him. "As soon as I'm ready. Madame Giroux thinks next spring. I have the brochure for the local spring music season at the arts center. They're inviting guest performances." She opened a drawer and withdrew it, slapping it down on the table.

He took the brochure and looked at the section she'd circled in red. A quick scan made it clear it was meant for high school, or, at best, college-aged musicians. Not a cellist who'd now studied her instrument for more than fifteen years.

"You underestimate yourself," he said tiredly.

That night when he passed her music room, he was sure he saw her face intersected by the strings. Near the peg box, they seemed to bite into her. Cruelly even. Should a string snap, she could be seriously injured. Her cello, one he himself had purchased from an excellent luthier, was taking on the size of a bass fiddle in his head.

***

Gigue

The Bach Suite was playing when Eli came back from Chicago. He could hear it on the street now that the windows were open. Several neighbors seemed to be listening from their stoops. He wished he could make Nan understand the pleasure they took in her music, the look of joy on their faces as they listened. Maybe then she'd find the courage to play on stage.

But, strangely, when he came inside, he found her in bed, the CD player turned off. She looked dead. "Men only kill the thing they love," went through his head. The poem Wilde had written in jail.

"Nan," he said softly. And then he said it a bit louder. "NAN."

She sat up suddenly—like a puppet whose strings had been yanked. And it was all right then. He lay down beside her and together they absorbed the silence, entwined their fingers, tangled the sheets, and slept. She seemed to sense they needed a rest from it—from whatever it was lurking in the music room. For a week or two, she left the house with him for various events. A concert, a play, a dinner with some business associates. She seemed normal if tired; their life was ordinary for once. But normal for most people wasn't normal for Nan when you thought about it.

And however he defined normalcy, this period was short-lived. He came home to silence again but knew his wife was in the house because her coat was on the coat rack, her keys on the hall table. At first, he thought the music room was empty. It took several seconds before he saw her face, looking plaintively out at him from behind the bridge of the cello. Her skin seemed to be part of the wood, layered onto it in some ineffable way. Marquetry perhaps. The cracked spacings had merged.

"How did you get in there?"

The strings, which cut across her face earlier, now seemed to imprison her. Her cries for help seemed to spring out of the blasted f-holes—cello-like in sound. The entire instrument was a prison. Why hadn't he seen it before? When had the cello taken control? When had she submitted to it? Why had he allowed it?

"Don't worry, my darling. It won't take more than a minute to free you."

He looked around wildly for a suitable implement to destroy the thing that jailed her, thinking suddenly how difficult,

I Bring Sorrow

how painful, how necessary such a separation was. Surely she would understand if she could speak, imprisoned, as she was, that he was doing it for her

A Lamb of God

The first time Kyle Murmer's mother tried to kill him, he was nine. But he couldn't remember a day before or after that when he didn't worry about it. At night, he asked God to smite her, but he had no hope this would happen. And it did not.

"Let me see your teeth." Her voice cut through the sound of running water in the shower as she shoved the plastic curtain aside.

Her left hand held his chin like a vise as the right one forced his mouth open. Her personal supply of dental tools twinkled fiercely from the transparent case that hung from her neck.

"People not much older than you have lost all their teeth."

The desire to bite down on her fingers was nearly overpowering as she pulled him out of the bathtub and onto the floor.

On days like this, when she got up early enough for a frenzied completion of household chores, she hadn't taken her medication. On good mornings, the ones when the perphenazine made her sleep late, his father fixed them a bowl of cereal and they tiptoed out of the house, sharing an embarrassed smile.

She was waiting for him when he came home from school in the October of fourth grade. Hair curled, makeup applied perfectly, neatly dressed in a khaki skirt and white blouse, she wrapped pantyhose around his neck. It happened with such speed and precision, he wondered if she'd practiced on the back of a kitchen chair.

"Where have you been?"

Her nails were inches from his face, and beads of spit, scented with dental wash, shot into his eyes. He wasn't surprised. His life seemed exactly like a place where such things might happen. A place where mothers might practice lassoing kids in their off-hours.

"At school."

"Liar," she said, dragging him around the kitchen by his neck. "The Devil has you in his grip."

"I was at school," he repeated, trying to wait out this bad stretch. Survive it.

That's what his father always called it—a bad stretch. Bad stretches happened regularly at the Murmer house. Kyle and his father were always waiting for the other shoe to fall—another phrase his father used a lot.

"They called and said you weren't there. Said your desk was empty, no coat on your hook."

"That was on Monday." His throat was so dry that his voice scratched it.

Her eyes looked like the dead blooms on an African violet and a sort of eggy smell began to exude from her mouth.

"You forgot to call the attendance line and they called here. That was on Monday," he repeated.

Her grip on the pantyhose loosened. Then she was sitting at the table, collapsed and sobbing. "Don't tell your father. I wanted to lift you up to God." She raised her arms and he tried hard not to flinch. Her arms dropped on the table with an awful thud.

But he did tell his father; how could he not?

"Let me see your neck." His father ran a light finger over the bruises. "Your mother means well, but she gets confused.

Must've been a hormonal thing. Maybe the thought of having another kid just broke her. Probably flushed her meds."

Another kid? No one had told Kyle. In fact, he understood none of what his father had said, but knew he'd have to be even more careful.

His father also told Kyle he'd also found signs she'd tried to kill the baby. "Concoctions she must have mixed at her office."

At the Church of the Living God, birth control devices were forbidden—an impediment to the holy duty of women to bear as many children as possible. Children were the lambs of God. Abortion would mean expulsion from the Church. With just one child, the Murmers were frowned on. Encouraged to do more for the Lord.

When Kyle was sixteen, his mother attacked him while he slept. Her fists were hammers on his head. She wielded a small knife and tried to carve Aramaic words into his forehead.

"The devil will flee once you're marked." She'd flattened a crumpled piece of paper with the proper marks to copy on his bedside table. A flashlight shone on it.

His mother was jailed for several weeks, and he went to school with two strange marks on his forehead. Nobody asked about them. Such things were not unheard of at his school.

"This can't happen again," his father said.

Kyle wasn't sure if his father meant the scarring or his mother's imprisonment.

Kyle began college in Ann Arbor and never came home if he could help it.

"I have to work at the library over the break," he told them. "I need to study for finals. I'm helping out at my church." The last was a lie. He'd given God a chance and wouldn't again.

"Kyle." It was his sister, Jolene, whispering on the phone. "Mom thinks I'm having sex. I don't—I don't even know what having sex means."

I Bring Sorrow

Lambs of God didn't need such information. Information led to experimentation, ruin.

"I'm locked in my room. She's looking for a way in."

He borrowed a car and drove home, feeling more and more nauseated as he neared the house. His mother was in the garage, looking through his father's tools.

"Kyle," she said. "Can you help me find something to jimmy a lock? I hate to use a blowtorch. The wood's a fine oak. Maybe we can remove it with a screwdriver."

Her eyes were fixed and dull, dead moths again. The torch was in her hands. "Jolene doesn't understand I'm trying to lift her up to God." She looked at him closely. "Like I did with you." She smiled beatifically.

He put out his hand, and she gave him the blowtorch. He used it without hesitation, watching her cheap acrylic blouse go up in a flash, her face melt away. Her screams seemed inconsequential coming from a black hole as they did.

She was cast alive into a lake of fire burning with brimstone.

He didn't try to deny it when the police arrived, didn't try to run or to hide. He'd heard about Judgment Day often enough to recognize it when it came.

The Higher the Heels

The Night Owl was a blue-collar bar, and although Cara Willis had discarded both that look and the social status, she often stopped in after work. She'd paid less than three hundred dollars for the navy suit she wore tonight, but it looked damned good, as did the one-hundred-dollar haircut, and the gym-trim body. The higher the heels, the higher your sales numbers, someone had told her ten years earlier when she first got her license.

The guy directly across from her at the horseshoe bar was exceptionally cute. She noticed this gradually since the lighting wasn't great. He was the type she was a sucker for, skinny build, wavy dark hair swept back, tight jeans, one discreet tattoo curling out of his tee shirt. He was drinking a beer. Perfect. Solitary whiskey drinkers were likely to be alkies. She made eye contact, and a few minutes later, the bartender delivered her a second G & T. She smiled encouragement as the guy began his slow slide around the bar. His approach was like a mating dance, and she felt pins and needles in her feet as she got ready to tango.

More than once over the course of her pathetic dating history, a quick trip to her place or his had resulted in disease, a missing purse, a cab ride home paid for by her, a black eye. And on one dismal night, she spent a half hour sticking an eyedropper filled with medicine inside a cat's mouth while the doofus she was with pried it open. She'd come away with some minor wounds, but her itch never got scratched.

New Guy arrived at the empty stool to her right.

"Joey Rinaldi," he said, not offering a hand. So he wasn't just dressed the part of a blue-collar guy. White-collars always went for the handshake. Sometimes they even moved in for a hug, a definite no-no.

"Cara Willis." She patted the stool beside her, and he took it, lazily sliding his ass back and forth. "Gonna sit down on that seat or polish it?"

For a minute, she thought he wasn't going to get it. Damn. Another double-digit IQ had slipped into her life. But then he smiled, showing white teeth. Relieved, she took a long sip. She had a penchant for choosing men of limited intelligence. So many good-looking guys were either gay or dumb. Did good looks accompany a low IQ?

"Hey, I remember you," he said suddenly, pointing a finger at her and shaking it. "Realtor, right? You were showing a property I thought about buying a year or two ago. Over on Washington Lane? Around eight hundred square feet? Needed a lot of electrical work? Remember? Come on—you remember—the wires were dangling?"

She did remember: a small storefront perfect for selling ice cream, which is how it ended up.

"The people that bought it sell TCBY."

"I repair jewelry," he said. "Make some from time to time too. I was thinking of starting my own business back then. That was before things went bust, of course. Now I just work for the man."

"The man?" She stirred the ice with her finger and licked it.

He shrugged. "Anyone other than me."

"And you don't like that, right?"

"Right." He twisted the ring on his finger. It had a blue stone and looked expensive.

"Did you make that?" She nodded toward his hand.

"Nah. It was a gift. I like to make more delicate things."

She never finished the second drink. It was inevitable since she was a sucker for scrawny guys with witty banter, and his came close enough.

Her place turned out to be the closer one. She was leery of following strange men home anyway. Their filthy apartments were a turnoff. Unnervingly clean ones were worse. One guy stripped the bed before she left the bedroom. Earlier, she'd thought their shower together was foreplay, not a prerequisite.

Joey was good in the sack. So good, in fact, it made her worry. She was a six plus at best. He was like a nine, she thought, looking him over in the lamplight. And half a dozen years younger than her. It was childish that she still assigned a number to men she dated, and that the rating was based solely on looks—at least at first. At some point, that first evening, she lost the upper hand.

Nine got up from the bed and roamed around, picking things up. "This you in high school?" He put the photo down. "So what's your story?"

She shrugged. "Nothing much to it. I sell properties—as you know. I belong to a book club and vote Democratic, but don't tell my boss. I like pistachio ice cream, summer carnivals with phony midway games and dangerous rides, and the Pixies."

"Like fairies?"

"They're a musical group. Or were."

No sign of interest. Or was he too young?

"Realtors must know more about what goes on behind closed doors than most people."

"That would be home sales," she said. "I rarely get involved in those. They're a pain in the ass because everyone thinks their home is worth more than it is if they're selling, and less than it is if they're buying. Businessmen are more realistic."

"I bet you made a pretty penny on the one I missed out on."

Cara shrugged. She couldn't remember what her commission was but certainly nothing special.

"So they put an ice cream parlor in that place?" He shook his head. "Ice cream that profitable?"

Why the hell was he so interested?

Reading her mind, he said, "It would've been perfect for me. A great space for a nice little pawnshop." He stroked the hair on his chest, and she shivered.

"Thought you said jewelry?" she said, pulling herself together.

"Same difference. People pawn jewelry more than anything else." He got up and started dressing. Not a ripple of flesh to be seen. Pity she couldn't say the same. She pulled the sheet up tight and stayed put.

"Maybe we can do this again?" He was combing his hair in her mirror and caught her eyes. "Dinner, movie, whatever."

"I already put my number in your phone. You really should keep it locked."

He flinched. "I don't keep financial information on it."

"Cara with an C," she said.

Cara fell hard. It happened when he showed up with a necklace one night.

"Did you make this one?" she asked, fingering the delicate gold chain.

He shook his head. "Part of an estate my boss bought. He let me have it for overtime he owed me. Like it?"

"Love it."

"I knew you would. It's kind of old-fashioned—like you.

Most women are wearing that chunky, clunky stuff now. I hate it."

She'd never thought of herself as old-fashioned. Men had a way of inventing her, she'd found. Was this true of other women, or was she enough of a blank slate to bring it out? Not long ago, a man had told her what he admired most about her was her ambition. Ha! Marry me and I will never work again, she almost said.

"Always on the job, right?" Joey jolted her back to the present. "Looking through your—what do you call it—listings?" So, again, a reference to ambition. Maybe it was true.

"Not all the time." He knew this by now, didn't he? They'd been out a dozen times. I like the Pixies, she thought. See that book on my night table? Remember our discussion about Tarantino?

He sank into the chair. "I've been thinking about that little business—you know, a jewelry store. Just need a little shop." He squinted. "Ever see another property like that one? About that size."

Mentally, she sifted through her listings and the ones cross-listed. "There's always something available. Maybe a little bigger or on a less prominent street. But close enough."

She lifted her hair for him to fasten the necklace.

"Sorry. I'm all thumbs tonight. There."

She got up and went to admire it in the mirror. It hung just below her clavicle. The stones twinkled. She'd never been given such a lovely gift. Nothing even close.

"Looks great on you," Joey said, crossing his legs and leaning back. "I knew it would."

"What are the yellow stones? Topaz?" It was an acorn pendant on the chain—one composed of yellow and white stones.

"They're yellow sapphires," Joey said. "The white stones are diamond chips."

I Bring Sorrow

"I thought so—the diamonds, I mean. It must have cost a fortune. How much overtime did you have to put in?" The acorn felt warm on her chest.

"More than enough—but hey, you're worth it." They exchanged a smile. "Anyway, Cara, I was thinking maybe you could show me a few properties. I'm sick to death of working for Bill Davenport. Maybe there's a spot I could afford."

"How much do you have to spend?"

He shrugged. "Probably not enough for anything fancy."

"Why do you have to buy a place when you could rent?" she said. "I have a lot of rentals on my books."

"So you'll show me a few? I'd like a space that wasn't stuck out in the burbs. Something classy. Maybe Victorian—to suit the type of jewelry I'll carry."

"Sure," she said. "I have plenty of those."

They made a date for the next Saturday, and she showed him five properties, three of them rentals. The current owners were still in two of them: a furrier and a religious bookstore. The other three sat empty. He went through each as carefully as a city inspector, checking the electricity, plumbing, exits, and windows.

"Any fit the bill?" she asked him later over coffee.

"I liked that rental on Ogontz, but I think the neighborhood's too iffy. Wouldn't want to worry about getting robbed all the time."

"Price is good though."

"Yeah, I could probably swing it. But let's keep looking."

Sometimes she thought he was more interested in her ability as a realtor than her talents as a lover. She did what she could to step up her game with a new hairstyle, a diet, and some new clothes.

Cara talked it over with a fellow realtor—the closest thing she had to a friend in the business—at lunch one day. "I don't know why I let myself get so over the moon about this guy. He's nothing special once you get past the looks. Unfortunately, I haven't been able to do that."

Pam looked surprised. "I never knew you to be so big on appearance. Remember that Paul you dated a few years ago—he was the homeliest guy in the world. But you were crazy about him."

"Well, we had a lot to talk about. That's what I liked about him. Turned out he was a jerk though." They both thought back on the cocaine habit that sent Paul off to rehab. She'd never seen that one coming. Breaking up with Cara turned out to be one of his twelve steps.

"With Joey, there's not so much to talk about. The sex is great, and he sure likes to look at my properties. And I mean actual properties when I say that."

Pam smirked. "So he's using you to get a good deal?"

Cara raised her eyebrows. "Maybe I'm using him to get a good deal too."

"Speaking of property, did you hear about the robbery in Jenkintown? A fur store? It was a new listing with Cambridge Properties. Looks like the burglar got in just before they closed on it."

"Think someone forgot to lock the door?" Cara had made that mistake once, but luckily the place was empty and another realtor turned up to show it an hour later.

"They can't figure out how the guy got in. Doors and windows locked, no sign of forced entry—is that what they call it? Maybe the realtor was in on it."

"Or one of the employees," Cara thought aloud. "Guy didn't haul out the furs, did he?"

Pam shook her head. "Just interested in the money, I think. They were dumb enough to keep the dough in a cash box someone could carry out."

I Bring Sorrow

Cara's phone rang then and it was Joey. Waving goodbye to Pam, she walked toward her car.

"How about a movie?"

"I have to show a few properties tonight to a newly minted dentist," she said. "Can we make it tomorrow night?"

"Sure. How 'bout I make you dinner?"

Joey liked to cook, although the cleanliness of his kitchen—and hands, for that matter—concerned her. Would he get angry if she suggested her place? Better to let it go. She was well stocked on Imodium.

The client fell in love with the first place she showed him. It was perfect for a dental office. In fact, it had been one before it turned into a spa. "I hope the smell of candles lingers for a while," he said. "A nicer smell than the one in dental offices." They made arrangements to sign the papers on an offer the next morning.

She stopped at a bar on the way home. It was one she'd never been in before on the other side of the city. It was larger and more upscale than the Owl and she took a seat at a table, not wanting to make conversation with strangers after a long day. She ordered a Blue Moon and a cheeseburger, pulling out her iPad to check the news.

She heard his voice before she saw him. Or rather, heard his laugh. She'd begun to turn—to peek around the large booth back—when she heard a feminine laugh respond to his. The bar was busy enough for her to risk a quick look. The twosome was seated at the bar, their backs to her. A woman, looking like the cat that swallowed the canary, sat there, dressed surprisingly like her.

So he had a type. Or was it something else, because at the woman's feet was a binder much like the one she was carrying in her attaché. The woman reached for it, opening it up on the bar. She couldn't hear what they were saying, but the woman was flipping the plasticized pages, stopping every so often to point something out. Was it just a business meeting? Was he having his place redecorated? Was he choosing carpeting, perhaps?

But then the woman leaned in. Way in. The bartender brought their drinks and they took a sip simultaneously, laughing. It was early in their relationship, Cara thought. The period when you laughed at stupid things. Was she being replaced?

After a few more minutes, Cara took the opportunity, during a particularly intense exchange, to sneak out. Clearly when she couldn't go to the movies tonight, he called in the second string. Or, perhaps, she was the second string. How many strings were there?

The next day, she expected him to cancel. But when no call came, she drove over to his place. The lobster was excellent and nothing seemed amiss. Twice, she almost said something, but figured he'd either deny the woman in the bar meant anything to him or it would lead to an unpleasant confrontation of some sort. And perhaps the woman was just a decorator. If this were a TV sitcom, she'd turn out to be his sister.

"Are you planning on redecorating?" she asked suddenly, without thinking.

"What?"

"I thought you might want to redo this room." She looked around. "Paint job's a little old. If you ever do want to repaint, I can recommend someone. Realtors always know a good painter."

"You know I rent, right?"

And, of course, she did.

On Wednesday, Cara attended an open house for a new listing—a medium-sized office complex, newly constructed. The listing agent gave each of the realtors a thirty-five-page handbook detailing its construction, the various ways it could be divided, and its architectural assets for prospective renters. As she was thumbing through it, waiting for the oral presentation to begin, the woman she saw with Joey two nights before walked into the room. Though she'd only seen the woman in profile, the color and style of her hair alerted her. Her laugh, head tilted in that same way, convinced Cara. Did Joey have a thing for realtors, or was she showing him property too? Her personal property or her real estate properties? Cara was jealous on all counts. Working her way around the table on the pretext of getting coffee, she overheard the man asking the woman if she was insured.

"You mean for a break-in while we're listing a property? Oh, sure. The company has a policy that protects us against accusations of theft, fire—you know."

"Did they figure how he got in yet?"

She laughed that laugh again. "It's an old building and one of the cops suggested he used the chimney."

"Wow! Wouldn't you need blueprints to make sure it was wide enough?"

"You'd think!" she said. She turned then to face the head of the table as someone cleared his throat. Swinging from her neck was what looked like a pineapple on a silver chain.

The meeting began.

It all clicked into place a few minutes later. While the gray-haired man at the microphone was talking about plumbing or electricity, Cara was thinking about chimneys.

"Hey, Joey. I have a nice property I'd like to show you. It's a classic—just like the ice cream shop. A converted Victorian. There's a law office across the hall. It's an elegant building."

"What's in there now?"

"Crazy luck, but a jewelry store. Guy's about to retire.

Maybe you can even make a deal for some of his inventory. I can mention it to him."

"Let's not rush into anything. I don't want to seem too eager."

Joey's voice was notably less blasé than usual. Perhaps she was imagining a tone based on what she now knew. But Cara was only partly convinced she'd gotten it right: that Joey used his relationships with female realtors to scope buildings out for a robbery. His entry might not always be through chimneys either—if it even was the chimney used in the fur store robbery. There were probably lots of opportunities to figure out ways into properties while the female realtor, enamored with his attention, was otherwise occupied. She remembered vividly how Joey went over a few of the places she'd shown him with a magnifying glass. He was thorough, all right. And skinny enough to use a chimney if he needed to.

The place she had in mind had a chimney. It looked very large from the roof but narrowed into an upside down V as it approached the first floor, each side servicing a different fireplace in the two separate premises. She wouldn't have known this, but the inspector showed it to her in detail when he insisted the soot inside it must be removed to avoid fires. Getting stuck inside might land Joey in jail. Or serve as some sort of revenge at least. Let's see him wiggle out of this one, she thought.

Joey followed her through the place, delight evident on his face. "This would be a perfect spot for me," he said. "When's the guy going to move his inventory out?" His eyes glinted with greed as they scanned the locked cases in the rear.

"You are excited," she said.

Thinking it over as carefully as her rage allowed, she figured the longest he'd be stuck would be a few hours, and he could use his cell phone to call for help. She could imagine people in the law office coming in and hearing his cries for help. If he managed to get out on his own, he'd be locked in the store, and he'd never be able to climb back up.

There were a number of things Cara hadn't counted on when she made her plans. He chose her cell to call for help, but she didn't answer, figuring he could darn well call another one of his female realtors. The phone rang a half a dozen times, and he left a message every time that she quickly erased. She'd be darned if his voice were going to seduce her again.

After that, Joey's cell phone had apparently dropped, and he was unable to make more calls. The law firm next door had closed down for a week's vacation while some floors were being refinished, so no one heard him yelling. The jeweler selling the property in the adjacent business came down with the flu and stayed in bed, his one employee already let go.

At some point, Cara figured, or allowed herself to believe, he would have gotten out, although she didn't hear from him. She dialed him a few times, and when it went to voice mail, she assumed he was pissed.

Her colleague, Todd Rumsen, found Joey. He was showing the property to a client about three days later when they both noticed a smell. Joey had been skinny enough to slide into one side of the V, where he was asphyxiated from the fumes from the refinishing product and from a lack of oxygen inside the chimney.

"Hey, you must have showed the guy this place," Todd told her later. "Your name was on his phone. He was probably calling you for help."

"We dated," she admitted. "And I did show him this place, among others."

"He asked me to show him properties," she told the cops later. "I didn't realize he was scoping the places out."

"He must have been looking for means of entry," the cop

said. "Too bad he picked this place and this weekend. That re-finishing application is toxic. When we first went in, you could still smell it."

She could tell there was a hint of suspicion, but when they matched Joey up with at least three other female realtors, their suspicions disappeared. The one she knew about passed her in the hallway at the police station, in fact. A man hung from her arm protectively. Close up, the necklace, which she was wearing again, was not much like Cara's at all.

Perhaps she had just been Joey's realtor. Cara tried not to think about that. She tried not to think about any of it. He was playing her the whole time, wasn't he? She could play too.

I Bring Sorrow

They Shall Mount Up
With Wings Like Eagles

They were traveling from Boston to Norfolk, but Gaylen couldn't remember exactly how this happened. Why Norfolk, or who came up with the idea of a trip at all? She couldn't say where in Virginia Norfolk was, so it probably wasn't her idea.

It was the sixties and sudden departures, or trying a new drug you'd never heard of, or skipping the entire semester's worth of chemistry classes just seemed to happen. Routine events seemed backlit by action going on a million miles away and not much worth bothering about. Almost daily, there was a new vocabulary to learn, or a fresh issue popping up, or an entirely different style of clothing on someone passing by. Like those crazy bell-bottom jeans with a flag on the butt that some skinny blonde wore only last week. Or vests. She hated vests, but damn if she wasn't wearing one right now, some sort of tie-dyed thingy with gingham patches. Gingham? Freaky.

It was like the earth had accelerated its spin and just staying anchored on a task or a thought was impossible.

No one knew her whereabouts right now, and that was pretty freaky too. There was no time to leave a note or make a call. If this bus they were riding slid into a ditch—conceivable since the rain was falling hard and the bus seemed pre-World War Two—her parents would be shocked to get a call from a distant hospital or a police station. Especially on a night when they assumed—if they thought about her at all, which she doubted—she was grinding her teeth in her dormitory bed in Massachusetts. They spent a lot of money imprisoning her in a Christian college where bed checks were not unheard of. Their college research last year had centered on non-academic issues like early curfews, dorm surveillance, compulsory chapel, and pledges not to drink, smoke, or have sex. She'd get married after graduation anyway, and it would be easier to land a nice Christian boy if she was a nice Christian girl with Christian college credentials.

"I'll be able to sleep better knowing you're in good hands," her mother said before driving back home two months ago. She'd been in a lot of hands lately but few of them were good.

It was easy to get talked into something like jumping on a bus and taking off for no stated reason nowadays. It all seemed pretty cool last night. Or perhaps it was she who did the talking—came up with this plan—she wasn't sure. Getting hopped up on phenobarbital was probably not a good move. But that was all Trixie had in her fake Capezio shoebox/drug chest.

"We finished the last of the pot," Trixie said, offering each of them the bottle. Trixie looked just like Joan Baez now that she'd straightened her hair.

"How much do I take?" Gaylen asked, shaking the bottle.

"It's just gonna make us sleepy," someone said. "My mother hasn't been fully awake since the Kennedy assassination."

"The ones your mother gives you don't do anything at all," Trixie sang.

"Hey, Grace Slick," the boy with the bare feet said.

"Well, duh," she answered.

Gaylen was on this bus heading south, and Nick was asleep on the seat beside her, propped against the window, his breath fogging the glass. The ghostly image of a name—was it

Bonnie?—lurked behind his smudges.

She'd never seen him asleep before, and it was not an attractive sight. His mouth lolled open and a patch of unshaven skin bore the remnants of the strawberry frappe he had at a HoJo's in Boston. Was this the boy who could sink a basketball from half-court? Was it Nick who made the girls squeal when he danced at a coffeehouse in Peabody? This guy with the pink moustache?

Stuff like that had faded into insignificance already. It was funny how things that looked cool on campus could look dorky once you reentered the real world. Being a good dancer hardly qualified him as a decent traveling companion. She could hear her father asking what his grades were like, who his parents were, where they went to church. She had no idea. Five weeks ago, Gaylen and Nick were only on a nodding basis, recognizing each other from glimpses across the quad, or due to the proximity of their seats in chapel. They hadn't even had sex, for the record. Even their kisses were chaster than she was used to.

Though this was a religious school, which should be above such things, the high school photos of incoming girls were stuck on a wall somewhere and Nick claimed to have noticed her back last spring. At first, this seemed like a compliment, but looking around her in assembly, it became clear that the most Christian girls worked hard at being plain. Her roommate, for instance, had grown her hair down to her butt because her church didn't allow women to cut it. This might have been attractive on some girls, but Ruth braided her hair in tight coils. The first time they met, Ruth was on her knees, hands pressed together. So it was no wonder Gaylin stood out. You only had to try the least little bit.

They were at a party last night and issues like the war, bourgeoisie values, civil rights, and university investments in the war machine led to the idea of taking off. All of them were in on it at first—escaping from this institution. Each had been urged, if not forced by fearful parents or their church, to enroll here. And what did they know of the place, living across the country like they mostly did? The photos in the brochure had been overly influential with Gaylen. Boston, only an hour away, made the school seemed glamorous. They must have used a whole different group of kids in those shots, she thinks, remembering the photos of the homecoming court and the autumn hayride. The hayride, two weeks ago now, featured the reading of favorite Bible verses as entertainment. Coming home, they sang hymns. Her attempt to include *This Land is Your Land* was pushed aside for a third rendition of *The Old Rugged Cross.*

It was the late sixties and restlessness was effortlessly evoked. All the wrong things were influencing her group of friends according to the sermons they heard in chapel every day. Church, Family, Country—that was the ideal. Strangely enough, the chaplain never mentioned school. Not even as an afterthought.

So the bunch of them had worked out their positions last night, war, no; drugs, some; sex, probably; racism, no, (but there were no black people on campus except for that one kid from the Dominican Republic to test their liberalism); women's rights, perhaps. There were disagreements over some issues, but even the Port Huron Statement had supposedly involved compromises, someone pointed out. The thing was that everyone seemed to be more informed than Gaylin. It was too bad she hadn't read some of the books they were waving around or gone to one of the endless rallies in Harvard Square. Or read the stack of *Boston Globes* that lay on tables in the foyer.

After this lengthy session—and she was exhausted by her

attempt to understand the references the other kids seemed to effortlessly make—everyone else went off to class, whereas Nick and she remained in a druggy discussion over what she now saw was a meaningless gesture—ditching school and seeing what was happening out there—out in the streets. The streets of Norfolk, apparently, for Nick. It wasn't even really about those issues they'd just spent hours hammering out. They both wanted out for whatever reasons you cared to list.

"So do you wanna just blow this place?" she or perhaps Nick had said. They were both pretty high by then. She thought of her dreary dorm room where Ruth would probably be praying for her safe return, her long white nightgown threatening to trip her when she rose.

Each morning, Gaylin found a Bible verse on her desk. Yesterday's had been "They shall mount up with wings like eagles; they shall run and not be weary; they shall walk and not faint." She brought this scrap of paper with her as inspiration.

She pictured her empty chair in Psychology 1, imagining the TA marking her absent. Would she ever return to her dorm room or classes? Perhaps this bus trip constituted her life from here on.

When was the last time she ate? While Nick drank his frappe and ate a burger, she had nothing, having blown her allowance. She knew from his wardrobe he had plenty of dough, but so far none had been spent on her. Maybe she needed to get behind that women's lib stuff so men couldn't get away with treating her like that.

She stuck a cigarette in her mouth, and as she began to let go of the lighter's flame, a hand from the seat in front grabbed her wrist. No—grabbed was too strong a word—he encircled it with his fingers. In the light, she could see he had a full beard, long hair, blue eyes. Next to him, a guitar case rested, neck up.

"Gotta light?" Smiling slightly, he held on to her wrist. She nodded and pressed the thumbwheel.

Simultaneously, they exhaled a stream of smoke

"Sleeping Beauty," he whispered, looking over at Nick. Nick seemed ridiculous to her now. Where was his beard, his long hair?

She must have showed her displeasure because the guy said, "Don't want to claim him now that he's drooling all over your coat?" Then he smiled.

Alarmed, Gaylen looked down. Her coat was a recent purchase from Filene's Basement, and basement or not, it had cost a lot. Nick shifted uneasily beside her, sensing disapproval. She put a finger to her lips.

"Hey, come up here, where we can talk." Standing, he moved the guitar case to the rack above. It seemed impolite not to take him up on it. The bearded man took up more room than the boy called Nick. Nick, who was running home to his parents in Norfolk.

"Where you headed?"

"End of the route," she said, stubbing out her cigarette. "Norfolk."

"Miami's the end of the line, sweetie."

She was startled, not knowing the bus went all the way to Miami. "How old are you anyway?" she asked. Maybe this guy was too old to mess around with. She had her limits. Probably twenty-five was it.

"Twenty-four. Pretty old, huh?" He looked at her closely. "Know what I just did?" She shook her head. "Took a bus from Baltimore to the Canadian border and then chickened out."

She frowned, not getting it. There it was again. Where had she been when all this information had been doled out?

He reached in his pocket and pulled out a piece of paper, turning on the overhead light when she squinted.

"Draft notice," he said, poking at it with his index finger.

I Bring Sorrow

"I'm in deep shit now. Be wading through rice paddies in a couple months."

His name was Robert Gottlieb. But before she could read the birth date, he had squirreled it away.

"You should've gone through with it, Bob."

Her voice sounded adamant, sure of itself, but she didn't know why. This was also how she got into trouble, pretending knowledge when she had almost none. She knew he was talking about Vietnam, of course—the war there— but not much more.

"Yeah, you're right. I'm thinking of getting off this bus and heading back up north. Got the address of a place to go in Canada. A dodger shelter." He pulled another paper out of his pocket. "Not sure how to get there from the border, and I can't ask them—the border guards, I mean. You're on your own till you get by them. That's what I've heard anyway." He sighed. "It's all a trick."

"I guess so," she said, not sure why this was true. "But you'll figure it out. Maybe get on another bus once you get inside Canada."

There was something very appealing about this idea. Maybe both of them could ride buses forever. She remembered seeing a movie in high school about how people used to ride on trains without paying. Scramble onto a boxcar as it pulled out of the station. Cook dinner over a tin barrel. But on a bus, the driver sat right up front, so this was probably not possible. She figured she had enough money for a cheap dinner and not much else. Certainly not another bus ticket.

"I could come with you," she said suddenly. Maybe her company would be worth the price of her ticket to him. He looked like he needed a friend. She sure did now that things with Nick had gone sour.

He laughed, but then saw she was serious. "Why would

177

you wanna to do that? Haven't you and this fine gentleman here some plans of your own?" They both looked over the seat-back at the sleeping Nick. Had he gotten his hands on more phenobarbital? "Didn't you have evening plans in Norfolk?"

She paused, trying to put it into words. "I'm not going anywhere really. This was just a way to leave…where I was." She hated college, hated the people in Salem, Massachusetts, hated her parents—maybe even her country. "Maybe Canada will be better."

"I really couldn't promise you that. But at least they're not in a war."

For a minute, she couldn't remember his name—the boy she'd come with. "Nick," she said suddenly. "He's the one going home to Norfolk. Not me. His parents will probably kick me out if I turn up. Maybe even call my folks." And this was true. Why would they welcome a runaway into their home? "Hey, isn't William Shatner from Canada?"

"William who?"

"Captain Kirk on Star Trek," she said. "You know—the TV show."

"I don't watch much TV."

"Yeah, it's pretty lame."

"Hey, the bus is stopping," he said suddenly, peering out the window. "We're in Wilmington, I think. Delaware," he clarified, seeing the blank look on her face. "You're not from around here, are you?"

Stepping past her, he removed his guitar case and a knapsack from the overhead rack? "You coming? You don't have to…" He actually looked worried she would.

"Gaylen," she told him hurriedly. She stood up too, looking behind her. "Live long and prosper, Nick." Nick didn't move. What a stiff. She picked up her knapsack and prepared to go.

But when Bob had moved on toward the front of the bus,

she stepped back, turned quickly, and removed the protruding wallet from Nick's bag. Nick's eyes fluttered for a minute but he quickly settled back into his deep sleep. She looked up as Bob stepped onto the street outside, watched as he looked back warily. Was he losing interest already?

"Hey, Bob Gottlieb. Wait for me." She flashed him a boob through the bug-splattered window.

Tossing the wallet into her purse and hooking the strap of the bag over her shoulder, she ran for the door.

As she passed the bus driver, he looked at her and said, "This isn't Norfolk, you know. You got a ways to go."

"Yeah, but I'm with him now," she said, nodding toward Bob as she flew down the steps. "That guy with the guitar."

"Are You Going to Take Care of This Guy or Not"

"It is easy to take liberty for granted when you have never had it taken from you."

Lou's last meal at Jackson was on the night of the first debate between Cheney and the Jewish guy. He'd barely scarfed down the food, shoved through the port, when the guard came back and yanked it away. He was being fed in his cell to avoid last minute altercations, standard Jackson protocol for cons who were short-time.

The guards herded the most docile prisoners into a common room where the monitors were tuned to the debate.

"Can't we watch the poker channel instead?" someone joked, getting his head clipped in response.

"Porn, porn!"

It didn't have to be a good joke to evoke laughter, and the noise level rose.

"Shut the fuck up," a kid said. "I'm trying to hear the old dudes." This brought another round of guffaws.

"Not that any of you can vote, but you might learn somethin'," a guard said. "Be a test when it's over—for the ones of youse who can write." It was the guards chortling now.

Lou returned to his cell later, impressed with the two candidates. All the—whadya call them—commentators—agreed. Grandfatherly types, they called 'em. Kind of man he should become if he didn't want to end things with a backdoor parole—the way he'd always expected to leave here. He was gonna change his ways, make his girl proud. Take his grandson, Jason, outside and toss some balls. He looked at his tank, remembering there'd be none of that. Did kids still play Uno?

He'd put a lot of mileage between himself and the past. Shove a stick up his ass and be upright. Be a Cheney and Joe What's His Name kind of guy.

"Except for the occasional heart attack, I've never been better."

The parole came through once he went on oxygen twenty-four seven—a special handling case, pain in the butt. Prison croaker put in the word after he got the cords to his tank tangled in a geezer's wheelchair for the umpteenth time. Cons spending most of their lives in prisons usually ran out of housing options. Relatives died, drifted, got displaced. But he had his daughter, Marcie.

Marcie set him up in the back room—the one used for sewing projects, storing junk, laundry. Air smelled of spray starch, fabric, moth balls. Her iron board and sewing machine loomed over him. When he woke and saw the shadow of the plank on the wall, he thought someone was coming to shive him. He'd learned to sleep on his back watching the door a long time ago.

Jason was sixteen now, too old for Uno. Looked at his grandfather like he carried a filthy disease. His son-in-law, Stuart, watched the machine sucking air out of the room like his own lungs provided it, like the tank was debiting money directly from his bank account. Winced every time Lou's cords tripped someone, when he had to use his inhaler, when he didn't stay out of the way, when he did his old-man business in the toilet, when he ate too much.

"I had other priorities in the sixties than military service."

Time passed. A lot of time. He was watching TV most of the day, following the news on CNN.

"Not even a beer when I get out of here?" he'd asked the croaker.

"You gotta stay on your toes," the guy had said, patting his shoulder. For what, he wanted to ask?

Terrorists, Halliburton, friends getting shot in the face, boys spending years in places he couldn't find on a map. WMD—that was the term Cheney liked to throw around. Old Dick didn't look so grandfatherly anymore—spent most of his time in some unnamed bunker watching George's back. Using that phrase over and over. WMD.

Lou's life had been ruined in Nam—that's where he'd learned to smoke, drink, take dope, kill, steal. Men like Cheney sent him there. Grandfathers, lethal ones, sitting on his draft board like a panel of executioners.

Soon Jason might be in a war too.

"Go f*** yourself."

One day the call came. Marcie'd bought him his own cell phone, probably so he didn't have to vacate his roost. Bought a second TV, had it installed on his wall. His situation was like the prison break room, but smaller and more humid. She'd begun bringing his dinner in on a tray. He'd love to live on his own—even Jackson looked kinda good. He and Cheney had that much in common—holed up in a goddamned bunker.

I Bring Sorrow

He'd no idea how Willie Sandy got his number.

"So they sprung you?" Willie said. Eleven years since they'd pulled the job—the one that got Lou thrown in the slammer. A jewelry store where Sandy's niece once worked. She'd told them about a slim skylight over the backroom, and a few weeks later they were removing the glass, sliding in around two a.m.

"No one knows about it," she'd insisted, thinking of her part of the take. "Hidden by a chimney and crappy tarp."

Inside, they smashed through the glass cases with a hammer. Then it happened. Lou cut his finger. Left a fuckin' bloody print behind. Cops picked him up within hours. Recovered the jewels in the trunk of his car. He swore he'd done the job alone. Since he'd mostly worked alone in the past, they bought it.

"Sharky still has the diamonds from that other job—the month before," Sandy told Lou on the cell. "Been sitting on those rocks all these years. Just fenced the gold."

"That don't seem right," Lou said. But why would Sandy lie?

Lou'd never been convinced the two men weren't in cahoots back then—that they weren't living it up while he festered in Jackson. Maybe they'd even engineered the bloody print on the counter after the alarm went off. These were the paranoid fantasies that years beyond bars put in your head. Fixating on revenge can make you nuts.

"Are you kiddin' me?" he said now. "You've had the last five years to run him down. Why you calling me after all this time?"

"Diabetes," Willie Sandy said. "Lost my feet a few years back. Some of that money sure would help me out."

And me too, Lou thought, but didn't say it. "How the hell can I track him down?" he said, looking at his tank. He couldn't bring himself to tell Willie about it. Seemed too pathetic—even to a man with no feet.

"I know right where he is."

"My belief is we will, in fact, be regarded as liberators."

Sharky Black got rinsed at the Dearborn Dialysis Center. "Takes till three. Follow him home or wait in his car—nineties Cutlass. Blue." Sandy told him.

"How's it you know where he's doing dialysis and the make of his car, but not where he lives?"

"Had that car forever. And I know a guy who knows a guy."

Lou sighed. "I'll have to follow him home, see where he lives, and get him next time. I'm not movin' too fast nowadays. Look, there's no guarantee there's anything left. Eleven years is a long time."

"Local fences claim none of the big stuff ever turned up." Sandy knew his fences—that'd always been his thing.

Lou borrowed Marcie's car for an alleged doctor's appointment and found the facility.

It was a good ten minutes before Sharky exited, got the car started, and pulled out of the lot. Lou followed him home Wednesday and was waiting for him on Friday.

"Bet you're weren't expecting me," Lou said, sitting in what was clearly Sharky's favorite chair, his mini oxygen tank in his lap, a gun in his hand.

"Geez, Lou, you scared me. Isn't that kind of dangerous?" he said, nodding at the gun. "With your tank and all."

Lou didn't answer.

"When you get out?" Sharky sank onto the sofa, tossing his car keys on the table.

"Few years back. Guess you know why I'm here."

Sharky nodded. "Too late, Lou. Sold the stuff."

"Sandy says he checked with every fence in the state. None

of it ever turned up."

"Didn't fence it exactly."

"What then?"

"Heard about the emphysema, Lou," Sharky said, looking at the tank again. "Not much they can do for it, is there?"

Lou shook his head.

"And no way Sandy can get himself new feet. Good chair's about it."

"He can live better with some dough. So can I."

"I thought about that. But when it came down to it, the money can help me best. Can't buy you new lungs or Sandy new feet. So I bought myself a new kidney. Just got the call—some kid who died in a car crash. Surgery's tomorrow. You can kill me, Lou, but you still won't get the dough and you'll probably go back to Jackson. Do you see my point? That money moved me up to the top of the list, bought me a few more years. Maybe more."

"Or maybe less." Lou pulled the trigger and watched Sharky slip onto the floor. If he'd known where kidneys were, he'd have plugged the bastard there.

He'd always figured on a backdoor parole, and fuck if it wasn't pretty much the same as the backroom one he had now. He turned the air back on and walked out.

"We must be prepared to face our responsibilities and be willing to use force if necessary."

We Are All Special Cases

Polly was lying on the bed, book in hand, when she heard Saul's footsteps on the uncarpeted stairs. He'd paused on the floor below again, probably fumbling for his key. They'd forgotten the European practice in numbering floors, and each time he came back to the flat, he stopped at the wrong door. If they'd remembered this detail last autumn—realizing they were on the fourth floor and not the third—they'd never have rented this place. Then she wouldn't have sprained her ankle on the final step, an irregular one, worn down from too many tourists with heavy suitcases. In theory, she loved Paris; in actuality, it was a strain.

"There's such a thing as being too fond of familiarity," her husband, Saul, had said when she raised a few doubts about the trip. "You're far too young to find change so difficult. Doing new things is like a statin for the brain." He was always full of observations like this, usually involving some inadequacy on her part.

Was fifty-five years young in anyone's book? But it wasn't really about age. It was primarily about her fear of flying. Since she'd completed extensive therapy over this issue, she never mentioned it, just loaded up on Xanax.

I Bring Sorrow

"Do you realize when we went to Brazil, you came down with a stomach virus? And in Kyoto, you lost your voice."

"Coincidences?" she said weakly.

"I don't think we've once left the States without some sort of mishap."

Was this true? Had she always been this awful at being in a foreign place? What about their honeymoon in Dublin? Food poisoning, she remembered. They'd put her on a drip at the hospital there. Fearing air bubbles would enter her bloodstream; she never took her eyes off the IV.

"That can't happen nowadays," the nurse had assured her. But she'd read too many novels to believe her.

This trip, Polly sprained her ankle the first day. Immediately looking to Saul for sympathy, she saw a flash of anger in his eyes, a stiffening of his back. He practically had to carry her down the steps to get to the pharmacy, and he did it wordlessly

"Stay off it for a few days," the Parisian pharmacist suggested in perfect British English. "You're in Paris for a fortnight, right? You have time."

Once, years ago, she'd sprained a second ankle by putting too much weight on it. That was in Montreal. She was particularly clumsy on cobblestones.

Thoughts of the past flew out of her head as Saul finally got his floors straight and the door opened. She heard him putting the wine in the fridge.

"Should I leave the cheese out?"

The flat was so small he didn't need to raise his voice. "I got some great Emmental. We'll have ourselves quite the feast tonight. Wait till I tell you about the Picasso Museum. It's practically around the corner. Maybe you can get to it in a day or two."

"Hope so," she said, putting her finger in the book. She paused, debating saying it. "Saul, it's still there."

He stuck his head in the doorway and sighed. "So back to that again?"

"Am I supposed to ignore it?"

"No, but you're letting it—if there even is an it—take over."

She knew he'd like to point out other examples in her long history of preoccupations, but he left the room instead. Flouncing back down, she opened the book and began to read. She hadn't expected to like this book, but, set in Paris, it was the perfect choice. The streets in the book seemed as real as what she saw out the window. Sometimes life seemed safer a book's length away. And safer yet when she was reading in her own bed at home. This bed was more like a futon. It seemed stuffed with grains of sand.

"I prefer it," Saul had said the first night. "Better for my back."

"Why not sleep on the floor if that's the case?"

She sat up, watching him prepare to settle in for a nap. "Could you just take a look? Please."

She watched from the bed as Saul, sighing and slump-shouldered, walked over to the window and threw it open. The noise from the sidewalk café below drifted up. Someone was playing a radio. Saul closed the window with a bang. "Ugh. I came to get away from American music. Good thing it isn't hot and we can close it. Bet that noise goes on until three."

Up on her elbows, she could see bright light flowing through the glass. "Do you see it? Is it still there?"

"Yes, yes, I see it. But it's definitely a costume, Pol. Not half as large as it looked last night either. The light behind the curtain probably magnified it somehow."

The wings had seemed gigantic last night, taking up half the window. She was awestruck. Saul—not so much. He always wanted to see things as benign, normal. He'd never have spotted Raymond Burr murdering his wife. A bank of lit windows, in fact, would have no draw for him. He'd lower his shade and ignore them.

"Look at it through the camera, Saul. You can see it better with the telephoto lens."

Her voice was too shrill, but why did he insist on diminishing the wings? Making them seem smaller, less magical? These wings were all she had of Paris, after all.

He followed her instructions, snapping a few pictures even. He'd tried this last night, but the light was stronger now. He looked at what he'd shot and shrugged. "Probably a dancer lives there. Swan Lake? Isn't there an opera about birds too?""- No one could dance wearing wings that big." She was positive, having taken dance classes for six years.

"Okay, so then it's a costume for a play." He put the camera down and came into the bedroom. "A masquerade. Trick or treat." He looked at her. "The doctor didn't send you to bed, you know. Just said stay off your feet. You could sit in a chair, at least."

"It was only a pharmacist. And it's months to Halloween."

It was now, in fact, May—the month they'd thought best for their twenty-five year anniversary celebration even though they got married in July. Paris seemed the perfect destination. It wasn't as foreign as most of the places Saul wanted to go. Just last year he'd suggested New Guinea.

"Do the French even celebrate Halloween?" He sat down on the bed, examining her ankle. "Swelling's gone down. Hurt still?" He pressed on it lightly.

"Not unless I try to walk."

"Maybe you should try to walk around more. I think most doctors don't believe in keeping off it after the first day or so. It stiffens up."

"It feels better when I don't put weight on it." Was she getting lazy? She couldn't remember the last time she felt like walking anywhere.

"How can you stand it, coming to Paris and hardly leaving this place? If it were me..." He paused and looked back at the window. "Maybe it's for a costume ball?"

Conciliatory, so she'd be too. "I guess I could hobble across the street for a crepe."

He smiled. "I'll open the wine."

She'd first noticed the wings after limping out onto the tiny balcony for some air last night. In one direction lay a noisy creperie; in the other, a pricey shoe store. But across the narrow street was a window much like theirs—except for the wings, seemingly suspended in space. Angel, swan, it wasn't clear.

"These flats are small," he said when she called him to look. "Maybe that's the only place to store whatever it is. Be gone by tomorrow."

But it wasn't. She'd looked at the wings so often today the impression had been seared onto her retinas. Television programs were all in French so what else was there to do? Read her book. Look at the wings.

When they got back from dinner—and Saul was right, it did feel good to get out despite the flights of steps—the apartment across the way was dark. And although she tried, she couldn't tell if the wings were still there. It felt like they were, but she thought that if she mentioned this to Saul, he'd scoff. Felt like it. An odd thing to say. How could you feel like something was there? Shadows, perhaps, a heaviness.

She couldn't sleep. Her ankle throbbed. She didn't want to drink more wine—he blamed last night's hysteria on it. She'd slept too much today, drifting in and out of sleep while Saul visited the Picasso, Musee D'Orsay, the Rodin Museum. He'd brought back postcards for her.

"Of course, you can look at practically everything online

once we get home. Not that it's the same thing." He said this as if she'd suggested it.

Tucking the book under her arm, she crept into the living room, turning on the lamp on the desk.

It took a minute to see it, and she would have expected to scream but didn't. The wings had migrated over the course of the evening. They had, in fact, traveled across the street to the inside of their window—not ten feet away from her now. Had Saul left the window open? No, the noise from downstairs would have been too loud to ignore even this late. The window had been opened by something else. She'd like to shut it now but stood frozen.

Now that the wings were close, she could see they were much larger than she'd even imagined. They were about her height but much wider. The wingspan must be ten feet. It wasn't a costume or anything like it. Whatever it was, and she didn't have the answer to that, it was quivering: alive. Although quiver was the wrong word because it implied some sort of hesitation or fear. It was undulating, heaving like a beating heart, perhaps.

When she looked across the street, the window was wide open, the curtains streaming outward. What had made it seek her out? Had it watched her as closely as she watched it? Had her all-day vigil encouraged it? Had they made some sort of connection?

Slowly, she drew closer to the wings, looking into its insect-like eyes on each side of its head. A moth, she thought, and a giant one. Its coloring was not the white it appeared to be from across the street, but something closer to a lavender-gray. It twitched, fluttered, surged. She put out her hand.

"Polly, are you up again?" It was Saul from the bedroom, his voice sodden with sleep. "If you got more exercise…"

"Just looking at the wings," she said, deciding not to tell

him of the immigration. She could hear his sigh, and she sighed too.

Suddenly, there was a fluttery movement and she was enveloped within the wings. Like a delicate embrace. Inside, the wings were not quite solid. She could see through them, out into the night, back into the bedroom. She'd never felt so safe.

"You'd better come into bed and get some sleep," Saul said, sounding sleepier yet. "You don't want to miss any more of Paris."

"I won't," she said with confidence.

Polly, securely cocooned, flew out the window and into the night.

The Cape

"You make me a cappa? Si?"

The man standing at the counter had entered the shop quietly, and the proprietor, Joseph Valente, whipped around, wondering if the bell usually triggered by the opening door had malfunctioned. Then he saw the gray-gloved hand holding it still. Joseph had learned enough Italian to know cappa meant cape. For the gentleman's wife, no doubt, for this was certainly a gentleman.

He looked familiar, but the tailor couldn't place him. He spoke with a thick accent, an accent Joseph's Neapolitan wife, Valentina's family shared. But no relative of his wife dressed like this, so elegant in his single-breasted dove-gray waistcoat with a prominent watch chain, a wing-collared shirt, and a silky black bow tie. He wore a homburg on his rather large head. Never had a man dressed like this entered Joseph's shop. And today was a scorching hot day. Joseph was suffering dressed only in a cotton shirt and summer trousers. But the man seemed unaffected by it.

Although Joseph Valente had made a cape or two for women, he'd never made one for a man, and especially not for a man who, from the cut of his clothes, was used to the finest tailoring available in a city offering the top couture outside of Europe. Mulberry Street would be slumming for his kind. All of these thoughts passed through Joseph's mind with lightening speed as the businessman in him answered.

"An opera cape, sir?"

Joseph's mind flew to his pattern books for men's clothing. Did he have a book with men's capes? Perhaps he could alter a cape meant for a woman—change the cut and collar a bit. A job like this one could bring in money. He'd have to be very sharp indeed to impress this man. But why was he here in the first place? How was it possible his shop had made itself known to this man?

In Italian, the man told him the cape would be for outdoors. Moving his fingers in demonstration, the man wiped his brow with a large white handkerchief. "Andare."

"You want a cape to walk outside?"

"Si. Fur cappa. Per inverno in da zoo. No vorrei prendersi un raffreddore." Catch a cold, Joseph translated silently. He doesn't want to catch a cold when he walks in the zoo. How odd. Was he a zoo administrator? Or perhaps a wealthy patron of the uptown institution?

The customer waved his fingers, like the pope or a king might, looking at Joseph as if the reason for such concern was obvious. Joseph smiled and nodded as if it were. Perhaps the man was suffering from consumption, although he looked too well fed to have a disease that left most of its victims looking, well, consumptive.

The man walked to the door and stepped outside, pulling a tiny case from his breast pocket and putting a lozenge in his mouth. The humidity from Tina's laundry business in the back of the shop took some getting used to. After years of proximity, he could still smell the noxious laundry powder and bleach. But the scent of a hot iron on a dampened cotton shirt held its own delights, which was what he smelled this morning. The Irish girl who assisted his wife was singing *Let Me Call You Sweetheart* in a lilting soprano voice. Joseph usually found her habit a pleasant diversion from his work. Today's customer, however, seemed unimpressed, even annoyed, as he re-entered the shop. He made a face demanding action.

"Theresa, we have a customer," Joseph called out. He didn't like to hurt her feelings, but the customer came first.

The singing ended abruptly and something clattered to the floor. The two men looked at each other, sizing each other up in some indefinable way, and then Joseph reached for his drawing pad and began sketching. After a few minutes, he turned the pad around and slid it across the counter.

"Something like this, perhaps?" He could have drawn a better cape if he hadn't been shaking with anxiety. Or if he'd ever seen a man in a fur cape just once in his lifetime. His fingertip added a bit of shading to highlight how the cape would catch the breeze.

The man looked at it carefully and nodded with a small smile. "And da fur? Che categoria?"

Joseph was flattered such an elegant man would ask for his opinion on this important question. Perhaps it was a test? And one he might fail. Closing his eyes, he sped through a virtual furrier's display catalog. Better to suggest the easiest pelts to obtain, the most familiar. He had done some stoles in mink.

"Mink, I think. And dark red lining would be elegant."

The man smiled. "Red. Is not—come si dice?—garish?"

Joseph nearly laughed. As if a fur cape on a man could be anything but garish. "Not garish at all. Moto elegante."

"Si. Uno minuto," the man said, turning the pad back so it faced Joseph. "Necessita un taglios per mie mani." He drew a finger along the sides of the sketched cape. "Qui penso."

A slit for his hands! "Normally a cape ties at the neck, sir, allowing complete mobility for your hands. You won't need a...slit."

The man shook his head. He looked Joseph right in the eyes for the first time. "Cucire un taglio?" He mimicked the action.

There was no arguing with a customer. "Certainly. A slit would satisfy that requirement."

The man fairly hummed with pleasure. He was probably imagining himself in this fine fur cape already.

"A black lining, yes. As long as I can acquire the proper materials, it shouldn't take more than a few weeks."

In truth, Joseph was a novice with fur. He used no regular furrier. Nor did he know what working with this amount of mink would entail. He'd suggested it because it was the fur he saw most often when he went uptown to look in shop windows. The one he had used for a stole or two. Perhaps his machine would need a special needle for the job—even a particular needle foot. Could he get such a thing on short notice? But he'd learn quickly, get what was needed at once, because the price of this assignment would keep his family in coal for the winter and put red meat on the table.

Perhaps there'd be money enough to purchase Mr. Hoover's new machine for Tina's precious carpets. She'd been swept off her feet, so to say, by a demonstration of its efficiency at a local fair. And if this cape suited his customer, perhaps his friends would make their way downtown. Or, even better, perhaps Joseph would make his way uptown.

"You'll never guess, Tina," he told her that night. "An elegant man came into my shop today and asked me to make him a fur cape. Me," he repeated, putting his thumbs under his arms. "He seemed to know my work." Was this true or had his head puffed up the way his mother always warned it would?

"Oh, Joseph, that is fine news. And where did this gentleman hear about you?" she asked, echoing his first thought and calling into question his last.

"I never asked him," he admitted.

"What is his name?"

"I never asked him that either."

"Oh, Joseph. What if you make the cape and he never returns?"

The excitement had apparently wiped questions like these from his head. He shrugged.

He could see the wheels turning in Tina's head.

"I wonder if it was that forest green dress you made for Mrs. Walton. It had fur trim around the hem and neck. Perhaps word got around."

He'd forgotten that gown. Mrs. Walton had worn it to her son's marriage to a society girl in Connecticut last winter. Perhaps that was where this customer saw it. Up in Darien, he thought. Of course, he'd hand-stitched that fur onto the neckline and hem. His stitches were so tiny that Mrs. Walton asked for a magnifying glass to see them. This gentleman must have attended the wedding too. It was settled in their minds.

The next morning, Joseph began his hunt for the proper materials. A furrier on Mercer Street had several nice pelts and was able to provide him with advice and the proper needle foot.

"For a man, you say?" Mr. Gross asked him.

Joseph paused, wondering if it was a good idea to admit to that given the gentleman's surreptitious visit. "For his wife, I imagine. A surprise, I think."

"She must be a large woman." Mr. Gross looked with interest at the measurements. "Enormous shoulders, hasn't she?" His hands indicated what might cause that feature and Joseph blushed.

The job went more quickly than he expected despite the handwork needed. The cape was ready in less than a month. Tina stood over him every night, offering her opinions on the alterations in the pattern he'd made. She found the perfect binding for the slits, in fact. It was a black braid with a faint gold thread running through it. Sturdy yet elegant.

"Is it really for a man, Joseph?"

"Yes, yes. And one I have seen before if I could just remember where."

"This cape will make you famous." She ran her hands through the fur again. "But why these silly slits?" She poked her fingers through the openings and wiggled them.

Joseph shrugged. "Rich people. Who can understand them? Something to make them stick out at the theater." That thought almost rang a bell.

"Stick out indeed," Tina said, wriggling her fingers through the slits again.

Enrico Caruso walked into the zoo in Central Park in November, 1906. Over the summer, he'd taken his exercise at the Bronx Zoo uptown, but the recent commotion over Benga, a pygmie who slept in a hammock in the monkey house, brought him down here. John Verner's exotic find had brought riff-raff into the quiet of the monkey house. Benga, famous for shooting arrows into the bull's-eye of a target set up amidst the primates, also marauded about the zoo on a hot day. He had a talent for finding a person who would find his attention repellent rather than amusing. On one distressful occasion, he followed the tenor himself, pretending to steal his cotton candy to please the crowd. Caruso would have no more of that attention. He did not go to the zoo to be part of the attraction. He would save that talent for the stage.

The zoo in Central Park was far less impressive but would do for Caruso's purposes and save him the longer carriage ride.

The cape was more glorious than he'd even anticipated. He felt embraced by the soft fur: warm and elegant. He strolled toward the monkey house, breathing in the chill air. Once inside, adjusting his eyes to the darkness, he spotted her. He preferred blondes, and this woman was ideal for his game in her thin winter coat. She stood in front of the orangutan cage, watching a female nurse her baby. Her intense interest in this activity gave him an advantage.

Caruso looked around. Although his fur cape allowed him to blend into the dark enclosure, he had to be sure that pesky guard had not spotted him. A few weeks earlier, the man had tapped him on the shoulder with his nightstick, warning him about standing too close to the women. He couldn't identify himself in such circumstances so he was forced to accept such treatment. With a bowed head, he moved away. Of course, the fur cape was still too warm to wear in October. Now it freed his hands to roam less conspicuously.

Caruso stood right behind the blonde, his knees pressed against her thighs. His fingers darted through the slits, grabbing a handful of the woman's bottom. Just as quickly, he stepped away. Her scream echoed through the empty monkey house.

"Sir," she said, spotting him in the dark. "How dare you."

He looked around to suggest another person might be guilty of the crime. It was then that the same guard stepped out from behind a pillar. He gestured to the famous tenor. Within minutes, the cop had handcuffed him and led him away. Luckily his cape made the cuffs nearly invisible.

"Joseph, Joseph," Tina cried, waking him. "You will never believe who it was that bought your cape."

Joseph was more asleep than awake.

"What coat?" he asked, throwing the blanket aside. His bare feet hit the chilly floor in a rush.

"Your cape, your cape. The fur one."

In a flash, Tina was standing at the kitchen table with the

New York Post spread open. Drowsily, Joseph made his way across the room. Had his cape turned up on the society page?

Joseph saw the face first—the face that had haunted him.

"Enrico Caruso," his wife said before he could read the caption. "He's been arrested for fondling a woman in the monkey house in Central Park." She giggled and then covered her mouth. "He told the zoo guard a monkey did it. A monkey named Knocko."

"I suppose it is possible," Joseph said. He had stood too close to the cages himself on more than one occasion. The creatures were always looking for food. Always trying to grab the loose scarf or hat.

"They are looking for the woman he...touched. Her name is Hannah Graham."

"I can read it myself, Tina."

"The police want to know where he acquired a fur coat with slits for his wandering hands," Tina continued despite his comment. "They think the tailor was in cahoots with Mr. Caruso. That's you, Joseph," she added unnecessarily.

Joseph's heart sunk. Was he now to be part of a criminal case? Would conspiring with a masher ruin him? How was he to know the nefarious purpose for the slits? Such an intention never occurred to him.

"He's going to have to go to court," Tina told him, unwilling to let him read a single word of the story himself. "But they're allowing him to meet his obligations at the Met."

"The Met's patrons run city hall."

This was a subject they often discussed. The city was run for the rich and by the rich. Only the crumbs from their table fell on the Lower East Side.

"Why would a man with good looks, money, and a voice like his need to find his fun in the monkey house?" Tina asked. "I can't believe you didn't recognize him. He's in the newspaper every day."

Joseph shrugged. "It's a game he's playing probably. A rich man's game." Although then he remembered reading that Caruso had been born in the slums.

"They're talking about closing it down," Tina read. "There's a petition by a women's group."

"The Met?" Joseph said, scanning the article for further mention of his cape.

"No, Joseph, the monkey house. You silly man." She paused, and then giggled. "Where will he ever find a place so dark?"

"The subway is finished, let him go there," Joseph said. "It's dark on those platforms. Darker than a monkey house."

He was angry for some reason. His beautiful cape had been merely a means to a horrible, reprehensible act. He was glad Mr. Caruso had paid him in cash the day he picked up the cape. It would be difficult to extract it from him now.

"What upper-class gentleman would use the subway?" his wife asked.

"What society gentleman would pinch a woman's bottom in a monkey house?"

The coming days were tense in the Valente household. Every time the bell rang, Joseph expected to see a uniformed policeman enter his shop. But such a thing never happened. Mr. Caruso paid a small fine and continued to charm opera lovers across the globe. The fate of the cape is unknown.

Patricia Abbott

How to Launder a Shirt

I can't stop thinking about my husband's new wife.

She must toss his shirts into a dryer because I haven't seen them hanging on the clothesline. In fact, the line is wrapped around one of the metal poles behind the house—as if it hasn't been used in years. She'd be surprised at the difference fresh air can make. Maybe Helene didn't grow up in a place where you could hang wash outside in the bright sunlight, capturing that scent. I bet she grew up in the city, where clothes hung outside sometimes had to be washed again. Or the feel of them, gritty and stiff, wasn't something you wanted on your skin. Funny how often Joe's skin was an object of concern.

Helene stands on our porch all the time. Joe never did like putting furniture outside, so it's empty—just like it always was. The floor still needs painting and has the same loose board as you step up to the door. He said a chair on a porch was an invitation for folks to visit, and he didn't care for strangers in his house. Nor on his porch.

I said "our" porch when what I really meant was "their" porch. No one ever talks about the difficulty of altering pronouns once a marriage is finished.

She stands there smoking as I did once—burying the butts

around the yard as I did too. She's probably hoping for a car to pass by. Or idly watching the brazen crows pick corn from the farm next door. Maybe waiting for an airplane to fly overhead. The days can be long so you try to break them up with almost anything. I still remember that—the way a ringing phone, the mail delivery, or a crop duster became something exciting.

If it's late in the day, Helene's waiting for the school bus to drop off my kids. I still think of them as mine, of course. Her hair, which is long, wispy, and reddish-blonde, blows prettily in the wind. The back of her hand shades her gray eyes when the sun starts to drop to eye-level. I kept my hair short after a few mishaps, so nothing could grab hold of it.

Towels—towels need a dryer with one of those little paper sheets to make them soft. Hang them on the line, and the wind can blow the softness right out of them. It takes a long time to learn which routine works best. Trial and error. But Joe isn't the most patient man. You'd better get your Ps and Qs straightened out fast where he's concerned.

Helene wears slacks—the dressy kind with pleats. Joe never liked me to wear trousers, as he called them. Said a woman with legs as good as mine owed it to her husband to show them off. I didn't mind. Well, yes, I did mind, but when a request—or an order—comes along with a compliment attached, what can you do? Joe had a specific skirt length he preferred. Too long and he said I looked like an Amish woman. Too short and I looked like a, well, you know. Since we didn't have a full-length mirror in the house, I figured he knew best.

I wonder when Joe started liking pleated slacks. Maybe Helene's legs don't draw men's glances. Despite what he says, it's just as well that they don't. That's one of the tricky things about Joe—he blames you for what happened when you were just following his orders.

Perhaps his new wife sends his shirts to a laundry. Maybe

that new place on Elm Street in Marine City tends to their things now. Chinese people are known for their skill in laundering shirts. If this is the case, Joe must've changed his mind in the last year or two because he couldn't tolerate commercially laundered shirts in my day. Said the chemicals they used were poisonous—just like that MSG they put in food. Told me the machine that tumbled the clothes dry was filled with other people's germs.

Joe was very particular about most things. His shoes always had to point north in his closet. Point them east or south and you were likely to spend some time in the closet with them. Forget to insert the wooden trees and...

Joe worked for—well, he still does, come to think of it—the Ford dealer in Warren. Sales were down to almost nothing that last year of our marriage. I kept telling him I could get a job and he kept doing what he did when he got angry. Now the car business is back on track, I hear. If things had recovered more quickly, it might be me looking for the school bus from the porch.

It's possible Joe's wearing wrinkle-free shirts now, although it would surprise me. That kind of shirt was around in my day, but neither of us was satisfied with the way he looked in them. They had the sort of sheen that looked like they'd melt into your skin if you stood too close to a fire. Actually, I didn't think they were bad, but Joe said he lost sales when he wore one. Said it looked like he couldn't afford anything better—or that no one was taking good care of him.

I felt my eye twitch as I watched him finish the knot on his tie the last day, wondering if I'd carelessly put too much starch in his shirt collar. It looked so stiff against his neck somehow. Joe's neck was tender, and getting the starch right took some doing. I can't tell you how many fights we had early on over those shirts. I wish I could warn Helene about that. I know it might be unusual, but I've grown fond of her over time and grateful for the way she looks after my girls.

Although the laundering of shirts seems like a simple thing, it's one that comes up every day. The care and maintenance of shirts involves equipment and processes that choke, burn, and electrocute. It's easy to fall going up and down the cellar stairs with baskets of clothes. One can strangle on a clothesline that twists cruelly on those metal poles. Things you care about like your good coat or the kitten that climbed up on the porch one day can turn up inside a clothes dryer without any warning.

I just can't stop thinking about my husband's new wife. She'd do well to get the procedure for the care of Joe's clothes sorted out as quickly as possible.

Unless, of course, she wants to rest under the back forty with me.

Patricia Abbott

My Social Contracts

Weddings after a certain age, say thirty-five or forty, often smack of a bargain. It may not be spelled out in a contract or even verbalized, but it's there. The mistakes made in earlier relationships make us turn a jaded eye on the next one. Fool me once or something.

My first husband, Leonard, suffered from a need to participate in various rituals, a psychiatric condition I'd not heard much of at twenty-three. An illustration: he spent considerable time deciding what type of tea to have before going to bed, making a ceremony of selecting, brewing, and serving it. Harmless, yes, but a wearying ceremony to observe at the end of a long day. That's what comes from marrying an older man. Another obsession: the music of Philip Glass, which had to be played during sex and on special occasion dinners. Thankfully, our evenings of both sexual activity and special dinners dwindled quickly, and Glass' compositions became a dim—or should I say din—memory.

Truthfully, I had little else to complain about with Leonard. He surpassed me in his obsession with neatness. In fact, he may have nurtured the quality in me, leading me to a full-blown compulsion. I remember marveling at the order in his

I Bring Sorrow

color-coded closet and bureau drawers when he invited me up early on and I took a peek.

But when he died suddenly, I found out all those little rites and rituals—most I have not shared here in the interest of brevity—had come at the price of an adequate inheritance. Never once did he allude to his dwindling portfolio. I am making myself seem more craven than I was: I loved Leonard in my own way, and he loved me in his. It just wouldn't figure into a romance novel.

I lived on his money for nearly a decade, but then it was time to figure out the next move. I was not the bright young thing of twenty years earlier, but my goal was a modest one. I was looking for a man with a steady job who wanted a stay-at-home wife but no children. And also a man requiring scant romance in his life and even less fussing over. I was particularly loath to do that.

George Starkey stood out. He was a successful car salesman who worked long hours and had needs I could satisfy. What I brought to the bargain was the maintenance of a clean house, good meals, and serving as a respectable escort at social functions. I detested parties, but I threw him first-rate ones at suitable intervals and sat with him in church each Sunday despite having no such beliefs myself. Salesmen need visibility in the community, and I understood my part of the bargain. I was still moderately attractive, and I gardened, cooked, and cleaned better than anyone, not that it seemed to mean much to him. To me, it meant everything. I am sure a shrink could tell me why, but I didn't examine my obsession, just indulged it with hours spent on my hands and knees with a scrub brush, at the stove stirring, on ladders cleaning windows, pulling weeds, reordering a closet or a drawer.

It wasn't expensive clothes or cars or travel I was after. I wanted what wives of a generation earlier had craved: a quiet, clean suburban existence and a house that invited, no, called out for, inspection. That was our deal, although it was never discussed. I doubt he was even aware of it. But to my mind, our bargain was written in stone. George gave me the money I needed to indulge this lifestyle for a good many years. He never complained and neither did I. Sometimes I wondered if we were both settling for less than we deserved, but I kept such feelings to myself.

The downturn in U.S. car sales came earlier than the one brought on by Wall Street. George was good at what he did, but even the best salesman cannot save a dealer who has pumped money into bad investments and luxury items rather than his business. And although George had changed bosses over the years, he'd landed at a dealership selling particularly undesirable cars when things went bust.

"I doubt we'll ride the month out," George said at dinner one night. "Plesper was holed up with his accountant all day. Better start tightening your belt." His elasticized waistband, something we noted together, made a mockery of this expression.

"I'm sure it will be all right," I told him, watching him push his peas onto his fork with his index finger.

Soothing George did not come naturally. I knew I should offer another sentence or two of commiseration but was stuck. So I repeated the same words, and thankfully he didn't notice. I considered patting his hand but the fork was still in it—with the peas as well—so instead I made that clucking sound that signals support.

"It's not going to be all right, Zelda. You might as well get used to the idea that things around here may have to change." He looked around the room for an example but couldn't come up with one. "No trips to Honolulu," he eventually said, which was quite amusing since we'd never been anywhere more distant than Cape May, New Jersey. To be fair, this was more my fault than his. Leaving the house for more than a day or two was very stressful. I too easily imagined the influx of dust, dirt, and decay and was unable to enjoy myself. And the thought that my quiet house might attract vermin—of both the human and animal kinds—doomed any hope of an enjoyable time.

"I won't pack my bags anytime soon," I said, striving for humor, which is another trait that doesn't come easily to me. He stared for a second—obviously reading it as sarcasm—threw his napkin down on the table, and sauntered off to watch TV.

George had worked so many hours over the course of our marriage that he had nothing to do with himself on the evenings he was home. I watched that night as he tried in vain to find something that would interest him on TV, finally settling on a show about people blindly bidding for unclaimed items in storage units. In a sense, that was what each of us had done when we married.

A few weeks later, George announced the final demise of Rader Motors. "Not even a package to grease the deal," he said. "Plesper's accountant announced it before we had time to take our overcoats off."

"Doesn't he have to provide severance pay?"

George shook his head. "Not if he doesn't have the money to do it. It's not like I'm working for a big corporation with iron-clad rules for issues like severance pay."

"You can collect unemployment until you find something else." I was anxious to be done with this. The dirty dishes in the sink beckoned to me.

He nodded. "That won't be much, and it won't last for long. Finding a job at fifty-eight will be tough. I've never worked for anyone outside the car industry and not many dealers are looking for salesmen now."

"A good salesman can always find work," I said in a final attempt to buck him up. "Every industry uses salesmen." I knew I should've probably supplied more succor here, but such a balm would've taken considerably more practice. I was used to dealing out a repertoire of clichés.

He shrugged, being a man of low expectations.

George was right though. His age went against him, although unspoken, of course, in every interview he was able to get. And that number was small. We were not on the verge of complete bankruptcy, but a few years of unemployment might mean selling the house and moving to a more modest suburb. He put this idea to me himself on many occasions over the next weeks, and the streak of cruelty in his voice was something new.

I looked around my house. I'd poured every ounce of creativity, love, and energy I possessed into our home. The curtains were handmade, the wallpaper chosen and hung by me. Every carpet had been picked with great care. The paint was nothing you could find at Sherwin Williams—I had it specially mixed. It was a perfect house and I was both responsible for and devoted to its flawlessness.

The more George hung around the house, the more that perfection began to show chips. Chips, dents, ashes, stains, burns, dirt he tracked in with his shoes—well, you get the sense of it. George was untidy. He never closed a door, drawer or cabinet. He never put his clothes into the hamper or into his closet. I'd always known this about him, but traits annoying in a man you had to deal with only a few hours a week became unbearable in one around most of the time.

"You never minded before," he said when I complained about the seven cabinet doors hanging open in the kitchen.

"What else do you have to do?" he said when I spent an hour rearranging the closet I'd only arranged a few days earlier.

I Bring Sorrow

"Why don't you put the recycling bin where I can reach it?" he suggested, patting the floor next to him when I swept the empty Heineken cans into a bag. He was driving me mad.

Weeks turned into months. Both George and I grew more irritable, and he began going to the local bar. I was glad for the hours of peace, but the expense of it and the condition he returned home in were unacceptable. If he was untidy while sober, inebriation proved fatal. And I was beginning to wonder if he didn't enjoy it. Complete idleness may have made a nice change for him.

I had some experience with remedying a situation like this one—a circumstance that threatened my carefully constructed life. Early in our marriage, George had stopped his car in a rural area for gas and come upon an abandoned dog. No collar, no license, but a friendly mutt. They took to each other and George brought him home. He was a small dog, nice enough as dogs go, and George named him Esso after the gas station where he'd found him.

Esso turned out to have some bad habits. He was clumsy, sloppy, and he barked too much. He liked to hide things, trotting after you as you searched for them. Once these annoying traits made themselves known, I saw nothing wrong with the dog spending most of the day in our yard. It was a pleasant fenced yard behind the house. But once outside, Esso either dug up my flowers or barked to be let back in. If I shut him up inside a room, he barked too. None of this barking occurred when George was home. When I tried to tell George about Esso's behavior, he was entirely unsympathetic.

"You can take care of a little dog, can't you?" he said. "How much trouble can he be?"

So, of necessity, I developed a plan. Esso loved to dig so I began standing on the other side of the fence with a nice piece of meat in my hand. Day by day, Esso got a little more successful in tunneling his way under the metal fence and out of the yard. When a perfect tunnel under the fence stood as proof, I bundled him in the car and took him to an animal rescue facility in a distant town. There the kind people assured me he would be easily placed given his friendliness.

"You can't keep him, huh?" the woman said. "Such a delightful dog."

"Allergies," I told her, wiping my nose with a tissue.

"Ah."

Surely dogs have been sacrificed for less than a person's sanity and the preservation of a house.

"Esso seems to have run away," I told George that night, showing him the tunnel with a flashlight. "How clever he was to dig his way out. He must have been practicing for weeks," I added, pointing to some other spots where the dog had been.

"He seemed so happy," George said, kneeling down next to the fence. "Do you smell anything?" I shook my head. The meat lay there for almost an hour while Esso dug his way under the fence so it wasn't surprising.

George spent days trying to find him, posting signs around the neighborhood, notifying the police. He met with no success.

"We'll have to look for another dog," George said when his hope dried up.

"Perhaps in the spring," I said. He forgot, of course. Those were the days when the auto business was flush.

Back in the present, George's behavior continued to worsen, and our arguments increased. One night he took a swing at me, and only a quick move on my part spared me a black eye. He apologized profusely, but the gloves were off. But an all-out fight might destroy the very thing I was striving to save—my home. Many women would have forced him to prepare his own meals, but the mess this involved made it impossible. Withholding sex was long gone as a punishment, and any silent treatment played right into his hands. He'd always complained that my only conversation concerned household matters and it bored him.

Things grew worse. As the money in our accounts seeped away, he continued to leave the house every night, coming home dead drunk around midnight. He was able to walk home, although the dirty and torn knees of his trousers made it clear he stumbled quite a bit. His breath in the bed next to me was noxious, and I began sleeping in the den. Something had to be done before he either sold the house out from under me or destroyed it bit by bit.

Since it was unlikely I could turn George over to a rescue center, my actions would have to be more drastic. I searched online for methods of murder, but all of them had limitations in either execution or detection. I certainly did not intend to trade my house, the very object that drove my actions, for a jail cell.

One night, more out of curiosity than as part of any plan, I followed George to his watering hole. I turned up, as near as I could estimate, about the time he usually headed for home. I watched as he sidled out the front door and around to the side of the building. There, under the glare of an enormous metal lamp in a little alcove, he relieved himself. The entire process must have taken a full three minutes. First his fat hand on the wall steadying his swaying body, followed by a fumbling search for the zipper, the long wait until the process began, the zip-up at its conclusion. He managed to smoke half a cigarette while this ritual took place. That almost made me angrier than the luridness of it all. Smoking! I thought I'd put that habit to rest years before.

I was sure Bub's Pub had bathrooms. Why would George choose such a well-lit spot? Because it was a little ceremony,

I suddenly realized. As drunk as he was, he would choose to lay down a routine for getting himself home. I'd heard or read that urinating outside was not uncommon for men. In Amsterdam, men insisted that peeing from the canal bridges was a God-given right.

While George slept a week later, I scouted Bub's wearing a wig and a non-descript outfit. The lamp George stood under every night—and I checked on that habit two more times—was just beneath the ladies' room window and affixed to the stonewall with a large metal plate. If I stood on the john and opened the window, I could reach the lamp. It was a huge fixture—surely weighing fifty pounds or more when you considered the base, the lamp, and the fanciful impediments soldered onto it. A large rusty cherub was attached to the base. A bird perched on the finial. It had to pre-date the current use of the facility because its elegance was certainly not contemporaneous with the pub inside. It was probably a brass fixture, although no one had bothered to polish it for years. Sticking my hand through the open window, I could easily reach it. The screws seemed loose and a bit rusty. Should this lamp land on an unsuspecting head, could that person survive? I certainly didn't want to tend to an addled George for a dozen years.

I actually did a trial run twice. I ducked into the bar just before George's departure, headed for the ladies' room—no worry about him seeing me, as drunk as he was—and practiced loosening the screws from my perch on the john in the left stall. The lamp's drop would be one of about twenty feet since the restrooms were located on the half-floor above the bar. In the several times I went there, there was never a woman there, although men seemed to exit quite regularly from the room next door. Apparently, George's proclivity for relieving himself outside was not universally shared. I'd have to be quiet, though, because the wall between the two rooms seemed thin.

I sound a lot calmer than I was. Even practicing the maneuver made my palms sweat and my heart pound. But day by day, George was making life impossible. And should we separate, I would get only half of a fairly paltry amount. Most importantly, I would lose the house. The house would be on the auction block within weeks.

I chose a night when the bar would be busy—easier to sneak in and out among a crowd. St. Patrick's Day, in fact. Green beer flowed from the taps like a river undammed. When the time for George's exit drew near, I took my place in the stall. I smelled his cigarette being lighted outside. He never looked up, never heard my hands fumbling at the window, and seconds later the massive lamp landed on his head the way I expected. I peeked out and saw a pool of blood beginning to form under his head. It looked black now that the light was gone. The cigarette still burned in his limp hand.

I nearly blew it, though—one of those things you just couldn't anticipate. As I let myself back into my house, I looked down and saw I'd tracked tar or some substance all over my carpet. I thought back over the evening. Had I left tracks of tar on that toilet seat? Tar tracks would certainly tip off the cops that the lamp's fall was not necessarily an accident. It was even possible I'd left a footprint in the stall or on the seat, really pointing a finger toward me.

Back I went, Goo Be Gone in hand. George was still lying in the same spot. I crept inside where the party was going full blast and cleaned off the toilet seat, which indeed showed signs of my visit. It took only a minute or so and I felt strangely exhilarated by my quick thinking.

Nothing went wrong after that. Not for a long time. A small group of family and friends buried George a few days later. No one suggested the accident was anything other than…accidental. The screws the cops found were rusty. The lamp was over seventy-five years old, it turned out, its weight considerable. And luckily, any number of people had observed George taking his nightly pee on other nights. "Yes, yes, he did that all the time," one of them chuckled and then frowned with embarrassment.

George left me a large enough inheritance to live on nicely. And once his Social Security kicked in, things would only improve. It was during one of my jaunts to the cemetery to scrub George's grave and headstone a few months later that I ran into trouble. A shady little man approached me as I knelt over the grave, scrub brush in my hand.

"I have this problem," he told me when I looked up. He was about my age but looked liked he spent almost no time outside.

"I beg your pardon."

"Yeah. I can't seem to do anything about it—my little ritual," he continued. "You'll never guess."

I looked around me for signs of what he was referring to. Perhaps he was the one who left the baby shoes on the benches I'd passed one on my way to George's grave today. Or maybe it was he who pinned queasy little notes to the headstones. Printed sayings a lunatic might think funny.

Like, "Here lies Anna White, silent at last. You can thank me later. All those who pass."

"Don't you want to know what it is?" He was crouching down, his breath in my ear. "My problem and where you fit in."

I didn't say anything. Better not to encourage him.

He reached into his pocket and took out a snapshot. "You'd better take a look."

I knew it was going to be some horrible photo. I just didn't know how horrible. I took a quick glance and gasped. The photo was of me, cleaning the toilet at Bub's. I was on my hands and knees, giving the john a good scrub. A look of determination distorted my face.

"How did you get this?" I whispered, looking around. "Are you a cop?" I knew he wasn't though. No cop dressed like this.

"That's where my little problem comes in—my little proclivity I think they call it. Sometimes, and it is often just after the infrequent woman enters the ladies' room that I find myself in the right stall in the men's room at Bub's with a camera in my hand. Well, an iPhone now. Smaller, you know. At home, I have an envelope full of snaps I've taken at Bub's over the years." He giggled a little. "A history of Bub's female patrons and the changing fashion in underwear."

"You're a pervert," I said, still staring at the snapshot. "How did you know I'd be here today?" I looked around to see if other men were hiding in the bushes.

"You stick to a routine. Thursdays at two, you come here. If it's raining, it's Friday. Found out the first week I watched you."

"You've been doing this for years? Taking these pictures?" I said, looking at the snapshot again. Why had nobody noticed the hole in the wall?

"Oh, yes, indeedy," he said. "For a long time, it was just a thing I did for my own pleasure. Never thought about a payoff. Other than the usual one." He giggled. "But all those years led up to the day I saw you scrubbing that bowl." He smiled. "And a pretty sight it was. I think they'd have to look into George's death again, should they see this picture. The cops, I mean."

I thought in vain for a way out. The snapshot was dated, which certainly left little room for doubt as to when he took it. He'd managed to get almost my entire face into what was essentially a profile shot. I looked deranged, of course. Like someone who'd just murdered her husband. The bottle of Goo

Be Gone rested on the floor.

"I must have missed you the first time," the man said. "Your big moment, I mean."

"I assume you want something from me or you would've gone to the police."

"Yes, indeedy." He paused as he put the snapshot back into his pocket, patting it. "Plenty more of those just in case you wondered. You know, George talked about you a lot over the months we shared a pint at Bub's. Even with my running into the men's room every so often, he managed to tell me what a fine housekeeper you were. What a great cook. Those are qualities not always valued nowadays. He thought it was all pretty funny, but I thought it was sweet."

I didn't say anything.

"Ever since my wife died, I've been all thumbs trying to keep things in order. Oh, yes, even perverts have wives sometimes. I hate disorder, but she was the one who took care of such things. You can't imagine how hard it is to learn to cook at my age."

I listened to this and a bit more about his late wife's abilities in various areas. "So you want a housekeeper." The thought of keeping two houses clean was exhausting. I was no longer a young woman and my standards were high. And I now had the graveyard detail too. It was only natural that my standards would slip given the increase in work. Could I live with that?

"Actually," he said. "I was hoping we could share a house. Maybe yours? George always spoke so highly of it. Truth be told, I'd be a bit embarrassed to show you mine just now." He looked at the pristine headstone. It was a work of art. "So, I guess I'm proposing."

"Proposing what?"

"Proposing we get married. One house would be easier to keep nice than two."

I Bring Sorrow

"You want to marry a woman who just murdered her husband?" I whispered.

"Look at it like this. I have the means to see such a thing doesn't happen again. It'd be like a contract—although unwritten, of course. My end of it would be to keep quiet; yours to take good care of me." He paused a second.

I was still dumbfounded.

"It'll be a lot better than you think. I am a lot more orderly than George."

"But you're a pervert."

He shrugged. "But the harmless kind."

"Is there such a thing?"

"I guess you'll have to find out."

Stark Raving

Less than year into her career as a mediator, Elsa Scotia saw the unfamiliar names of Mr. Edward and Miss Alice Starkey on the day planner. Mediating was a late career move for her that played well into her talent for problem solving. She assumed the Starkeys were coming in over a dispute about the disposition of a will. Mediation of wills was often contentious, but since it was about possessions rather than people, no swords had been drawn in her office yet. If words could kill, however, there'd been some near misses.

"Husband and wife?" Elsa asked her assistant.

Doris fanned through the papers in the file. "Siblings. Their attorneys recommended mediation rather than a courtroom to settle their disagreement."

"A will, is it, then?"

"Yep," Doris said, coming up with the relevant page. "There seems to be only one area of contention. Financial matters, furniture, the house, and cars—all that's complete."

"So what's being disputed?"

Doris paused, scanning the page. "Alma Starkey's collection of Beanie Babies. Alma's their deceased mother."

"Her collection of what?"

"Beanie Babies." Doris looked up. "Kids collected them in the nineties? My daughter had quite a—"

"I know what they are. But aren't the Starkeys adults?"

I Bring Sorrow

"Edward is fifty-four; Alice, fifty-two."

"Edward?" Elsa said with a frown. "A grown man who cares about dolls?" She walked over to her computer and googled "Beanie Babies." She looked up. "Their value's been declining since around 2000. Practically worthless."

"Perhaps the Starkeys think differently," Doris said.

Elsa shrugged. "Should be fun meeting these two."

"Or not," her clerk said.

"Or not," Elsa agreed.

The brother and sister who walked into her office a few hours later could've been twins—even twins of the same sex. Both had seen significant declines in the hormones that differentiated them earlier. They were short, nearly the same height, round, and wore bobbed hair the color of hay. Their features were soft, their eyes nearly colorless.

Simultaneously, they thrust out right hands that could have been stamped from the same cast. Without meaning to, Elsa pulled back, a bit repulsed. The Starkeys seemed used to this reaction and slipped into chairs, waiting expectantly. Almost invariably, any group entering Elsa's office took seats as far from each other as possible, but Edward and Alice Starkey sat side by side. Obviously, their close relationship had survived the issue of the ownership of the Beanie Babies.

"I see the major portion of your mother's estate was settled without dispute," Elsa began, flipping through pages.

Alice nodded. "The rest of it was just about things. We've always lived in the house, shared the car, and sat on the same furniture: Edward, in the club chair, me, on the loveseat. We will simply continue as we always have. He, in the blue bedroom; me, in the yellow."

The lyric "Same as it ever was" ran through Elsa's head.

"Our last argument over household matters was when I wanted to paint my room apricot," Edward said. "Back in

1995, I think."

"It's always been blue," said his sister, "and still is."

Elsa took a cleansing breath as she imagined their life. "So what makes the Beanie Babies a particular source of friction?"

The siblings looked at each other at length. Finally, Edward said, "We have different plans for the Beanies."

Perhaps one of them wanted to pass them along to a charity and the other to younger family members, Elsa thought. Dispositions could be fractious.

"I intend to play with them," Alice said. "I want to cut those darn tags off and put the Beanies in chairs, beds, a dollhouse. I've made clothes for them over the years, collected appropriate furniture." She paused. "The Beanies have been Mother's prisoners for twenty years. I was never once allowed to handle one."

Edward bristled visibly. "And I plan to maintain them just as Mother did. With their swish and tush tags intact, with their fur completely blemishless. That's what Mother expected when she bequeathed them to us. That's what we promised her," Edward added, glaring at his sister.

"It was a promise she extracted under duress," Alice said.

"How many Beanie Babies are we talking about?" Elsa asked, reminding herself that they'd been adults even when the craze began. It was much like her experience with Barbie dolls. Regrettably, she'd been a teenager when Mattel introduced them.

"Over five hundred," Alice said. "Every Beanie that Ty made. In triplicate at least."

"Ty was the name of the manufacturer," Edward said. "Mother has—had—five Garcias, the bears, for instance. And ten Princesses. She was extremely intuitive about which ones would increase in value."

"Mother even collected the counterfeit ones," Alice said.

"She had quite a thing for Tabasco the Bull."

"But they have no value now, right?" Elsa said. "None at all?"

"Exactly right," Alice said. "So why not play with them? I've been yearning to hold one in my hands for twenty years."

"Piffle," her brother said. "You were far too old even then to play with toys."

"And you're off the rails if you mean to stare at them forever. They're worthless, Edward. Mother made the wrong decision in collecting them." She looked at Elsa. "She did the same thing with Cabbage Patch Dolls. Her intuition, such as it was, was extremely fallible in the long run."

"But if there're five hundred, why can't you both do what you want? Divide them in half." It seemed obvious to Elsa.

"They all want—or should want—to be played with," Alice said. "How would we decide which ones to keep encased? Or should I say imprisoned." She looked at Elsa. "The glass was even tinted. You could hardly get a decent look at them."

"Very few children were allowed to play with their Beanies. That's why so many still have their tags and are pristine. Beanies would be nothing more than a pile of dirty fur otherwise." Edward's sniffed. "If playing was all you wanted, ordinary toys would suffice."

"Beanies are ordinary toys. They always were."

"Things come back into vogue, Alice," Edward said. "And why does a woman of your age want to play with stuffed animals?"

"Why does a man of your age want to stare through glass at them?"

"Do you have any idea about how to settle this?" Elsa asked. It was suggested in her manual that she put this idea on the table. Let the contentious parties offer ideas.

"Indeed, we have," Edward said. "We want you to come to

the house, build a bonfire, and burn every last one of them."

"It's the only thing to do," Alice said. "I can't bear seeing them in those dreadful cases and Edward can't bear seeing me handle them."

"I'm not sure Beanies will burn. Aren't the beans in plastic sacks?" Her five minutes worth of googling had netted her this information.

The siblings looked at each other and shrugged.

"Look, I'll send someone to pick them up and dispose of them in an environmentally friendly way. Is that acceptable?" Both of the Starkey children nodded.

"It's only fair that Mother paid a price for her obsession," Alice told Edward a few days later. "For the last twenty years, she used those Beanies to drive a wedge between us. Playing us off one against the other. Interfering with our relationship."

Edward nodded. "Watching that man carry the boxes out the door was one of the best moments in my life. That mediator will see that they are disposed of correctly. Even if they can't be burned."

"Yes, it was nearly as satisfying as watching Mother swallow that cup of tea."

Alice watched as Edward smoothed the wrinkles in her skirt, his hand lingering familiarly. "Every sip was a step on the path to freedom. She could've outlived us both on pure vitriol. Evil woman."

"Speaking of tea, shall we have some? It's Oolong today," Edward lifted his cup and Alice tapped it lightly with hers.

Three weeks later, five hundred Beanie Babies, their tags cut off by Doris to prevent future hoarding, were on their way to Afghanistan where Elsa's nephew handed them out to waiting village children. No one once considered putting them behind glass.

"My aunt says the people who owned these toys wanted to burn them," said the soldier.

"Some people should be thrown in jail," said his companion, watching two little girls wrap their beanies in keffiyehs. "Look at those smiling faces."

Old Friends

"Shit, shit, shit, shit, shit," Henry swore through clenched teeth, "You're sure this is the right road, Gillian?" He grabbed for the sheet of directions, peering blindly through the tangle of green.

"Frances says it's a very narrow lane." Gillian whipped off her sunglasses and lowered the window. The pungent smells of midsummer flooded the car.

"Blair Witch territory is more like it." Henry groaned as the Subaru pitched rightward. Seconds later, both ducked instinctively as a branch scraped menacingly across the windshield.

"Can you picture those two living out here?" Henry reached out the window to remove forsythia clinging stubbornly to the wipers. "What were they thinking?"

"And what in the world do you do here in winter?" Gillian shook her head in disbelief.

"Nothing. Dan said it's strictly a summer place."

"I'm not sure I'd survive here any time of year," his wife said. "Do you think they have Wi-Fi?"

"They should have warned us if they don't. I need to be able to contact my editor."

"Oh, they must have it. He has departmental duties, right?"

They continued to creep along until, quite dramatically,

the trees cleared and the Liebold house appeared. Frances came rushing through the door with Dan a step behind. They were wearing swimsuits, brave apparel for people in their fifties. Neither face was visible beneath gauzy beekeeper hats.

Gillian swatted Henry with the map. "Not a word," she warned as he choked back a laugh.

"Welcome, friends!" Frances called out, yanking the car door open. "Breaking news! We have our own pond now. Dan found it a few days ago when he was picking berries. We've spent two days clearing away the undergrowth and picking up beer bottles and condoms. Must have been a lover's lane once."

Henry had already noticed the red welts and deep scratches etching their upper bodies. "You always hope that phrase speaks to flowers and tender letters. But it never does."

"We've just had a dip," Frances said. "Yikes." Her feet danced impatiently on the gravel path as she swatted a mosquito. "Uh-oh, they're out already! Never mind, it's just a scout. You'd better hurry if you want a swim before the serious invasion."

For the last hour, Henry had been hoping their arrival would coincide with cocktail hour. Instead, he'd now be forced to strut about in a swimsuit. His only suit was from the late W years, and he wondered if the elastic would hold. Obama had not been kind to his waistline.

Wearing an ankle-length terrycloth robe lifted from the Marriott Marquis in Chicago, Henry headed for the pond. Screams revealed their location. He guessed it was a pond, although mud hole might be a more accurate description. Nasty things would ooze between his toes. Probably there'd be glass and metal fragments to cut him too. Steeling himself, he headed in, his predictions immediately met.

Frances bobbed around him like an air-filled water toy. Was her splashing, clearly directed at him, an expression of hostility or did she intend it as flirtation? He splashed back finally, with the heavy-handed push of the rough middle school boy he once was. She fell over backwards, Dan turning just in time to witness her plunge.

"Steady, Lovage. She can be an annoying old thing, but she's harmless." Dan's tone was jovial, but a hint of menace filtered through. Frances came sputtering up, uttering what was surely a curse.

Embarrassed, Henry swam off—or would have if his trunks hadn't refused to go along. Gripping the waistband, he climbed out of the water where Gillian handed him his robe.

"Told you to buy a new suit," she hissed. "Quite a display out there."

It was hard to take her reprimand seriously when pieces of rotting vegetation climbed her legs like tattoos. Her skin was slick, a look he didn't associate with potable water, and her hair was plastered to her scalp, oozing a gelatinous substance.

"Yuck," Dan said, coming up on them. "Franny's having the water tested, but we haven't received the lab report yet. I'm not optimistic based on what I've seen today."

How like Dan, Henry thought, to offer this information now that the damage was done. Who knew what species of bacteria was making its way to his lungs, his stomach. A gentle burble brought their attention back to the pond where Frances floated serenely on her back.

"She only sees the good in it," Dan said in a solemn voice. "Ponds, that is."

After they showered, Henry got his long-awaited drink. Glass in hand, the two old friends circled the cottage, taking in its construction.

"It's first rate on insulation and windows," Dan told him, "triple this, and quadruple that. But it's rather characterless, isn't it? And I loathe the way no two rooms are on the same level. I'm always stumbling up the steps, or putting my foot down on air." He pointed to a fading bruise on his shin.

"What's there to do here?" Henry asked him. "Do you have any neighbors? Where's the next town?" He couldn't remember passing one in the last hour of the trip. "What about a library or a bookstore? A restaurant?"

"Oh, there's a town of sorts about eight miles from here. Franny says we can do it on our bikes, but we haven't tried yet. Too busy sorting things out."

"You mean the Citgo station and grocery store where I turned off the interstate."

"That's it. There's a post office there and a DVD red box. Not too up to date, right? We'd have to drive ten more miles to a real town."

Taking pity on him, Henry said, "Still, the fresh air and leisure time will do you good. You've been working too hard on that book."

Dan had been working on the book for the last decade. It was a comparison of Richard Nixon and Richard III. Others had written on the subject in the interim, but Dan didn't let this deter him.

"Did I tell you I'm to be chairman next year, Henry?"

"You did, Dan. Congratulations! How long is the commute from here?"

"Commute? Oh, this place is just for the occasional long weekend or the odd week in summer. Baltimore's still our home."

"And New Brunswick's ours," Henry said inanely. It was far too late for either of them to be from somewhere else. They were stuck where they were, for better or worse.

"So what do you think of the place?" Frances asked, husking the corn with a ferocity that seemed to come over her in waves. "I can't believe I found it. I had to force the realtor to show it to me."

"It's delightful," Gillian said, basting the chicken. "You were lucky to find it." Sniffing suspiciously, she asked, "Is there something hot in this marinade, Franny? Henry can't eat red pepper, you know."

"Well, I don't think so," Frances said, sniffing too. "I threw a bunch of things in. But I don't think we even have red pepper out here. It must be the cinnamon basil you smell. I've got oceans of it growing in the garden."

"You don't think you'll be bored up here? Take me away from the bookstores, the movies, the restaurants, and I'm finished." Gillian picked up her glass of Chardonnay, draining it. "I couldn't survive without my dance series at Lincoln Center."

"A pretty long trip from New Brunswick, no? Anyway, I grew up in the country. There's a cycle to country life that's reassuring. The season dictates your activity. For instance, right now it's all about berry picking and swimming, but soon it will be time for apple cider, pumpkin carving, and caulking the doors and windows."

Gillian had forgotten just how banal Franny's conversation could be. When Henry had put forth this observation last night, she'd denied it.

Franny began placing the marinated pieces of chicken on the grill. Each piece trembled as she tossed it breast side down. "Anyway, Gillian, I'm sick to death of living in the city. How long can I look at the concrete stoops of Baltimore? What kind of people don't bother to plant grass? Some might say it gives Baltimore distinction, but it's a merciless surface to me."

"You're not happy there?"

"I might have thought so once, but since the kids went off to college, I've hated it. It's stinking hot in the summer, much worse than New Jersey. And winter's no picnic either."

Gillian got to Baltimore fairly regularly, and, weather-wise, it seemed much the same as New Brunswick.

"What about Dan, is he happy?"

"Well, you know Dan," Frances said enigmatically, running down the steps to the basement for the roll of extra-long aluminum foil.

Which was quite true, Gillian thought.

Gillian headed out to the deck where Dan sat on an Adirondack chair with a badminton net rolled out before him.

"Thought we might try this after dinner," he said, trying to thread the net through the pole. "Never much liked the game though. How do you avoid bruising your forearm with the serve? Mine gets red and—"

"Isn't that volleyball? Anyway, will you please shut up for a minute? Your wife will be back here any second." She looked warily back at the house, and then continued quietly. "Dan, are you planning to be up here every weekend? Because if you are, I don't know how we'll see each other this summer." She looked around, trying to locate Henry. "I was counting on the weekends at least. Henry will be in his sweltering archives most of July and August."

Without looking up, Dan said quietly, "I wasn't consulted on Frances' purchase of this place. She took money inherited after her mother's death and bought the house without even telling me." He threw the end of the net he was holding down, trying another section. "Never mentioned her house hunting till the deed was done. Hugging trees was not my idea."

"When you should be hugging me. Think she knows about us and that's what it's really about?"

"If she knew, I'd be dead. Here she comes."

He threw the net down and ran over to help his wife. She

was carrying a large tray of condiments, bread, salad, a pitcher of iced tea.

"The chicken's almost done," she told them, sliding the tray onto the table. "Where's our Henry? I asked him to pick mint and pointed him in the right direction." They all looked over to the tiny garden. No Henry.

"I'll find him." Gillian sighed and walked back toward the house. If she knew Henry, he'd found a dark corner and fallen asleep. Set him down anywhere and he was off. It made him seem like a very old man. She couldn't wait until he took off for his archives next month. The eight-week separation every summer was saving their marriage. Where was he?

"Doesn't Henry look older? When did we last see them?"

Dan stood at the grill turning ears of corn. "Must be a year or two."

Although Dan scrupulously refrained from criticizing his old friend, he had certainly noticed how old Henry looked. His friendship with Henry dated to grad school. Henry's doctorate was in history, and Dan's in political science. They both left Columbia at the same time, marrying women they met there. It was the custom then.

Oddly, Dan's affair with Gillian started the same summer he married Frances and the year after her marriage to Henry. It sounded positively sinister or sick now, but it was just one of those stupid late seventies things. The two of them had been thrown together once too often at those strange academic parties where pairings and unpairings unfolded in every bedroom. It was very difficult not to have sex with every woman you met. People expected it of you, even when it was inconvenient. Which it was with Gillian, considering he was within weeks of marrying Frances.

"You must have noticed it, Dan," Frances went on. "His

face is a series of pouches. Whoops, here they come." She began taking the pieces of chicken off the grill. "Now, who needs a refill?"

*   *   *   *

The Lovages beat the Liebolds at badminton. No one remembered the rules of the game but, assuming it was much like Ping-Pong, they adapted. Then they collapsed onto deck chairs, contemplating the evening ahead.

"I brought a couple of movies along. I've got *All the President's Men*. Or we could play poker or hearts," Dan offered. "Oh, or charades if it's not too retro."

"Oh shit!" Frances said. "We're out of beer. Someone forgot to make a run." She glared at her husband. "It won't be much fun without alcohol. Whatever 'it' is."

Dan shrugged. "Sorry. I can be back in ten minutes. Anyone care to come along?"

Henry was snoozing on the chaise lounge and didn't answer.

"I guess the antihistamine knocked him out," Frances said. "It did the trick, didn't it? He's breathing more easily. He really is allergic to red pepper! I thought we were going to have to perform a tracheotomy and was looking forward to it. Sharpening those knifes at the hardware store yesterday would have paid off."

They all looked at Henry, admiring his ability to sleep so deeply after the scare he gave them.

"Well, I wouldn't mind a drive into town," Gillian said, rising. "I feel like a Snickers bar. How about you, Fran? Coming along?"

"No, someone should stay with Henry. And I'm going to call home. My mother-in-law's housesitting, and I want to make sure she hasn't burned the place down. She's always dozing off in the armchair with a Marlboro in her hand. Does anything look worse than an old lady smoking? I mean, who smokes nowadays?" She waved them away.

"I guess there's no way we could have a quickie," Gillian suggested after they'd pulled away.

Dan looked doubtful. "I should've planned better beyond running out of beer. I think we're too old to do it in a backseat this shallow and low. I don't bend in too many places anymore. Or if I do, I don't bend back again." He turned around to reassess the backseat of his Prius. "And the woods are too dense around here to get out of the car. Plus, they're full of poison ivy and strange, almost mythical animals. Did you ever see a possum? Ugly suckers!"

"I wanted to suggest taking our car instead, but it sounded bizarre."

He reached over to stroke her thigh. Why was it so much silkier than Franny's?

His hand felt unbearably thrilling on her bare skin, and she shuddered. "I'm willing to try the ground. How can I be so hot for you after so many years?" she wondered aloud. "Maybe I can straddle you." When her thighs proved too long for that maneuver, she climbed off. "You know, I haven't felt like having sex with Henry in ten years. I'd like to think he noticed, but I doubt it."

"If you'd married me, it would be Henry you were hot for."

"That's a shitty thing to say. Do you believe that?"

"I don't know. But it's strange we continue to remain married to people we don't love. If we were both available, the sex might lose its energy. Maybe we're addicted to the danger."

Gillian didn't answer him, wondering for a minute if he had someone else back in Baltimore. Then she discovered her seat went all the way down.

"Clever girl," Dan said, loosening his belt.

I Bring Sorrow

"Clever girl," said Henry, from his prone position on the sofa. Though his eyes were closed, he was wide-awake. "I was wondering how you'd find a way to get them out of here. What if he'd thought to buy beer? Where would we be then?"

"You make it sound like we're having an affair, Henry."

They both cringed as Henry reached for his scotch.

"Should you be drinking after all that antihistamine?" Her concern surprised them both. Embarrassed, she quickly added. "Do you have it? They'll be back in a minute." Her hands perspired with excitement and she wiped them on her shorts.

"Would I come without it? I must warn you again, Frances, this is the last payment. I'm prepared to resign my position at Rutgers and hang wallpaper rather than continue. I refuse to allow your extortion to become the defining experience of my life."

"Oh, don't be so dramatic. That ship sailed long ago. It was your suggestion, after all. Way back when." She put a hand on his cheek. "Keep the little typist happy."

He slapped her hand away, getting up. A moment later, he shouted from the bedroom, "My jacket must be out there. See it?"

She looked around, spotting it on a doorknob. Springing to her feet, she found the breast pocket and pulled out the long white envelope. She ripped it open immediately and was counting the bills when Henry returned.

"So that's it, Frances! I think fifty thousand dollars is enough. With the incredible investments you made during the nineties and again in the last few years, my little faux pas bought this summer place. Who knew when I pledged you my royalties, that book would be so successful."

She laughed. "Nice for both of us. And your threat rings a little hollow. You couldn't stand being someone as anonymous as a paperhanger. You don't even have the clothes for it," she said, stroking his linen shirt. "Of course, plagiarism has a certain cachet nowadays with book tours and talk shows."

"Oh, we've been through all this a million times. Could you stand being publicly labeled an extortionist? Or even more to the heart of it, could you bear for Dan to know that about you?"

"It might make me more interesting. You and I could appear on the circuit together. Each of us pleading their case. If you just hadn't been too lazy to research your own dissertation, Henry! Or if you hadn't thought I was too uneducated to see the parts you'd stolen."

"Didn't you ever wonder if I might kill you? Put an end to blackmail in that time-honored way?"

She was fumbling in her purse, and for a minute, Henry thought she might be about to pull out a gun. But she removed a pack of cigarettes. "Funny how only the silly little typist spotted it in all this time. I'd have thought scholars would be pouring over your work. Looking for every nuance, every resonance. And no, I never thought you had the gumption to kill me. It was laziness that got you into trouble and laziness that kept the checks flowing."

"I got rid of the worst of it by the time the book came out, and I've never repeated my mistakes in subsequent editions. It would be hard to prove any of it now."

"Maybe all scholars do it. A line here, a paragraph there. Except poor Dan, of course. He should have found someone to plagiarize." She lit a cigarette and went to stand by the window. A small fan blew the smoke away.

"Christ, he still won't let you smoke! It's your house, damn it. Tell him to fuck off."

A minute later, she stabbed her cigarette out in the philodendron, tossing the butt out the window. He smelled rather than saw the mouth spray she applied. Sighing, he lay down on the couch again, their business completed.

"He's the most boring man in the world," Gillian told Dan, her head on his shoulder as he drove as quickly as he dared. As much as Gillian claimed she didn't love Henry, maybe never had, Dan noticed his name was never long from her lips.

They'd been gone over an hour and were still miles from home. Their lovemaking took a very long time. First, he was slow to arouse: the woodland noises distracted him. Then he was slow to finish. And around the main event lay several smaller failures. Such a locale for sex was better left to teenagers who did such things more easily. To top it off, the damned convenience store was closed, leaving no choice but to drive to the next town.

"I can't imagine how Henry's students keep their eyes open. He quotes himself, for God's sake. 'As I wrote in the first volume of my study on Robert E. Lee...'"

"Still, he's had a sterling career," Dan said, counting off the books Henry published. "Seven, if I didn't miss one." Why did they always talk about Henry, especially after sex? He was their joint guilt, their joint regret. Perhaps even their joint obsession.

Gillian stroked his cheek consolingly. "Everything went into his career. He didn't have enough juice left to satisfy a wife. The great man—that's how he thinks of himself. The great man gives a lecture. The great man writes a book. The great man takes a piss."

"He couldn't help but think favorably about himself when success came so easily. Publishers stood in line for his second book. His first, which was not much more than his dissertation goosed up, was reviewed in the *New York Times*, for Christ's sake."

"So what?" she said harshly. "He's never made a dime off of

any of them. At least, that's what he tells me. Every time I think we're getting ahead, the money disappears."

"You're awfully hard on him, Gillian. He's basically a sweet guy. Look at how well he took that frightening allergic response. I thought I was going to have to slit his throat and insert a straw. And academics rarely make any money on books. They sell a thousand copies if they're very lucky."

"I'd think it was Henry you wanted to fuck if I didn't know better."

But Dan wasn't listening. His one book sold two hundred and ten copies. The remainder of the first printing sat moldering in his basement in cardboard boxes, the bottoms damp from the spring rains.

"I guess it's very hard loving a good man when I feel so evil all the time." They pulled up to the house and she followed him inside. "Don't forget the beer, Dan."

*   *   *

"I knew I was in trouble when I didn't feel the next step," Henry said, rubbing his twisted ankle. "Did you find an ace bandage, Frances?" This was so delightful, Henry thought to himself. I can just sit back for the next two days and do nothing. The three of them were buzzing around him like honeybees. Let them play childish games and swim in that cesspool.

Frances looked in the medicine chest, knowing very well they had no ace bandages. Hopefully, Henry was not the litigious type. First the red pepper and now this. Could they be held responsible for the architect's whimsical design? she wondered.

"I can make one out of an old towel," Dan suggested. "At least it would immobilize it." He began to shred it into long strips, almost whistling with delight. How obliging that Henry had chosen their moment of return to twist his ankle. Frances had not even commented on their tardiness.

I Bring Sorrow

"You've certainly had an exciting evening," Gillian said, handing her husband a glass of water. A bag of ice, deemed too cold by Henry, lay melting on the table. "Do you ever wonder why so many things happen to you, Henry? Nobody is more prone to accidents." She looked at the two men for confirmation. "It must mean something psychologically, honey."

"I can't think of what." Henry and Dan said this in unison, but nobody except Gillian noticed. How queer we all are after twenty-five years.

"Come on, Gillian," Frances said, rising to Henry's defense. "Lay off the poor guy. It's my fault about the pepper, and we're always stubbing our toes and banging our shins on these steps." Frances put an almost proprietary hand on Henry's shoulder. What a witch Gillian can be. Poor fool had no idea what lengths Henry had gone to in order to keep her.

"Yeah, I'm just a poor schlub. An old shoe," Henry said. And one you'll have to wait on for the rest of the weekend.

For a second, Gillian wondered if there was something between the two of them: Henry and Frances? Was it too much to think they had also engaged in a long-term romance? There was an air of intimacy in Frances's touch. But a second later, Henry shrugged her hand away, his lips twisted in distaste.

It was just too ridiculous, Gillian decided. From the beginning of their friendship, Henry and Franny had never quite clicked and she doubted they'd ever had a private conversation. Perhaps he'd never seen Franny as more than the woman who typed his dissertation.

"Well, it's great having you guys here," Dan said, helping Henry into the bedroom. "We'll go to a movie in Mt. Pleasant tomorrow. That'll keep you off the ankle, Hen. Sorry I won't get the chance to get even in volleyball."

"Badminton," his three companions corrected.

"It'll be time to go home before we know it," Gillian said,

almost to herself. "I've got to get back to my desk by Tuesday morning."

"Now I hope this won't be your only trip up here this summer," Frances told her. "You're welcome anytime, you know. Dan and I can never get enough of you two. Isn't that right, honey?"

"Oh, and us too," Henry said drowsily from the couch. Gillian nodded her agreement.

Fall Girl

When I was twelve, my mother shot a soda-pop salesman she'd known less than eight hours. Daddy had purchased the gun a few weeks before, telling her it was to keep us safe now that they were divorced. He taught Mother how to load, fire, and clean the gun. He also installed locks on our new apartment door and windows. Afterwards, he slipped three keys off the ring and pocketed them, flipping the remaining ones on the table. Mother eyeballed this maneuver, but let it pass.

"Now where's my jacket?" he said, beginning to roll his shirtsleeves down.

Mother grabbed his blazer from the back of a chair and handed it to him. Slipping it on, he smoothed the lapels, tugging his shirtsleeves down from the wrist. Despite his labors, he looked crisp and elegant, and I longed to throw myself at him and beg him to stay.

"Do you really think we're unsafe in a neighborhood bookended by a John Wanamaker's store and a Bonwit Teller?" Mother asked as he headed for the door. He didn't answer. Didn't even give her a glance.

And perhaps Daddy was right—maybe there was a dangerous, if undetectable, current coursing down the street, because it was only a few weeks later that Jerry Santini, a man Mother met earlier that day, walked out of our bathroom, saw my mother removing bills from his wallet, and headed for the phone, mumbling something about "thieving bitch" and "not getting away with it."

Mother, adept at both identifying potential danger and acting quickly on it, moved toward the drawer where the gun was kept, planning only—or so she insisted later—to scare Jerry Santini.

"I figured he'd take off when he saw it," she told me.

But stymied by our Ericafone, a Swedish import with the dial on the bottom popular at the time, Jerry was too sluggish for her swift actions. She caught him in the chest, the ribs, the thigh, emptying the entire chamber, in fact. He'd been shooting his mouth off about what he was going to do to her when she started pulling the trigger.

My mother almost always acted on instinct, especially in tight spots. So however it happened, whatever state she was in, and whatever Jerry Santini said or did or didn't do, Mother killed him, emptying the gun of bullets, letting it clatter on the hardwood floor.

There wasn't much Jerry did know after only an hour or two's acquaintance. Mother met Jerry Santini at a shoe repair shop. She was always a sucker for a man who took care of his shoes, and Jerry wore an expensive pair of well-polished, buttery-black wingtips. There were no holes in his black socks, an item she examined carefully over the top of the wooden stall. She was disproportionately impressed by such touches, often judging people solely on their appearance. So she invited him to come up to her apartment where she served him stuffed figs, cocktail nuts, dates, and several dry martinis before taking him to bed.

My mother's apartment gave the impression of belonging to a wealthy woman who wouldn't need to rob a soda salesman. Having her child sleeping in the next room would also seem to preclude her undertaking a robbery, much less a shooting.

I Bring Sorrow

After shooting her date with a degree of marksmanship no one would've predicted, Mother rushed into my room and shook me.

"Look at the marks, Christine," she hissed.

Only half awake, I badly wanted to see at least a blossoming of bruises. But her neck was white and blemishless.

Seeing my disbelief, she dropped onto my bed and began to sob, claiming through her tears that no one ever took her side. It was then that she confessed she might just have peeked inside his wallet, an action she'd been forced to take given our current position.

"Your father's stingy. How can we be expected to live on…"

I did feel responsible once I understood. If it weren't for me—for her reluctance to leave me alone even at twelve—Mother and her date might've gone out to a nightclub or theater, where she wouldn't have been tempted to rifle his wallet. Or she might have been able to steal the odd twenty dollars less conspicuously—blaming its loss on a waitress or busboy should it be discovered. Or maybe they would've gone to his apartment, where no gun conveniently waited in a drawer. My role in this debacle was growing large.

I hadn't heard the ruckus in the living room because my mother had turned on *Saturday Night Live* before Jerry and she made love, and it was still playing. I'd slept right through the skits about bumblebees and cheeseburgers, the lovemaking taking place in the next room, and, even more blessedly, the gunfire. Only Mother, screaming in my ear as ABBA sang SOS during the musical interlude, was loud enough to wake me.

I was still clinging to the hope her imagination had gotten the best of her—or, at the very least, that the wound was not the fatal one she reported when we finally walked into the living room. She continued to jabber away, pretending we were looking at some ordinary thing—like a broken vase or a ruined piece of furniture—so the oddness and horror of finding a dead body in my living room didn't immediately sink in.

The room had the dreamlike atmosphere of a scene from a B movie, like the ones we watched on late-night TV. How could the dead body on the floor be genuine when the rest of the room was still the familiar place where I'd watched Mary Tyler Moore a few hours earlier?

"He seemed like such a nice guy." Mother sounded surprised by this sudden change in personality—as if he'd pulled something over on her.

"How many times did you fire the gun?"

The blood was shockingly red. Our black and white TV had shielded me from the truth. The black blood on TV was somehow less startling—less of a life force, more like sludge.

"Six?" She paused for a second. "Look, I fired until the gun was empty—like I did at the shooting range, the one your father took me to."

Mother didn't know Jerry's last name until we examined his wallet more thoroughly.

"Santini," she said triumphantly, his license in her hand.

But Mother continued to forget Jerry Santini's name every time she was asked in the weeks ahead—I never once heard her get it right. More often than not, she called him Joey Spatini, confusing his name with a packaged spaghetti sauce popular at the time.

Sprawled on the fluffy carpeting, an item Mother made my father buy as part of their divorce settlement, Jerry Santini was certainly dead, putting to rest any notion Mother had exaggerated or misunderstood the outcome of their tête-à-tête. It was almost impossible to stop her from immediately spraying the area with rug shampoo.

"Hey, you're not supposed to touch anything," I said, clapping my hand over the nozzle. "They can find things out from his blood."

It was before the science of blood splatter or DNA, but there was still information to be gleaned from it. Blood type, at least.

She turned toward me, the can still poised. "Just what do we want them to find out, Christine? It was an accident. You upset me when you insist on seeing this…mishap as a crime. Make sure you use the word accident when they come—the police or whoever. First impressions last longest, you know."

I was speechless.

"And look," she continued, "we have to protect ourselves, not make the case for the cops. They'll be trying to pin it on me—us."

Us? Us?

Mother's voice trailed off as she stepped back from the body. She'd already linked me with the events. Perhaps I saw us as linked too. It was our apartment, our life. I should have been more vigilant in protecting her—us.

"I'm gonna call Cy. He'll know what to do."

"Not Daddy?" I whispered.

If she'd kept the door locked as Daddy suggested, we wouldn't be in this mess. Military training and running a business had prepared him for tight circumstances. His shirt would never wrinkle, his pants would retain their pleat. Surely this meant something.

"How could we possibly call your father, kiddo? Look what's lying on our rug. Think Hank would be able to see past that?"

Her voice had regained its normal strength; the power in the room subtly shifting back to her. I nodded, still transfixed by the pooled blood and the man I'd never set eyes on before.

He was naked except for a pair of extremely tight briefs.

The bottoms of his feet were pink and plump, like he'd never spent much time on them. Good attendance to his feet seemed essential to the story, and I couldn't see his face at all—squashed into the rug as it was. I could see he boasted a nice head of steely black hair and wore it long in the back.

Cy Granholm, the man Mother went to call, had loomed large in our life lately. In the last three months, he'd handled Mother's divorce, gone to court with her on a speeding ticket, and twice filed papers demanding an increase in child support. Mother had begun calling him at his home with domestic and household troubles: questions about financial matters, advice on how to fix the gurgling toilet.

"Cy!"

I heard Mother on the phone in her bedroom. There was gaiety in her tone—probably a quality she'd cultivated long ago and couldn't discard now—even though it was unseemly.

The treacherous Ericafone still lay on the living room floor. If the incident had happened in the bedroom, the use of her baby blue princess phone might have saved Jerry's life.

"If it's not too late, I could use your help, Cy. No, no, you'll have to come over here." She laughed a little, pretending, if only to herself, that it wasn't too awful, that nothing was greatly amiss. "I'd rather not explain it over the phone."

So two hours after the soda salesman's death, I told two police officers I'd found Jerry Santini strangling my mother in the living room and pulled the gun Daddy bought for us from the drawer.

"I held the gun in my hand," I said, caught up in the excitement of the scene and more than half believing it. "Confusion ensued and the gun went off."

Nobody flinched at my words. I was the sort of twelve-year-old who might say such a thing. "I was barely aware of doing it." The idea of his murder being dreamlike seemed like a good way to go.

Cy nodded in the background as I said exactly what he'd instructed me to say an hour earlier, telling the police as little as possible. I was perhaps a bit shrill in my delivery, but shrillness established my immaturity. Reticence was Cy's advice for any situation allowing it—and ladylike tears, if needed.

I didn't mind lying for Mother, and it turned out I was pretty good at it, and would get even better in the years ahead. When Mother lied, she prattled on. I was the essence of brevity, my tears restrained. I looked to her for approval, but she kept her eyes pinned to the wall behind me where a chartreuse and aqua ceramic señorita and señor danced the tango. I was on my own.

Our apartment had a hushed air over the next hour despite the host of men who were carrying Jerry Santini off, examining the carpet, looking for the bullet casings, powdering the place for fingerprints, talking to Mother and me, snapping their cameras. A child murderess merits solemnity. Nobody pushed me beyond my practiced confession on that day or on any other day over the following weeks. Ordinary men, even cops in 1975, didn't anticipate a mother asking her child to lie—even after the Johnny Stompanato case.

To be honest, I can't remember either Mother or Cy Granholm directly asking it of me—the lying or taking the rap. Cy's attempts to cobble a convincing story from Mother's words had gone awry every time.

"You seem amazingly cavalier about what's taken place here tonight, Eve," he said. "You did kill the guy. Right? Unloaded the entire gun into his gut?"

"Truthfully, Cy," her eyes fluttered, "I don't remember a damned thing. Not until Christine was standing here beside me." She looked up then, her lashes damp, her lips slightly parted. "And what else could I do?" she added, forgetting herself for a second and changing her tone. "For a lousy twenty bucks, he was willing to see me hang."

"You sound like a cheap prostitute, Eve," Cy said, frowning.

"He didn't even buy me dinner. I fed him, in fact."

Cy and I sighed simultaneously, fearing she'd indeed hang if she made such comments. So after that display of ineptitude, I stepped in with my special skill set. Everyone believed me—seemed eager to, in fact. My statement was met with subtle sighs of relief, of feet shuffling noisily in tight shoes, the funny crinkling noise nylon stockings used to make, the slight inhale of breath when what I was saying became clear, of the squeak of chairs as people sat down and started to write, with relief the entire sordid episode could be wrapped up quickly.

No one would have to haul Mother off to jail. No one would have to press up against her body in that see-through negligee Cy had made her continue to wear. No one would place cuffs around those fragile wrists or push her head down as she entered the police vehicle.

No, nothing bad would ever happen to Mother. Not when I was pathetically willing to be a good daughter and serve up my story. Not when it was clear I'd misunderstood the adult events transpiring in the next room. Got it wrong when I'd come in on a scene and mistaken ardor for violence. Mistaken shrieks of passion for those of fear.

There was no trial since I'd pled guilty, just a cozy hearing in the judge's chamber. The story never appeared in any newspaper—if it spread at all it was over the telephone, in whispers in grocery store checkout lines, behind closed doors. The judge gave me some stern admonitions and scolded my parents for keeping a loaded gun in the house. My father assured the elderly adjudicator the gun hadn't been loaded when he put it in the drawer; the bullets were in a separate package, the safety on.

I Bring Sorrow

"I never once touched the dreadful thing," my mother averred, unmindful of the distressed motions from Cy behind her.

But a forensics report, read aloud by the judge, contradicted what she'd just said, announcing a stray fingerprint had been found on the gun. Mother instantly recalled taking the weapon from my hands.

"Christine was nearly paralyzed with terror at what she'd done. I had to pry it loose from her frozen fingers, terrified it'd go off again."

I nodded my agreement as Cy signaled her to stop speaking with a jabbing slash of his hand. I could see the indecision in Mother's eyes because she thought her account of the events was going well, and she didn't like ceding her minutes on the stage. A collective sigh drifted across the room, all of us enervated by what we'd just heard.

At that moment, I could almost remember pulling the gun from the drawer. I could feel Mother's hands on mine, prying the gun loose. I watched, transfixed by my imagination, as the revolver fell to the floor emptied of bullets. I think we all saw it her way for a minute; the drama of her account was compelling, convincing.

I wondered if all the hearings taking place in the judge's chambers were set pieces like ours was. Were there rehearsals to keep things from getting out of hand in some cases? Jerry Santini had turned out to be an exceptionally solitary man. No family members or friends came forward to ask questions, to demand justice, to weep for their loss. Whereas Daddy's family rallied around us.

Mother and I shared moments of intense intimacy for years to come, but none would ever match the neon brilliance of the night she killed Jerry Santini. How could they?

I was eventually ordered to see a court-appointed shrink. I

began my therapy the next week, the doctor's eyes wide at the idea of treating a child murderess.

"Where shall we begin?" he asked me.

I could feel Mother in his outer office waiting. She'd curled up cozily on his salmon-colored sofa. A copy of *Glamour* rested in her hand, the scent of her Mitsouko perfume drifted through the door. She was everywhere—my mother. And I knew my lines well by then—she didn't have to worry about that.

About the Author

Patricia Abbott is the Edgar, Anthony, and Macavity Award nominated author of the acclaimed novels *Concrete Angel* and *Shot in Detroit*. She has published more than 100 stories in print, online, and in various anthologies. In 2009, she won a Derringer Award for her story "My Hero". She is the author of two prior collections of stories: *Monkey Justice* and *Home Invasion*. She is the co-editor of Discount Noir. She makes her home in Detroit.

Visit her online at pattinase.blogspot.com and follow her on Twitter at @Pattinaseabbott.

CPSIA information can be obtained
at www.ICGtesting.com
Printed in the USA
BVHW03s2142200318
511127BV00001B/112/P

9 781943 818877